I0592475

PARALLAX ERROR

SUSANNA ROGERS

Bucher & Reid

Bucher & Reid

Cover by Amygdala Book Design

978-0-6481868-7-8

DEDICATION

To my buddy, James
Still the best

ALSO BY SUSANNA ROGERS

INFILTRATION SERIES
Infiltration (Book 1)
Regeneration (Book 2)
Validation (Book 3)

CHAPTER ONE

Middleton, California

Three months ago...

Where does it start? Where does it end? Sometimes the answers seemed so far away but I was sure everything started somewhere.

Coffee was a good place to start, so I got the breakfast things ready while Mom was still in the shower, then padded to the living room to get my history book.

I glanced through the window, then stopped, did a double-take. A guy was waiting by the side of the road in front of the Johnsons' place, hands in the pockets, a dark gray hoodie pulled over his head. A weird place for anyone to be standing. There was nothing around, only houses with tidy yards, no bus stop, nothing.

By the time I got back to the kitchen, Mom was at the table. We'd had a huge argument last night because apparently I hadn't done a good enough job of cleaning the bathroom. She'd taken my laptop and phone away from me for the night and I'd let her. Anything to stop her ranting and calling me names. She could go on for hours.

Longer sometimes.

My computer and phone were at one end of the table. I didn't dare touch them in case it set her off again, though I was dying to check if there were any messages from one person in particular.

Mom smiled as she looked up. "Morning, honey."

Such a relief to see her smiling and in a good mood. I'd got my looks from Mom, the fine lips, dark blond hair and brown eyes. I'd seen pictures of my so-called father but didn't know much about him even though I'd always wondered.

"Hey, Mom," I said. "Did you sleep well?"

"Depends on what you call well." She sipped her coffee, then slammed the mug on the table, coffee sloshing over the edges. "You forgot the sugar again!"

I flinched, my nerve endings skittering, then jumped up toward the cupboards behind her. "Sorry, I'll get it."

"You're useless, Sasha." She nudged me out of the way as she reached for the sugar jar in the overhead cupboard. "Don't bother."

There was no point trying to talk to her when she was like this so I stayed quiet, edged back onto the chair and opened my book. Cereal stuck in my throat, I forced myself to keep eating.

Mom peered at me over the top of her glasses. "So that book is more interesting than I am?"

It made no difference that this was a history book for school and most of the time she was nagging me to do my homework. It also made no difference that I'd been wrong about her mood and this morning she wasn't in the mood for light conversation.

Frustration simmered inside me. That was the thing.

6

Didn't matter what I did, I could never win.

"Are you feeling okay today, Mom?" I asked in a small voice.

She rubbed her temple with one hand. "I've got another headache."

I didn't know if this was *another* headache or the same one that had been continuing for a few days and didn't think it a good idea to ask.

"Sorry to hear that," I said. And I was. I just couldn't stand it when she took it out on me. "Will you be going to work today?"

She stared at me, daggers in her eyes. "Of course I'm going to work. We wouldn't have this house or anything else if I didn't go to work."

It wasn't so much her words as the snarl in her voice that got to me, felt like a stab in the gut. Still, I didn't let my feelings show. Leaning over my bowl, I had another mouthful of cereal and swallowed the resentment.

"I'll do the cleaning up." I tried to sound upbeat.

"That new school is expensive, you know," she said. "The mortgage doesn't pay for itself and neither do all the costs for that school. It adds up."

She was right. I'd started at Morton College after getting a scholarship but that didn't cover the cost of books, uniforms and other bits and pieces, though luckily the laptop was included as part of the deal. I had a part-time job and would have contributed, except Mom didn't let me. It also didn't seem to count that I was getting the most outstanding test results Morton had ever seen.

"It's not easy on my own," she added.

I bit my lip, stopped myself. What about me? Didn't I count? I pitched in, cleaned, cooked and did other things.

"Have you taken anything for your headache?" I asked.

She grunted. "Leave me alone."

If only I could leave, get away from everything. Instead I got up and cleared the table as quietly as I could, then took my history book and headed back through the living room. Stopping in front of the window, I saw that guy was still across the road.

He pulled the hoodie off his head, revealing short dreadlocks that looked out of place, as if he'd been whipped out of the mean streets of downtown LA and dropped into the middle of suburbia.

I stepped closer. Couldn't help it. The guy's lips curled to a smarmy smile and even from across the road, the glint in his eyes was clear. He curled his index finger, motioning me to come to him.

I froze. He was staring right at me through the window. There was no mistaking it.

He lifted one hand to his throat and made a slashing movement as if that was what would happen if he got his hands on me.

Fear ripped through me. I stumbled back, stepped to the side so he couldn't see me. Had I imagined that? My heart raced, my skin suddenly clammy while I stood there in shock.

Seconds later, I was back in the kitchen, leaning over the table. "Mom, there's a strange guy across the road." She didn't move so I grabbed her arm. "Come and see."

"I told you I'm not well," she shouted. Always shouting.

I tugged her arm harder. "Quick, before he goes."

Trudging behind me on her way to the living room

window, she swore and muttered, then stuck her head next to the glass. "What guy?"

Just my luck, he wasn't there any more.

"There was a guy out there, looking at me, and he did this." I mimicked the throat-cutting gesture with my hand.

"What is with you? You're always thinking about yourself." The tendons in her neck were straining as she yelled, "I don't have time for this."

"It's true! I thought he was going to come and get me. I was so scared."

Mom's upper lip curled in disgust. "You're always scared."

It sucked the air right out of me, my chest ready to cave in. I'd been through so much at my old school and it hadn't stopped after I shifted to Morton. The bullying was never going to stop. Didn't she care? Why couldn't she understand? Who else was I supposed to tell if someone was threatening me?

Damn it, she always thought the worst of me, that *I'd* done something wrong, that I was either imagining things or had brought them upon myself.

She shook a finger at me. "Don't even think about staying home today. You're going to school."

Tight-lipped, I stared at her. I might be going to school but I couldn't leave through the front door so that guy could follow me, or worse. I'd learnt a lot at my old school about staying away from trouble.

I squared my shoulders, turned and walked away. I was upset and shaking on the inside but couldn't let it show because that'd only make things worse.

Sometimes my own mother was as bad as the bullies at school who could smell weakness from a mile away, then they'd pounce.

I was weak. She'd told me that often enough. I was a lot of things, none of them good.

At least I had one person who believed in me and I was dying to talk to him. Sometimes I thought I shouldn't complain to him so much about my mother and about other things too, but he always listened. Always knew exactly what to say too.

One true friend. That wasn't too much to ask.

CHAPTER TWO

I steeled myself because I still had to get to school. Had to get past the guy with the hoodie and dreads, and no way could I go out through the front door.

I waited until Mom was in the bathroom then scaled the back fence, which was tricky enough because I wasn't particularly athletic, then hoped my neighbors didn't see me traipsing through their yard.

Still on edge, I stayed off the main road as I headed toward the bus stop, then it hit me. What if the guy knew which bus stop I used? Fear rippled through me. Mom was right. I was always scared. And useless. Still, I didn't have time to waste. The next bus stop was a lot further so I had to run to make it in time.

I was still panting as I got on the bus and took a seat half-way down the aisle next to a younger girl who looked like a pretty safe bet. As usual I took a book from my bag so I could ignore the other kids on the bus who were much better at ignoring me than I was them. Being left out was better than being hassled. I'd learnt that the hard way.

It would've made a huge difference if Alec could've caught the same bus as me. Though he only lived in the next suburb, he was on a different bus route, worst luck.

Five minutes later, Madison Frost and Aisha Johnson walked down the aisle, smashing into my shoulder with their bags, giggling as they passed. I kept my head down.

It must've been my lucky day because some boys at the back of the bus called out for the two girls to join them. A pang of jealousy shot through me, not because I wanted to be like them, but because I'd love to have friends calling out to me to sit with them. Not something Madison or Aisha would ever think about.

By the time the bus pulled up outside school, I was dying to get into the open air. I was surrounded by kids in pale blue and gray uniforms like mine and could disappear, which was exactly what I wanted. The uniform wouldn't have been so bad except for the navy and white striped tie which was plain embarrassing. And also mandatory.

I perked up as soon as I spotted my two friends sitting on a bench in a courtyard near our homeroom. Alec Hooper had striking black hair and was six feet three inches tall so he was hard to miss even sitting down. Penny Novak had one hand on her eBook reader which seemed to be her new best friend. The two of them appeared to be deep in conversation, a serious one judging by the looks on their faces.

Alec looked up at me, not that my face was much higher than his when he was sitting. "Whassup everybody?"

So much for the serious conversation. He'd got that saying from watching the host of a fight show he loved. He'd never been in a fight himself and wanted to keep it that way but got a kick out of watching this program with his dad and big brother. Entertainment for the whole family.

"Actually, something is up," I said.

Sliding beside Penny, I leaned across and told them about the guy with the hoodie and how I'd snuck out the back door and used a different bus stop.

"Was that overkill?" I asked reluctantly.

That was the problem with being constantly criticized by my mom, or one of the problems. I didn't know where I stood and couldn't trust my own judgment. I was even starting to wonder if I'd imagined the whole thing.

"Better safe than sorry," Penny said.

The two of us I looked vaguely similar though her hair was cute mousy brown whereas mine was not-quite-blond. We were both slim and flat-chested as opposed to tall and sinewy with big boobs like Madison and Aisha. At least we weren't mean. Penny wore glasses so you'd think she'd have copped the worst of the bullying but for some reason she didn't. It was as though those girls could sense I was under pressure and would go in for the kill.

"What did your mom say?" Alec asked.

I shrugged. "Not much. You know what she's like."

Though I'd never given my friends the full story about my mother, they knew she was hard to get on with. I didn't have the full story myself. Sometimes I didn't know what the hell was going on.

"Are you going to call the police?" Penny asked.

Another shrug. "No point, not if my mom won't back me up. Who's going to believe me?"

Alec leaned over, his arms resting on his thighs. "You can always wait until the guy beats the shit out of you, then go to the police."

Penny turned to face him and we both stared. Gave him 'the look'.

"What?" He threw his hands up. "I'm only trying to help."

"Maybe it'd be better if you didn't," Penny said.

"I won't let anyone hurt you, Sasha." Alec turned to me. "Fighting is my specialty. I know how it's done."

It was honorable of him to say that but I had a feeling that if things came to the crunch, he wouldn't be much help.

"Watching fights is your specialty," Penny said to him.

"A guy's got to start somewhere." He wasn't fazed. It was one of the things I liked about Alec. You could say whatever you wanted and he'd never get upset.

Penny turned to face me. "Keep an eye out for this thug over the next few weeks. Make sure there are witnesses, other people who see him as well. You always carry your phone with you, that way you can call for help."

"You can call me any time," Alec said.

Penny gave him 'the look' again. "I meant the police."

At least these guys believed me. Having a couple of friends made a huge difference. It beat the hell out of spending every lunchtime in the library on my own like I had at my old school.

Besides, Penny was much nicer than my previous friend Molly who was so competitive she wouldn't even pick me when she was the basketball captain choosing the team. That was because Penny had the great advantage of being every bit as lousy at sport as I was.

"So what were you guys talking about before I got here?" I asked.

"The news was all over FacePlace." Penny's tone indicated I was supposed know what she was talking about. She looked at me as if I was an idiot. "You mean you haven't heard?"

"About Domenic Simms," Alec added. "He was from your old school."

There'd been over a thousand students at Southern Hills High and the name didn't ring a bell.

"He committed suicide." Penny lowered her voice. "Sounds like he'd been bullied for years until he couldn't take it any longer."

Suicide. Sadness flooded my chest. I had a pretty good idea what the poor kid must have been through, the taunting, the bullying, the way it never stops, the way no one else will stick up for you. None of the other kids would help anyway, not at the time, not when it mattered.

I knew about bullying in all its magnificent forms – name calling, being pushed around, spat on, talked about, left out, laughed at. The amazing thing was that there were so many ways kids could go about it from face-to-face to behind your back or on FacePlace or even completely anonymously.

"According to the reports, this kid Domenic washed down a heap of pills with a bottle of bleach," Penny said. "It wasn't the first time he'd tried to kill himself either."

"How old was he?" I asked.

"Fourteen."

Two years younger than us. What a waste. A goddamn waste.

Then it came to me. A picture of a boy's face flashed in my mind. I remembered some guys from my previous math class who'd pointed at him and laughed, saying he was an even bigger loser than me. I'd only found out his name later.

"I knew him." The words slipped from my lips.

Penny put her hand on my knee to comfort me. I tried to explain that even though I hadn't exactly been close friends with the kid, it was still a shock. And it was.

Alec was listening too but he'd taken out his smart phone, his pride and joy, purchased after many hours of working at a fast food joint. He looked up Domenic's FacePlace page and showed it to me. Sure enough, it was him.

Alec shook his head. "I don't believe this."

"Don't believe what?" I asked.

"Most of the messages are tributes." He stared at the phone, fingertips on the screen. "They might be corny but they're saying nice things about the guy. Then there's, *I'm glad he got the job done properly this time.* Closely followed by, *The world's a better place without him.*"

Domenic Simms was just a guy. He'd lived and breathed and had a life once. He didn't deserve this.

This was too close to home. Too close altogether.

Alec's upper lip curled in disgust. "I can't believe the crap people come out with on FacePlace. As if it's okay to be bitchy because you're on a computer."

"People come out with a lot of crap in real life too," Penny said.

And if these two had known me a year ago they'd have seen the same sort of comments on my FacePlace page. At one stage I couldn't get the stuff down fast enough.

We sat in silence for a while, then the bell rang and we stood. Madison and Aisha sauntered toward us, both of them looking like they'd just walked out of the beauty salon, Madison with her wavy blond locks while Aisha had straightened her long black hair. I had no clue why she went to all that trouble when her African-American hair looked sensational.

"Speaking of being bitchy…" Alec muttered.

Penny whacked him on the arm.

Madison turned to her friend. "Those three look like they've been to a funeral."

"I wonder whose," Aisha added. They both giggled.

Penny stood. "Haven't you heard about the kid at Southern Hills?"

Madison rolled her eyes. "Everyone has. It's public information." She looked down her nose at me. "He wasn't a friend of yours, was he?"

"No," I said.

"Of course." She grinned. "You don't have any friends."

A wisp of anger curled in my stomach. She didn't care, not about a dead boy or me or anyone else.

I motioned towards Alec and Penny. "What does that make them, then? Are they invisible? Figments of your imagination, maybe?"

For once I had a reply. Even if it wasn't the wittiest retort in the world, at least I'd managed to come out with something.

Hand on her hips, Madison sneered. "I thought you were supposed to be smart. Turns out you're just a smart ass."

Aisha grabbed her friend's arm and said over her shoulder, "It won't be long until even those two losers don't want to hang out with you either."

The two girls ambled away.

"Hey," Alec yelled. "We are *not* losers."

Madison and Aisha laughed and kept walking.

Penny frowned. "Alec, why do you always have to be

so confrontational?"

He spread his hands. "Me?"

"You said they were bitchy."

"They *are* and they didn't hear me say that anyway."

"There's no need to be rude.

"Of course." Alec shook his head sarcastically. "There's only one way, the Penny Novak way."

"I'm just saying there's no need to stoop to their level."

"I have to stoop to get to anyone else's level," Alec said, his shoulders suitably hunched.

He could always make me smile, yet another reason to adore him.

"He's got a point," I said.

"We've got English next and we have to sit in the same room as them," Penny said as the three of us headed for class.

Alec shrugged. "What's the big deal? It's not like they'd want to sit with us anyway."

"That's not what I meant." Sometimes Penny wouldn't let up. "Maybe if you were a bit nicer, they'd reciprocate. Instead, you egged them on."

"No way." He shook his head. "Those two can be nasty without any encouragement at all."

I stepped into the classroom ahead of the two of them. Penny was plain wrong. Maybe I should've told her so and stuck up for Alec. I took the easy path instead, grabbed a seat near the front, waited for my friends to join me and moved on to something else.

It took us a few minutes to notice there was no teacher. The kids got noisier, rowdier, some sat on desks, others wandered around.

"We can't afford to miss another class." Penny drummed her fingers on the desk.

"But we haven't missed any classes this semester," I said.

She looked annoyed. "You know what I mean, Sasha."

I did. Penny wanted the best academic results possible and despite all the reading she did, English was her weakest subject, meaning she was less than brilliant at it. Sometimes I even got the feeling she was jealous of my marks.

A paper plane sailed overhead in an arc, high at first until it lost gravity and flew straight out of the open door. The class cheered, me included.

At that moment, Mr. Di Giuglio, the physical education teacher walked into the room, pushing a trolley with a television set on it.

"I just dodged death." He reached for the cord behind the TV set. "It's not every day I nearly get hit by a plane."

That raised a few laughs.

"Ms. Dyson is sick so we're going to watch a movie instead," he said.

Cheers.

"Has anyone ever seen M*A*S*H?"

Moans.

I wasn't sure what the fuss was about or why the others would object to what was effectively a free period.

While Mr. Di Giuglio plugged in and switched on the set, he told us a little about the movie. Since this was supposed to be English class, I wondered why he hadn't chosen *Anna Karenina* or at least *Twilight* or something based on a book. For all I knew, maybe it was.

The opening credits rolled, the theme music mournful

even though this was supposed to be a comedy.

A couple of the kids down the back starting singing. Taking the piss, actually.

"*Suicide is painless*," they sang in high-pitched sarcastic voices until Mr. Di Giuglio told them to keep it down.

The movie started, but the music stayed with me. It wasn't the lyrics so much as the tone, something about those minor notes that grabbed me in the gut and stayed there.

We only watched half the movie before the bell rang and it was pandemonium again. Chairs screeched on the floor and voices were raised. Kids pushed each other as they scuttled out. A few more missiles sailed through the air.

Waiting until the crowd had passed, I looked over my shoulder. Madison was walking side by side with Finn Masters. A cooler sixteen-year-old boy did not exist. Maybe I shouldn't have been taken in by the olive skin, blond hair and stunning green eyes, but I was. Yes, I was that shallow.

Madison was chatting. Her specialty. Finn took her arm to steer her clear of a girl who'd stopped in front of her.

But he was looking at me.

My heart raced. I didn't know what to do. I never did. I smiled at him the way any friend might, except I was never going to be his friend and I was desperately hoping my face wouldn't turn red.

Finn looked away. As if I wasn't there.

I covered my mouth with one hand. How could I have thought I'd win him over with a smile? A guy like him was never going to look twice at someone like me.

Penny pointed to the top of my desk. "Look, Sasha, you've got a chocolate."

A *Baci*, no less. The name meant kisses in Italian and the chocolates had cute little sayings inside about love and kissing.

I smiled, a genuine one this time. Someone must've dropped this on my desk while I'd been ogling Finn.

Then I saw what I should've seen in the first place. The wrapper looked as if it had been screwed up, then smoothed out to cover something. There wasn't going to be a chocolate in there. This was a trick.

A pang in my gut, I looked around the room, wondering who had left this little surprise for me.

I scooped the item up, stood and started walking. "Let's go."

The wrapper probably had a turd in it. That was the kind of thing a lot of kids would find funny. Hilarious. The pinnacle of wit.

Penny and Alec were right behind me, arguing as usual.

"What was that on your desk?" he asked me.

"Nothing," I said. "I'll catch you guys at lunch."

"Okay, I've got drama next," Alec said.

When I'd first met him, it had surprised me that someone who was so good academically would also be good at acting. Now there wasn't much about Alec that surprised me at all.

The two of them kept arguing and I headed for the girls' bathroom. Inside one of the cubicles, I put the lid down, took a seat and stared at the supposed *Baci* chocolate in my hand.

My hand was shaking. If I was a stronger person, I

would've thrown that thing in the trash and not given it a second thought. But I wasn't strong. And I had to know.

I opened the wrapper. No chocolate. Instead there was a grubby eraser inside. A mean prank.

Alec had been right all along. People could be nasty without any encouragement at all.

A small piece of paper with neat printing in block letters was wrapped around the eraser, just like the little messages about kisses inside *Baci*. Someone had gone to a lot of effort.

A note: *Suicide is painless. Try it.*

This was never going to stop.

CHAPTER THREE

The Primary

Nothing stops.

It hasn't stopped now.

I open my eyes but everything stays blurry. My head sways on my shoulders and a face in front of me comes into focus slowly, the face of a boy I've never seen before. He's shaking me awake.

I should get up. I should do something but I can't. I'm listless. No energy. As if the blood has been drained from my body. Maybe it has.

And I remember everything. It all comes back to me, so shocking it takes my breath away but it's definitely my breath and my body and that's what matters. I'm in one piece and so grateful I can't believe it.

The guy leaves his hands on my shoulders and now that he's stopped rocking me there's something soothing about his presence. It must be the warmth in his pale eyes because it's certainly not his cropped sandy hair.

"Are you okay?" he asks.

"Much better now you've stopped shaking me," I say.

I sit slumped against a wall, my knees up in front of

me, the ground hard below. No, it's not the ground. These are ceramic tiles and I'm indoors. The smell of lavender rises from the floor as if it has been recently cleaned.

Looking around, I see a desk, a bookshelf, a wall covered in plaques. Must be an office. I've been in the principal's office often enough recently and this room has the same air of importance.

Suddenly, it hits me that I'm still here. Except I'm not here. I'm somewhere else and that's okay. I can do this. I can work it out. A wave of renewed energy surges through me.

The guy stays crouched in front of me as I peel his hands from my shoulders. Sure, he's good looking but he's also acting a bit too familiar for my liking.

"Where am I?" I ask.

"Mason's office," he says, as if that answers my question. "What are you doing in here?"

In here? As opposed to where? I've definitely never seen this guy before. I wouldn't forget a face like that in a hurry.

"Who are you?" I ask.

"It's me, Remy." He stares, puzzled. "Remy Christensen."

"Nice to meet you, Remy."

"Is that a joke?"

His stare is intense and concerned. He takes my hands into his, getting a lot more cozy with me than he should. It sends a shiver up my spine.

"I'm not laughing," I say.

"Sasha, that's not funny."

I jerk my hands away. Nerves settle in the pit of my stomach. "How do you know my name?"

"Don't be ridiculous. Of course I know your name."

My mouth drops open and I hold his gaze. Weird is being taken to a different level. The downy hairs on the back of my neck stand on end. Something is wrong, more wrong than usual.

Suddenly blood rushes through my body. Where I was listless before, now I feel ready though I'm not sure exactly what for.

I lift my hand to brush my hair back from my face, only to find it's already been pulled back into a ponytail. I look down at my arms resting on my knees and wonder why I'm wearing boots, khaki pants and a black tee shirt. These aren't my clothes.

I pinch the skin on my wrist. It hurts as I give it a little twist. I'm here. I can feel it.

Letting out a long sigh, I lean my head against the wall behind me and fold my arms. They feel strong and muscular, my bicep flexing beneath one hand. Looking down, I notice my breasts seem bigger and wonder how that could've happened. Must be some bra I'm wearing.

"Come on, Rodriguez," Remy says. "You've got to snap out of it."

"Who's Rodriguez?" I ask.

"You. You're Sasha Rodriguez."

Relief washes over me. He has me mixed up with someone else. We'll be able to sort this out and maybe then I can get out of here.

"You've made a mistake," I say. "My name is Sasha Pierce."

He looks bewildered. "No, it's not."

"I think I know my own name."

"Sasha, please tell me you're mucking around."

I hold his gaze. I'm getting good at that. Then I decide a staring competition might not be such a good idea.

My eyes flit around the room. "Do you want to tell me where we are?"

"I told you. Mason's office. You've been here loads of times."

I grit my teeth, hope my nerves don't show because this is getting harder to handle by the minute. "Let's start again and maybe you can tell me what's going on."

Remy jumps to his feet and stands back, one hand covering his chin before he lets it drop. "This can't be happening. This is bad."

I don't want to ask more questions. I just want this all to go away. I press my eyes shut, cover my ears and sit back on my haunches, curling myself into a ball. I must be dreaming, having a nightmare or some weird waking vision. This will go away. It has to.

I open my eyes. Remy is still there. The room is still there. I struggle to my feet and face him. Though I know it can't be the case, I feel stronger than ever before. Taller too.

"Slap me," I say.

He steps closer. "Are you sure?"

"Slap me and it'll shake me out of this. Just do it."

His hand lands. My cheek burns. Though he has done exactly as I asked, it still shocks me.

"Ow!" I cover my cheek.

His eyes glimmer with concern. "Sorry, Sasha, you know I'd never hurt you on purpose."

He seems genuine but I don't know this guy. I don't even know where I am. And I have to do something.

I walk to the other side of the desk on shaking legs and

lean over, looking for clues. A computer and a document tray with some papers sit on the immaculate desktop along with a black diary, the current year embossed in gold on the front. I open it at the page marked with a burgundy ribbon, check the date and find it's correct.

I take a deep breath. "Let's try again. Where are we in geographical terms? This is California, isn't it?"

"Yes, it's Planalto," he says.

"Never heard of it. Is it near LA?"

His brow furrows. "No, LA's not there any more. This is Northern California. It's too hot in the south anyway."

That doesn't make sense. I stop my eyes from widening because I don't want to give too much away.

He ambles around the desk closer to me. "Sasha, I'm getting worried. Are you feeling all right?"

I step away from him and look at the plaques on the wall. I'm half expecting school certificates and awards of academic achievement, only to find they appear to be military plaques.

One award catches my eye. Not the award exactly but the mirrored surface on which the writing is etched.

I look into the mirror.

And someone else stares back.

Panic rips through me. My heart is in my throat. No, I'm not going to have an anxiety attack. That's not going to help.

Deep breaths. In through my mouth. Out through my nose.

"You don't look so good," Remy says from behind me. "Are you okay?"

I don't answer.

Staring into the mirrored surface, I lift my fingers to

my face and a hand appears in the mirror covering the strange girl's cheeks. I open my mouth. She opens hers. I lift my eyebrows. She lifts hers.

She's very exotic looking, I'll give her that. Her black hair is pulled back into a ponytail revealing striking blue eyes, olive skin, high cheekbones and a full mouth. There's an air of confidence about her and that's what gets to me. Confidence, the one thing I wish I had.

Stunned, I keep staring as if this is a science experiment and the answers will miraculously come to me. I lift the plaque and check the other side before replacing the item on the wall.

"Come closer, Remy," I say. "Put your face next to mine. Now poke your tongue out."

As he does this, I start pulling faces, then shifting out of the way of the glass surface. Each time, the girl in the reflection follows my every movement. As if that's me in the mirror.

"What are you doing?" he asks.

Fear slices through me like a knife, so deep it takes my breath away. I don't know what I'm doing, where I am or how this can possibly be happening. Except I have a horrible feeling I do know what's going on.

I'm in someone else's body.

Except that's not possible. Maybe I'm in a coma. After what I went through, that'd make more sense. And if I'm in a coma, none of this is really happening.

"What's going on, Remy?" I ask.

He turns to face me. "Sasha, you're freaking me out."

"That makes two of us."

"Let's start from the beginning. What's the last thing you remember?"

My stomach lurches, dread sinking deep into my bones. I can't tell him that, not when I can't even face it myself.

I was in trouble before. Big trouble. Only I have a feeling that was nothing compared to what I'm up against now. And this isn't the time for the truth.

"I don't know," I say. "It's a blank. You said we were in Mason's office. Who's Mason?"

"General Mason."

I screw up my face. "As in the army?"

"Not exactly. You really don't know?" My blank expression must be answer enough for him because he adds, "This isn't the army. It's The Primary."

"You'll have to spell it out for me, Remy. What's The Primary?"

"A government installation. We're prime candidates, the most highly skilled in our field, hand picked from The Ghettolands to be trained in close protection."

I'm still wondering what The Ghettolands are, when I ask, "What's close protection?"

"We're bodyguards."

Remy looks the part, from the khaki pants tucked into his combat boots up to the black tee shirt stretched across broad muscular shoulders. We're dressed the same but that doesn't mean anything.

I cover my mouth. "*We* are bodyguards? Remy, you might be a bodyguard but there's no way I can possibly…"

It's too much for me and I explode into nervous laughter. This is too ridiculous for words. I'm a schoolgirl from Middleton, California, a scholarship student, a nerd, a misfit.

Remy puts his hands on my shoulders. "Sasha,

something happened to you and you're in shock."

I nod. "Yes, I'm in shock."

"Oh my god, you've got amnesia."

"I don't... No...Yes."

Even though my legs are still shaking with fear, my mind seems to be working. Amnesia, that's much more believable than the truth.

Because I'm pretty sure I've suddenly woken up in somebody else's body, and no one is going to believe that. I'm not sure I do.

Remy would think I've gone loopy. Maybe I have. Maybe I'm so far gone I'm in a mental institution and I don't even know it.

At least this amnesia story will explain a multitude of sins. I'm smart enough to get through this. I have to be. It's the one skill I've got because none of my skills are physical. I am absolutely one hundred per cent not a bodyguard.

"Can you remember anything?" he asks. "How old are you?"

"Sixteen," I say. "Did I get that right?"

"Same as me." He nods. "Do you remember anything else? Who you are? Where you came from?"

"Look, let's go find this General Mason or a person in charge and tell them what's happened. Maybe someone else can help me."

Horror in Remy's eyes. "No, you can't tell them you've lost your memory."

"Why not?"

"We've got to get you into training."

"Training?"

"For the tournament tomorrow."

"Tournament?" I step back. "You've got this all wrong."

"Sasha, you have to fight tomorrow because you have no choice. Tomorrow you're going to win. Today, you're going to train."

What's he talking about? I can't fight.

Anger wells in my stomach. Suddenly I don't like him using my name, being so presumptuous, telling me what to do.

I push him in the chest. Hard. It comes out of nowhere, unlike anything I've ever done before. And it makes me wonder if I'm mistaken.

Remy stumbles back and grins. "See, you've still got it."

"Got what?"

"Your survival instincts, your fighting skills. All those years of training are still inside you. They have to be."

No, that's not what's inside me at all. He has no idea. Still, it sounds as if he cares and maybe he does.

"Come with me." He takes my hand. "Outside. I'll show you."

He leads me out of the office down a long white corridor. I can tell he's trying to help so I follow.

Remy throws open a set of double doors leading outside and I expect the sun to come streaming in. Instead, thick dark clouds loom overhead, hanging low in the sky like a black ceiling. It's not cold, though. Far from it. The air feels clammy, thick with humidity and crackling with electricity. A sheet of lightning flashes in the distance.

We wander into a quadrangle. At one end, a small group of girls dressed in shorts and tee shirts jostle with each other for the basketball as they shoot hoops. Nothing else out here looks even vaguely normal.

Flat-roofed, utilitarian, concrete bunkers dot the area. They seem distinctly unfriendly and don't resemble the houses, apartment blocks or suburbs I'm used to.

I point as we walk. "They look like bomb shelters."

"Of course," Remy replies as if that explains everything.

He leads me along a concrete path past a grassed area, the only green I can see. There's a climbing wall at one end, an obstacle course at the other and in between several groups of kids about my age are doing pushups, boxing drills and sprinting exercises. It's more boot camp than summer camp.

What is this place? Remy described it as a government installation and that's what it feels like. This isn't home. And it isn't fun.

It certainly isn't Middleton. This isn't my world.

Remy stops outside a door marked 'Arena', opens it and pushes me ahead of him down a corridor with rough, formed concrete walls. They sure like their concrete around here.

Soon enough, we're inside the building in what appears to be a training room. The smell of sweat hangs in the air, mixed with that of stale bacteria. The air is still so I wonder why no one has opened a window. I look around. No windows, no distractions.

Punching bags line two walls, while at the far end an octagonal cage takes pride of place. Blue padded mats cover the floor which in turn is covered by young people around my age. Guys in white karate suits roll and wrestle on the floor while others punch the bags or pads being held by another person. Some appear to be hitting each other, or sparring.

This is definitely not the place for me. I want to go back home, back to my old life, or what's left of it.

Looking down, I remember how good it felt last year when I'd slept over at Molly's and we snuck out at midnight to the burger place and how those older boys had talked to us. I remember lying on the grass beside Alec and being warmed by the sun. Warmed by his friendship too. That's where I should be, not here.

I let out a long breath. "Remy, this is all wrong."

"You've got to train. Tomorrow you'll be fighting in a cage like that one."

No way. That's not going to happen. "Why would I do that?"

"For your country." The look on his face tells me he's serious. "*Country above all else.* You know that."

I shake my head. "I have to tell someone I've lost my memory and that I can't do it."

He steps closer, his hand on my arm. "If you don't do this, they'll get rid of you."

"Fine, I'll go somewhere else."

Anywhere has to be better than this. Remy has mentioned The Ghettolands and though the name doesn't sound appealing, maybe someone there will help me sort out what's going on.

"No, that's not what I mean," he says. "This isn't about losing a fight. If the authorities think you've lost your memory you'll be useless to them. They'll eliminate you."

Eliminate. He means kill.

My gut clenches with fear. My pulse races. What kind of place is this?

I look at the other kids training on the mat. I'm not like them. I'm not a fighter. Nowhere near it. I could probably fight my way out of a math competition or a spelling bee, but not a ring. And I don't dare even look at that cage at the back of the room.

Blood pounds against my temples. The words thunder in my head: *I don't want to die.* I need to get back home. More than anything, I want to live.

Remy looks me in the eye. "Sasha, tomorrow you're the main event."

CHAPTER FOUR

Tomorrow…I can't take it in. I shouldn't even be here today.

This whole situation feels so surreal that part of me doesn't believe it's really happening. Maybe that's why I go along with it. Also, I don't want to let Remy down when he seems to be on my side.

I turn to him. "Where do we start?"

He nudges me towards the rear of the room where shelves line one wall. Remy grabs several items, shoves a pair of navy shorts into my hand and points toward a door on the other side of the room.

"Get changed," he says. "You can leave your shoes in there."

I slump onto a wooden bench in the girls' locker room, unlace my boots and drop them onto the floor. I hold my hands out in front of me. They're trembling. My hands or Sasha Rodriguez's hands, I'm not sure whose.

A panic attack is on its way. I know the symptoms. These are the first tremors and the earthquake is yet to come.

Nausea rises inside me. My heart races, banging against the walls of my chest. The first time this happened I felt intense fear, thought I was dying, having a heart attack. Now I know better.

Focus. I suck in a long slow breath through my nose. Count to five. Hold it in for two more counts, then breathe out slowly through my mouth. Count to five again. *I can do this.* I focus on my breathing and do it all over again until my heart rate slows.

There's no point fighting a panic attack. That only makes it worse. The trick is to ride it through, and I've got off easy this time, probably because I've had so much practice.

I drop my head into my hands. I've faced many things worse than panic attacks. Much worse. But maybe not worse than this tournament thing.

I pull myself together and come out to join Remy at the edge of the blue mat.

"Are you okay?" he asks. "You seem kind of sweaty."

"Fine," I say.

He passes me two long strips of black fabric. "Hand wraps. Copy me."

I'm much slower than him as I wrap the fabric around my hands and knuckles.

"You need wraps to protect your hands because you hit hard," he says.

"I do?"

"Believe me, you do." He motions toward the mat. "I'll give you the run down. We do mixed martial arts here, a combination of stand-up and ground fighting. Kickboxing is your strength. It's a combination of kicking, punching, elbows and knees. Between your hands, legs, elbows and knees, that makes eight weapons."

"I have weapons?"

He nods. "You've also done a lot of grappling and ground fighting. It's the one martial art where size doesn't matter. Supposedly. It's about jostling for position, looking for leverage, and trying to get your opponent into a submission."

I have no idea what he's going on about. "A submission?"

"That's where you get the other guy in a choke or a hold where you're just about to break their bones and they have to tap out to signal the end of the fight."

I can't quite get my head around this. "So I'll be fighting?"

"Today you're training. Tomorrow you're fighting and you're going to be good at it." He grips my shoulders. "You *are* good at it."

I've never been able to hurt anyone even when they've lashed out at me. What's more, physical education isn't my strong point. I played basketball for a while but the other kids didn't want me on their team. Also, I'm not sure basketball skills are easily transferable into the boxing ring. Only this isn't a ring. It's a cage and that has to be worse. Much worse.

"We'll see." My voice quavers.

"You're still Sasha. You've got the same physical ability, motor skills and muscle memory regardless of whether you can remember anything else or not."

I'm not that Sasha. I'm a different person. I stay tight lipped.

Remy's fingers dig into my shoulders. "You're still smart, aren't you?"

I shake him off. "That's one thing I've got going for me."

"Good."

His eyes light up. "I'll grab the Thai pads." He heads for a pile of equipment by the wall and tosses me a pair of gloves. "Listen to me, copy what the others are doing, and I'll explain this bit by bit."

I pull the gloves on. "Sure."

Nearby, a huge guy with short ginger hair kicks the pads, each strike pushing the pad holder back. The guy is about my age and twice my size with a giant dagger tattooed on his back.

"You're a monster!" the pad holder yells.

Is that a compliment?

The big guy grunts with each strike. Drops of sweat fly from his head. The word Neanderthal comes to mind. I'm relieved when they settle at the rear of the room, then freak at the thought that that's what I'm supposed to do.

"Don't worry about him," Remy says. "We'll take this one step at a time."

I'm not planning on worrying about the big dude. Because I'm not planning on going anywhere near him.

I do as Remy instructs and kick the pads, tentatively at first, then harder. I can't believe it. *I can do this*. No one is more surprised than me. Remy was right. I'm in Sasha Rodriguez's body with her muscle mass, her physical skills. And it feels good. Weird but good.

It isn't me, yet it is.

Next Remy shows me how to throw punches, knees and elbows. It's all coming back to me or at least that's how it feels. These must be Sasha Rodriguez's physical skills I have, because they sure as hell aren't mine.

I feel as if I can take on the world. It's inside me. The skill. The power.

After countless rounds of going hard on the pads, Remy lets me take a rest. Very kind of him.

I slump over, my hands on my knees as I suck in deep breaths. "Sasha must've been doing this for a long time if she got this good."

He crouches beside me. "Sasha has been training for years. All her life, if I'm going to be honest."

"I didn't think this stuff came out of nowhere."

Remy holds my gaze. "Sasha is you. *You* are Sasha. You can't talk about yourself in the third person. You'll give yourself away. Someone will notice. Then they'll check you out and you'll be done for."

What about tomorrow's tournament? That sounds a lot like being done for. Isn't he worried about that?

Maybe I'd be better off trying to escape, run, hide. I'm a lousy runner but I could probably find a way. Then I'd be on my own again. A shudder shoots up my spine at the thought.

Remy paces the floor in front of me. "You can't go anywhere. You know that, don't you?"

I straighten, wondering how the hell he knows what I'm thinking. Is he telepathic? Is that something else I don't know?

"Sasha, I know the way you work," he says. "You run on instinct first and then think later. It's not hard to work out. If I were in your position, I'd probably want to run too."

"That's not fair," I say. "I don't know you at all."

He steps closer. "But you can trust me. Deep inside, there must be some small part of you that remembers. Please, Sasha. You have to do this."

Desperation in his voice. I wish I could help him but

there's no one left I can trust and I feel more alone than ever.

"Security is tight until after the tournament," he says. "After that, things will go back to normal. You can't leave. You can't go anywhere, not without permission and they'll never give it to you."

"Maybe I can hide."

"Lift your shirt," Remy says.

I screw up my nose. "What?"

He motions toward my waist and I raise the hem of my tee shirt, shocked to see a toned six-pack midriff so fabulous it makes me think perhaps there are some perks to being in this body after all. I also have a strange ink and metallic item embedded in my skin. It's huge. Goes from one side of my body to the other. I swallow. It looks like a tattoo, only very sci-fi.

Remy lifts his shirt to show me his. "We've all got them."

"What are they?"

"Electronic locator tattoos. There's nowhere you can hide with one of these. Our superior officers can always find you. And I guarantee that by tomorrow, they'll be looking."

"It's really a tattoo? I can't get rid of it?"

He shakes his head.

I can't run. I can't hide. That doesn't leave a lot of options. At least I have this strong, highly trained Sasha Rodriguez body to go along with her intense, hard ass life.

But I need more. I need to get out of here. I need help. My shoulders slump as I start shaking inside and out. Tears sting at the back of my eyes. I hold them back because somehow I know it would be bad, very bad, to cry in this place.

"I want my mom." My voice cracks.

Remy shakes his head. "Your mom and dad died when you were ten."

His words bring me back to the present. If that's where we are.

He says, "You've got a little brother, Joey, and you love him more than anyone in the world. After your folks died, you looked after him as best you could. You did it tough. Lived on the streets. A few months later your aunt took the two of you in but you didn't last long. You've been at The Primary ever since. Joey's still with your aunt."

"A little brother…"

"You've got lots of friends here too but they're giving you space to focus on your training," Remy says.

Friends? That'd be nice for a change. Remy puts the pads down, reaches for a pair of gloves by the wall and pulls them on. "Time for some sparring."

It isn't enough that I've spent the past hour smashing the pads, that I'm about to crack, that I don't know what's going on. Now he expects me to spar.

He gets into a boxing stance. "I'll talk you through it."

"You don't understand."

He jabs me, the strike stopping an inch from my nose. "Come on."

The next punch lands gently on my cheek. I lift my hands to my face.

"Good, you've got your guard up," he says.

Do I? He hits me again, brings me back to *now* because *now* is all I've got. I let Sasha's instincts take over. *Ride through it.* I step back to evade his punches. I shuffle to the side, keep covered, stay out of his way. I slip from side to side, keep my head moving so he can't hit me. *I can do this.*

"Now hit me," Remy says.

He has to be kidding. Hitting the pads is one thing and hitting a person is another.

Remy jabs me in the face, one, two, three times. "I'll make you want to hit me."

I don't have that much of Sasha Rodriguez in me. I don't want to hit anyone. I can't.

Remy comes at me with a barrage of punches to the face, the body, kicks to the leg. I cover as best I can. Blood pumps through my veins. Anger wells in my stomach. Rises to my throat.

I hit him back. Sasha Rodriguez takes over.

Remy doesn't let up. Relentless, that's what he is. Only now I'm hitting back. I spot an opening. See his chin. He lowers his left hand ready to strike. I slip his shot and throw a big right hand.

Remy drops to the ground, lands on his butt. I've hurt him, knocked him out, done something terrible.

I crouch in front of him. His head is in his hands, his elbows resting on his knees.

I place my gloves over his. "I'm so sorry. Are you okay?"

He looks up at me, a glint in his eyes. "That was shit hot."

That's not exactly how I'd describe it. Still, the words bring a smile to my lips.

He rips off his gloves, hands them to me, tells me to leave mine at the side of the room. Remy is still sitting when I get back and join him. I'm glad this is over.

"Now I'll show you how to wrestle and get some Brazilian Jiu Jitsu submissions," he says.

My face falls. Back to submissions again. And I'd thought we were done.

Still I listen to Remy's instructions, let Sasha Rodriguez's body take over and go with the flow. Chokes, arm bars, sweeps, it all comes naturally to me. Sasha may have spent years working on her ground game and now I'm reaping the rewards. If you can call it a reward.

When we're finished, I slump onto the mat while Remy puts away the equipment. When we were training I was in the zone in my own little world, not paying attention to anything around me. The room is still full. People have come and gone and everyone is still training.

Someone charges at my waist. A man. I smell aftershave mixed with sweat. Feel muscular arms around me. In an instant, he's on top of me and in this room full of martial artists there's nothing unusual about that.

He doesn't yet have his full weight on me. I don't hesitate. Don't think. A hip escape to leverage some space, a sweep to spin him over so our positions are reversed, then he leaves his arm free so I grab it and get him into an arm bar. He taps out. He has no choice.

Letting go, I shuffle away from him on my backside. My eyes are glued to his.

I was good. I can't believe it.

And I still don't know what's going on. The man is old enough to be my father. His face is weathered, his dark hair cropped short, his hazel eyes sharp and he's grinning as if he's the one who's just won.

"Why are you looking at me like that?" he asks.

Because he's twice my size. Because it's not okay to jump me. Because I'm suddenly coursing with anger.

Remy appears, his hand on my shoulder as he

crouches beside me.

"Mason," he says in a loud voice. "I didn't know you'd be joining us today."

I have to be careful. So this is General Mason? What would Sasha Rodriguez say to him? How would she respond?

She'd be cool, confident, cocky. The opposite of me. Being in her body gives me a little of that confidence.

"You're lucky I didn't break your arm," I say.

Mason laughs. "You can break all the arms you want tomorrow. Tomorrow will be the real thing."

Great. Just what I want to hear. What about my arms? Will they get broken?

"You're not worried, are you?" The General takes my hand to help me up. He leans closer and quietly says, "You're not still mad at me about what happened before."

What happened earlier? Sasha would have a smart answer, the sort of thing I can never come up with quickly enough.

"Should I be?" I ask.

"No, you're my prize student. After this, your career will be made. We need more people like you." He extends an arm to Remy. "And you too."

We act like one happy family, only I don't believe that for a moment. I'm not sure what to believe. I've taken everything Remy has told me as the truth, but he has kept me away from everyone else in this world and I have only his word for it.

I fold my arms. "What if I refuse to fight tomorrow?"

Mason laughs again. "We both know that won't happen."

"What if I had some illness or disease? Or if I was no

good to you any more?"

"That's not funny, Sasha."

"It's not meant to be. It's a question."

His face clouds over. "You're like a daughter to me...but there are some things that even I can't protect you against."

My mouth twitches. Everything Remy has said is true.

"You've trained hard." Remy's voice. "You can do this."

Mason looks me in the eye. "Do you want me in your corner for the fight tomorrow, is that it?"

"No," Remy says too quickly, then adds, "I'll be there. Best to stick with what's familiar."

Mason whacks me gently on the back. "There's no need to worry. Broken bones can be mended."

As if that's supposed to make me feel better.

"Country above all else," he says, then leaves.

"Mason taught you everything you know." Remy frowns. "Did something happen between you and him? Why were you in his office?"

"I have absolutely no idea," I say. "I've never seen him before in my life."

Desperation claws away inside me. I want to get through this. I want to win. To survive.

How can I have taken my life back home for granted? Why didn't I show more backbone? Why didn't I fight then when it mattered?

Instead I did something terrible, made one enormous error, and went through a huge trauma. That's what propelled me here. I might not know exactly what's going on but I've worked that much out.

And I suspect Sasha Rodriguez also went through

some shock or big event. If I can find out what had happened to her, perhaps I can find my way back to Middleton.

Because that's what I want more than anything else – to go home. Doesn't matter that it's not much of a home.

In the meantime, I have to take things one step at a time.

I look around the room. "Who do I have to fight, Remy? Is it one of the girls in here? Surely they don't want me to fight a boy. It wouldn't be a fair fight, even if it was against a guy my size."

His lips part as if thinking of a reply and I know the answer isn't going to be good. A horrible thought crosses my mind.

"Not you," I say. "Surely I'm not supposed to fight you."

He shakes his head.

"Then who?"

He motions to the back of the room.

The huge ginger-haired guy who'd sprayed sweat all over me while kicking the pads earlier is training or wrestling or doing some sort of drill. His trainer stands opposite him, egging him on. The big guy lunges at his trainer, wraps his arms around his legs, picks him up and throws him to the ground.

He looks as if he's going to pummel him. Two other guys step in to hold the big dude back. An enormous roar like that of a wounded animal fills the air. The sound is coming from him. He shakes the other guys off and stomps around the room, banging his chest, yelling, "Yes, yes."

No…no…

He's human. And he's a monster. And I'm supposed to fight him.

CHAPTER FIVE

Middleton

If there was one good thing about working at the supermarket two nights a week, it was getting paid. I liked having money for books and the occasional movie ticket or to buy myself some cool clothes from time to time. I needed all the help I could get in the cool department.

The other good thing about the supermarket was that the people here liked me, everyone from the managers and full-time staff to the students like me who came in as needed.

All except one. There was always one.

So far, it'd been a good night at work. I'd spent two hours stacking the shelves which meant I had minimal customer interaction except for stepping out of someone's way when they wanted something on the shelf I was filling. What's more, people seemed to think I was doing them a huge favor when I did.

Then Joshua Phillips turned up, the one staff member I tried to avoid. He was my age, same school, same grade, only he hung out with the in-crowd. We hadn't worked the same shift for a while and now, unfortunately, he must've been told to stack the shelves in this aisle.

"Hi," I said.

His lips spread to a smarmy grin. "I heard about your little run-in with the eraser."

A pang shot through me, dread sinking deep into my stomach. The eraser, the note suggesting suicide, all things I didn't need to be reminded about. I didn't want to go there, not again, not ever,

"If you didn't appreciate the note, why didn't you just *rub* it out?" Josh laughed. "Wasn't that what the eraser was for?"

Turning toward the shelf, I said under my breath, "Yeah, it was a lovely gift."

I should never have reported the incident. You'd think after everything I'd been through I'd know better but, just this once, I'd hoped I might be able to get through to someone so they could see what was going on. The principal had tried to find out who was responsible and then word had got out. If I'd kept it to myself, the whole world wouldn't know and I'd be better off.

"You're very sensitive today," Josh added.

I stood on a crate to reach for two jars of asparagus that were in the wrong spot. There was a stepladder further up the aisle but I didn't need to get up that high.

"What's the matter?" Josh asked. "Don't you want to talk to me?"

Suddenly, he rammed me in the hip. I slipped off the crate, holding onto the shelf to break my fall. I landed on my feet, mostly. Meanwhile, the jars of asparagus smashed onto the floor, making a huge racket.

I stared at Josh, my mouth open.

His expression was slightly surprised as if he hadn't

expected my fall would be quite so spectacular, then he composed himself.

"You should be more careful," he said, clearly back to his normal self.

I didn't know why he hated me. Didn't know why any of the kids did.

Thoughts banged around inside my head. What did you do that for? Who do you think you are? What makes you think you're so special? All things I didn't say.

Instead I stood and stared and took it. Angry and helpless. Mom was right. I was useless.

Josh pointed at the broken glass, liquid and smeared asparagus on the floor. "You'd better clean that up."

His words took my breath away.

Suddenly our supervisor, Russell, appeared at the end of the aisle. Some of the girls at work had nicknamed him the vampire because his skin was so pale it looked like he'd never seen the sun. Still, I'd never been so happy to see him.

"What's all the racket?" he asked.

"Sasha broke some jars," Josh said.

Russell looked at me. "Are you okay?"

"Yes," I said. "I'm sorry."

Sorry, I was always sorry. Why did that word come out of my mouth so often? How was this my fault?

As much as I wanted to tell Russell what had happened, there was no point. No one had seen and no one would believe Josh had pushed me on purpose. He'd insist it had been an accident and I'd end up looking bad. He might even tell Russell about the eraser incident and I didn't want that.

"No problem." The supervisor shifted his gaze to

Josh. "Can you clean that up please? Sasha, you're needed on register three."

Josh stepped forward, sidestepping the mess. "It's okay. I'll go on the checkout."

Russell put his hands on his hips. "No, you can clean up."

"But she's the one who made this mess."

"I want someone on the register who will actually serve people," Russell said.

"You always favor the girls," Josh mumbled.

Russell stepped closer. "What was that?"

Josh turned to the shelf and reached for some cans. "Nothing."

It felt good to have someone sticking up for me for once. The supervisor stood there for a moment and I left before he changed his mind.

Josh was right, though. Russell did favor the girls. He also made lots of sexual innuendos and sidled up to us if he had the chance even though he was much older, probably around thirty. It's what was known as harassment.

Still, for once this had gone my way and that beat the hell out of having my nose rubbed in the mess.

I headed straight for the register and took over from Marie, an older lady who was knocking off for the night.

Glancing up, I smiled at my first customer even though he looked about a hundred and smelt like a brewery. You got that sometimes on the night shift.

He didn't smile back. Most people were pleasant enough but there were always one or two who were grumpy or rude or sometimes just plain psycho.

I picked up the items from his basket of groceries and

scanned them, only for the man to snatch a package of butter out of my hand.

"That's meant to be on special," he said.

"I can get a price check if you like," I offered.

His face contorted into a scowl and he looked ready to explode. "I don't have time for that." He waved his hand for me to continue.

I scanned the final items. "That's eighteen dollars and sixty cents."

He slammed the butter onto the counter. "So you're not going to give me this for the discount price?"

"Sorry, sir," I said.

That word again. I was always sorry.

The man handed over a twenty and waited for his change.

"Bunch of goddamn thieves, that's what you are," he muttered under his breath as he left.

Yep, that was me. On top of everything else, I was a goddamn thief. I knew I shouldn't let it bother me but it did. I was tense, my shoulders rigid. It was going to be one of those nights.

I got back into the rhythm of things fairly quickly, the rhythm being that it'd be quiet for a while and then all the customers would come through at once. Wasn't that always the way?

During a quiet patch, I glanced up to see Finn Masters walking through the supermarket, looking cooler than ever in a pair of ripped jeans and a tee shirt with a skate motif.

I smiled at him. Maybe I was a sucker for punishment.

Finn grinned and headed toward my checkout. "Hi, Sasha."

He knew my name. Either that or he could read my

name badge.

"Hi." I scanned his Coke and chips, wishing I could think of something to say but all I could come up with was the total price.

He handed over the correct amount in change. "See you at school."

I watched the back of Finn's blond head as he walked away and called out, "Sure, see you."

So this was what it was like to be treated like a regular person. Such a relief. It may not have been a hugely meaningful interaction but it hadn't been painful like so much else that happened to me.

If Finn would talk to me, maybe other kids would too. It'd make a huge difference if a few other people talked to me, acknowledged me, maybe stuck up for me. What's more, it had felt good to be at the receiving end of that smile.

I looked up, saw a face I'd seen before.

And froze.

Swarthy skin, dark eyes, short dreadlocks. It was the guy who'd been watching me that morning at home a few weeks ago. What's more, he was still wearing the same gray hoodie.

My heart thumped in my chest, my mouth suddenly dry.

I should never have let myself get lulled into a false sense of security by seeing Finn. I should've been on my guard. If I expected the worst, maybe it wouldn't be such a shock when it happened.

My stalker was going through a register at the other end of the supermarket but his eyes were on me. Suddenly he switched on a smile for Tim who was serving him.

Tim looked the other way to tend to the next customer, and the guy with the hoodie shifted his gaze back to me. The smile turned to a sneer. He walked away from the checkout, his eyes glued to mine as he headed past me on his way to the door.

Finally, he was gone. My heart racing, I leaned against the counter to steady myself.

What was that all about? I'd only seen him once before. I didn't even know the guy but he knew where I lived. Knew where I worked.

And he was closer than ever before.

Another customer turned up. I had to serve her. There was a rush of people and I had to serve them too. It was the same thing over and over again, the same mindless work. Mindless was okay. Mindless, I could handle. Except that guy's mean eyes and face kept flashing in my mind.

I wondered if I should tell Russell about my stalker. That's the thing about mindless work – you still have plenty of time to think – but without evidence I decided not to bother. The guy with the dreads was smart. We had security cameras covering the checkouts but he'd done nothing that could be construed as threatening. Besides, there'd been plenty of times at my old school where I'd had 'evidence' and it hadn't made any difference.

One thing was for sure, nine o'clock couldn't come fast enough. When it finally did, I closed off my register and deposited the drawer from my till in the secure area. I couldn't wait to get out of there.

On a good night, Mom came to pick me up but she was going through a bad patch and this wasn't a good time. I'd be walking home and tonight of all nights, I shuddered at the thought of being in the dark, being followed, maybe worse.

Russell followed me as I passed through Tim's register to say goodbye.

"You leaving now too?" Russell asked.

"Yep, I'm starving," I said. "Can't wait to get home."

That was the truth. I was desperate to get home as fast as I could, and not only because I hadn't eaten. I also had homework to catch up on though, realistically, that wasn't going to happen. If I could get through to Brody, I'd start telling him about the things that had happened, he'd start asking questions and then I'd never get anything else done. He'd make me feel better and that was the main thing.

Russell edged closer to me and raked a hand through his dark hair. "Would you, ah, like a lift?"

If he was trying to be suave – and I think he was – he was failing dismally.

I kept my head down. "No thanks."

"You sure? It's no trouble. We can stop and get something to eat on the way if you like."

He was a grown man, supposedly. He was also my boss. I didn't know what he was thinking, only that this was never going to happen.

"No thanks," I said again. "My mom's probably got my dinner ready."

Russell shrugged. "What can I say? Next time you might be the one cleaning up the mess in aisle nine."

So much for him sticking up for me. The sliding doors leading out of the store opened and we stepped out. The unmistakable reek of cigarette smoke cut through the air. I turned toward the smell.

And saw him.

The guy with the dreadlocks was leaning against the

wall at the end of the building, one leg bent, his foot resting against the masonry. Waiting.

My heart thudded inside my chest, my skin suddenly clammy. I couldn't walk home alone, not with that guy around. It would've been asking for trouble.

And I sure as hell couldn't call my mother. Anything was better than getting her riled again. She already thought I either attracted trouble or created problems out of nothing.

Russell motioned toward the car park. "You sure I can't tempt you?"

I nodded. "Actually, I'd appreciate a lift."

His eyes lit up and he reached across, preparing to put his arm around me. "I thought you'd never ask."

I moved away. "Let's get this straight. I'd like a lift home. Nothing more."

He put his hands up defensively. "No problem. Follow me."

I had to admit Russell looked kind of innocent and most of the time he seemed harmless.

Meanwhile, the guy in the hoodie hadn't flinched, hadn't moved except to draw back on his cigarette. The end glowed red. It made me wonder if I might be imagining the whole thing. Was I going crazy?

He was there. I wasn't imagining that part.

Russell swaggered through the car park with me at his side. He pressed the remote unlocking mechanism for his car and the tail lights of a battered black Jeep Cherokee lit up. It figured he drove a big car, a truck.

He opened the passenger's door, ushering me inside. "See, I won't even touch you."

I edged onto the seat and told him where I lived. As

Russell reversed out of the parking spot, I looked around for Mr. Hoodie. Not there any more. I was safe.

Russell drove off onto the main road but didn't stay on the straight and steady. Minutes later, he pulled up outside a brightly lit liquor store.

"What are we doing here?" I asked.

"Don't panic." He opened the driver's door. "Just making a quick stop."

"I thought you were driving me home."

"I am. I want to get some beer and maybe a bottle of wine. It won't take long. Why don't you come in with me?"

Because I'm sixteen. Because I don't want to have a drink with you. Because I need to keep my wits about me.

I looked straight ahead. "I'll wait here."

"Fine, play it your way."

Russell closed the truck door and went inside the liquor store. I glanced around the parking lot. There were a couple of parked vehicles, no people, certainly no suspicious characters. It didn't take Russell long to make his purchases, then he was back in the truck.

He nudged my leg as he leaned across to place a six-pack and a large bottle in a paper sack at my feet. "We can pick up something to eat on the way and go back to my place if you like."

I could jump out of the car before it was too late and walk home. Or run. But I wasn't going to do that when the guy in the hoodie could be lurking somewhere and he knew where I lived.

I edged further away from Russell in my seat. "Look, you're my boss and you're too old for me."

"I'm not old." He spread his hands. "I'm twenty-six."

Exactly as I'd said. Old. I didn't think he'd be the type to jump a girl but he also wasn't taking the hint. I had to be clear.

"I'd like a lift home," I said. "That's all."

Russell drew back his hand. "Hey, I was just making a suggestion." He started the engine. "Of course, I'll take you home. What sort of guy do you think I am?"

My shoulders scrunched, I sat jammed up against the door while we drove in silence until eventually Russell turned onto my street.

"Can you take the next left and pull over please," I said.

He slowed down. "I thought you said you lived on Brewer."

"I do, but my mom won't like it if she hears a strange car pull into the driveway and then I'll have some explaining to do."

That was an understatement. She'd freak out if she discovered I'd accepted a lift with someone I didn't know or, more accurately, someone *she* didn't know. She didn't trust my judgment. Never had. And I could never explain this to her.

Russell took the first left as I'd asked. "So it's better to drop you off around the corner and have you walk the rest of the distance in the dark where you might get attacked, rather than take you to your front door?"

He sounded concerned rather than sleazy which made a pleasant change.

"Yep, that's right," I said. "I normally walk home anyway. It's no big deal."

No, the big deal would happen if I gave my mother the slightest excuse to go off at me and that absolutely wasn't

58

going to happen tonight.

Russell pulled over around the corner. "It's not too late to change your mind."

"No thank you." I opened the car door. "But thanks for the lift."

"Your loss."

He smiled as if he'd done his good deed for the night. I was certainly glad he didn't get to do the deed he'd first had on his mind. This was typical. I hardly had any friends, certainly not a boyfriend, and the one guy who was interested in me was a creepy old dude nearly twice my age. Just my luck.

I closed the door of the truck behind me and Russell took off, presumably heading for home. As I walked toward the corner, the unmistakable smell of cigarette smoke hit my nostrils. My gut clenched immediately.

I knew. Before I even looked up the street, I knew.

Outside the Johnsons' house, the end of a cigarette glowed orange, then faded as the cigarette was lowered. It was a beacon, a tiny distinct signal, a warning sign.

I could make out the short, messy dreadlocks in the dim light clearly enough too. Slowly the rest of the picture came into focus.

I knew danger when I saw it.

And there he was.

The guy in the hoodie.

CHAPTER SIX

The Primary

Remy and I are in a back room of the Arena before the tournament. The walls and floor are concrete and it feels like that's what's in my stomach. Concrete.

I spent last night in Sasha Rodriguez's room and right now, I'm grateful for the small amount of sleep I had because I'm going to need my wits about me.

Remy sits on a chair opposite me, winding on my hand wraps to make sure the job is done properly. I've plaited my dark hair into a full crown braid in readiness for the fight, just as Remy told me to. I'm wearing martial arts shorts and a fitted sleeveless tee shirt which show off my muscular physique. I look the part. It's something, at least.

"You can do this, Rodriguez," he says.

I'm not Sasha Rodriguez. I never have been. I'm Sasha Pierce, a schoolgirl from Middleton and I'm stuck in a nightmare. It's not even my nightmare. It's someone else's. No wonder my heart is racing, my skin sweaty.

Remy has been so kind to me that I don't have the heart to say any of that to him. He wouldn't believe it anyway. Besides, it'd be the world's worst timing to tell him now.

A blond girl about my age heads toward us, threading her way past two guys shadow boxing and a young girl in a bright costume who appears to be a circus performer limbering up. I've given up trying to work out what kind of tournament this is or what's going on.

The blond girl smiles and waves so I smile back rather self-consciously. She's dressed in what appears to be the unofficial uniform around here, black pants, sneakers and a tee shirt, her hair pulled back into a ponytail.

I lean closer to Remy. "Who's that?"

He crouches in front of me. "Bridget Simpson. She's your best friend. Play along with this. Don't let on about your memory."

I glare at him. "You just said she's my best friend."

"You two had a falling out. I don't know what went on but I'm surprised she's even here. It's not safe to tell her."

Remy stands and turns, hands on his hips, looking casual. "Bridget, I wasn't expecting to see you here. How'd you get in?"

She shrugs. "The usual way. I was cleared for entry."

In an ocean of people who are all pumped for the tournament, practicing their moves, talking each other up, her calmness stands out. I could use some of her reserve.

"I'm here for Sasha," she says. "I thought you'd be pleased to see me, Remy."

Calm and confrontational, now that's quite a combination.

"It's not that," he replies. "We're trying to focus for the fight."

"That's why I'm here too." She crouches in front of me, her hands covering mine, her forearms resting on my legs. "You've got to relax, Sasha."

"I know."

Every muscle in my body is tense. I'm so far from relaxed it's not funny.

She tilts her head higher and whispers in my ear, "I forgive you."

For what? What have I done?

"Remy's right," she adds more loudly. "You've got to focus, go in there and show them what you're made of, give it everything you've got. You can't think about anything else."

I nod. "Thanks, Bridget."

"This is for your country." She pauses. "And yourself."

She gives my hand a squeeze, turns and leaves. Meanwhile my insides twist into a knot. I have friends here, people who are behind me, willing to go out of their way to wish me luck, and somehow that's the saddest thing of all. Even when I had friends back home, no one was willing to bend over backwards for me.

Remy slips on the pads and motions for me to move to one side and warm up. I punch the pads. I kick them. Panic shoots through me because I'm supposed to do that to another person.

His eyes hood over. "Now I want you to hit the pads like you mean it."

This time, I smash them. I go with the flow and let the kickboxer within take over. Because if I don't, I'll end up battered and bruised and maybe worse.

"You're a warrior, Sasha," Remy says.

"I know I worry too much but you can't blame me."

He laughs. "No, you're a *warrior*. You've done it harder

than me. I've got a family back in The Ghettolands. You don't. You've always been on your own and fought for everything you've got."

"You told me I had a little brother."

"Don't even think about Joey," he says. "This isn't the time. Right now, winning is the only thing that matters."

A muscle in Remy's jaw flinches. He's keeping something from me. My gut cramps up.

"This isn't a fight to the death, is it?" Dread fills my stomach. "It can't be."

"No." He slips off the pads. "The referee will stop it before it gets to that stage."

"So I won't get hurt?"

Remy's lips go thin. "You'll get hurt, all right. That's the whole point. That's what makes it a spectacle."

My heart races. "But the ref will stop it?"

"Yes, only he'll be outside the cage."

Nausea rises to my throat, my pulse races and my skin goes clammy. I know the symptoms of a panic attack better than most. *No way, not now.* I count to five and breathe in slowly.

My body is shaking with fear, my head spinning, but I can't let myself fall apart. I don't want to get hurt. Don't want to die. Desperation drips from me. A desperate desire to live.

I have to save something for the cage. This is for Remy, for me, for Sasha. I owe it to her to take care of her body.

Still, I can't believe any of this is happening. I'm not sure what's real any more, only that I have to follow my gut.

"What's the point of having a ref if he's not in there

with us?" I ask, surprised at how calm I sound.

Remy grips my shoulders. "One of you will get beaten and battered. Make sure it's not you. Close your eyes."

"What?"

"Do it." I obey and Remy starts talking to me, pumping me up for the event. "Pummel him. Hammer him. He's not better than you. He's bigger and he'll take advantage of it. So make him pay. Hit him back. Hit him harder."

Easier said than done.

The next minutes go by in a blur. Officials come in and we follow them into the stadium. I don't know how many people are there and I don't care. I'm frisked and checked and prodded, Remy at my side, while I stare into the black octagonal cage where my opponent paces the floor looking very much the part of The Monster, the dagger tattooed on his back a message especially for me.

Blood pumps to my muscles. My stomach churns. But for once in my life, I don't feel like I'm about to fall apart. I feel pumped. I'm scared, yes. I'd be stupid not to be.

Use the fear.

Make it work for you.

It's so clear to me. I know what I have to do. What Sasha Rodriguez would do. I become someone else. I become her.

Someone leads me into the cage. It's the referee, a man about the same size as my opponent. He closes the door of the cage behind him as he leaves. Through the throng of the crowd, I hear a soft tinkle as it latches shut, a small sound for such a big moment.

Then my world shifts into slow motion. The cage suddenly feels like exactly what it is. A cage.

A voice comes over a loudspeaker. I make out the words, "The President will now address the crowd." A spotlight shines on a group of men in suits in a VIP box in the audience.

One man stands to acknowledge the audience. The President, I presume. Someone hands him a microphone and the crowd goes quiet.

He gives a short speech and at the ends says, "Country above all else."

His words don't make sense to me yet the crowd applauds. They seem to approve.

I stare across the cage at my opponent as he storms from one end to the other, then back again, the floor reverberating with each step. He's so huge his arms don't brush against the side of his body as he paces.

Yet inside I feel strangely calm. Sasha feels calm. The calm before the storm.

More announcements, more words spoken that don't make sense. Then the crowd goes quiet and I know what's coming.

Blood rushes to my muscles. I feel the power inside me. *You're a fighter. You can do this.*

As The Monster steps closer, I take up a fighting stance and wait for the bell to signal the start of the fight.

He swings at me wildly and I slip out of the way. That's when I finally hear the bell. The fight hasn't officially started yet and already he's broken the rules. An enormous "Ooh" rises from the crowd. Anger burns inside me.

The Monster sends in a straight left hand. I shuffle out of his way. Two more shots follow. If this didn't feel real before, it sure as hell does now. I cover but even through my guard, the punches hurt as they pound against my head.

I slip out of his way. He's bigger than me but I'm fast.

The crowd is going crazy, chanting something, I can't make out what.

I kick The Monster in the thigh, surprised I can do it. His lips curl to a smarmy grin. I kick him again. My heart is racing so fast it lurches in my chest.

He lunges at me so I slip out of the way again. A sneer on his face, he comes at me, his punches big and fast and hard. I smell his sweat. My forehead throbs. So does my ear. Blood drips onto the floor. I don't know what's going on.

Hit him back.

His hands are down. I land a big right hand on his jaw. And it rocks him.

A roar rises from the crowd.

Hit him again. I kick him in the thigh. Chop, chop, cutting into it like a tree. He stumbles back, wobbles. Blood sprays to the floor. Where is it coming from?

Suddenly, it's not him I'm kicking any more. It's every kid who's ever taunted me. It's that man who did those things to me. It's that woman who beat me up. It's every bad thing that has ever happened in the world.

I kick The Monster again. In the ribs this time. I hear a crack. The sound sends my heart rocketing.

He hunches over. I press a hand to the side of my head, feel something sticky and look at the blood on my hand. A big mistake. I shouldn't have waited. I should've gone in for the kill because that's what The Monster is about to do.

He lunges at me, takes me to the ground. His weight is

on top of me, my chest crushed. I roll. Go with the flow. I'm on top. His arm is free so I grab it, get him in an arm bar, a submission. I have him now.

The crack of bone fills the air. I'm sure I've broken his arm but still he won't tap.

"Bitch," he yells.

I am that and so much more.

Power surges inside me. I'm going to win. Back home, I'd been taunted, blackmailed, taken for granted. I'm not that girl any more.

Today, I'm going to win.

I can't force this guy to give up but I can do something else. I spin around until I have his back. I'll choke him out.

I wrap my right arm under his chin across his throat, my legs around his body to control him. He's big and sweaty but I have time on my side. He isn't going anywhere. I hold onto my left shoulder with my right hand, push my other hand onto the top of his head, and squeeze. Remy showed me this yesterday, the rear naked choke, and I'm a quick learner.

The big guy goes limp, suddenly even heavier in my arms. He's out cold. I hold on a little longer to make sure he stays down.

As I get to my feet, over the roar of applause, the crowd starts chanting my name. *Sasha, Sasha.*

I glance at the cage door, still locked. I'm not waiting for anyone. I run to the wall of the cage, hoist myself up and jump to the other side. Remy is ready for me, and presses a towel to one side of my head.

Inside the cage, The Monster groans and rolls over.

Outside the cage, the referee grabs my arm and raises it in the air. Where was he when I'd needed him?

My towel falls to the ground. It's covered in red stains. I must be bleeding. That was why Remy pressed the towel to my head.

Meanwhile the crowd is on their feet, their arms in the air, yelling and screaming. I don't get it. I'm not a hero. This isn't entertainment. This is my life, my wellbeing, and I didn't choose to be here.

The next thing I know I'm sitting in the same room at the back of the stadium, only this time I'm surrounded by people.

Remy is there. He's always there.

A medic shines a light into my eyes, then examines my head and asks dumb questions about whether any parts of my body hurt. All of me hurts. Can't he work that out? What sort of doctor is he?

The liquid he swabs onto my scalp stings so I figure it must be antiseptic.

"You won't need stitches," he says, and leaves.

"Yeah, the other guy needs you more," someone yells at the doctor.

People around me laugh.

A girl my age crouches in front of me. "Sasha, you were sensational in there."

I wonder if I know her.

A guy behind her adds, "We knew you could do it."

Then the small crowd parts to make way as General Mason strides forward. The people around me nod acknowledgment and step back. Mason stops at my side and looks around. He doesn't need to say a word. The crowd disperses.

He presses my hair back on the side that's not covered in blood and leans closer. "I'm glad you've come around."

To what? If only these people would spell it all out to me.

"I won." My shoulders slumped, I look up at him. "I've done what you wanted. Can I go home now? Please. Can you send me back?"

He frowns. "Sasha?"

Remy puts a hand on my shoulder. "She got knocked around and doesn't know what she's saying."

Mason nods, holds my gaze. "You did well tonight. The President himself was impressed. He'll remember you. That's really something."

The words are meant to inspire me but I feel nothing. The President might remember me but that doesn't mean he'll do anything to help me. He sat and watched a teenage girl pitted against a guy twice her size. He's not the solution. He's part of the problem.

Mason curls his fingers in a fist. "Country above all else."

But I wasn't fighting for my country. I was fighting for my life. Can't he see that?

"Sasha, we all know how ambitious you are, how talented, and how hard you train. Tonight, you made me proud. I couldn't be more proud if I was your own father."

I don't have one of those back home, or here for that matter, and I'm not convinced Mason is on my side. Something about him reminds me of my mom and the way she only boasts about my achievements in front of other people.

"I taught you well." He turns to Remy. "You too. You're becoming an excellent teacher."

I sit there in a daze until Mason leaves, then Remy tells me to have a shower. There are a couple of other women in the locker room and, though they talk to me, I don't understand what they're saying. While I'm in the shower, the pain starts to set in, the cuts on my face stinging, my ribs aching, heart sinking.

Afterwards, we head for the accommodation quarters where I spent last night in Sasha Rodriguez's room which is now my room. Though I desperately need a good night's sleep, the thought of that room sends a shudder up my spine.

The problem is that after lying on the bed in a cold sweat for several hours last night, I actually got some sleep. And if I'd slept, then that means this whole situation can't be a bad dream. Because you can't have a dream where you go to sleep. They don't work that way.

So I'm not going to wake up and find this was all a dream. There's not going to be an easy way out.

Now the tournament is over, I have to think about what to do next. And to think straight, I'm going to need some sleep.

People are still spilling out of the arena, some of them heading for buses in a parking lot we'd passed, others staying on foot. Passers-by shake my hand and congratulate me as if I'm some sort of celebrity. It's like being in a bad dream.

I squeeze Remy's arm as we walk. "I don't want to go back just yet."

He takes me around the corner to a bench near the climbing wall I'd seen yesterday. It's quiet here. It has rained while we've been indoors and the smell of mulch rises from the grass beneath our feet, much more pleasant than the odor of hot wet pavement elsewhere.

He brushes water from the bench. "It's wet. Not much

we can do about that."

I've been squashed by a guy twice my size, punched in the head and bled all over the floor. I'm certainly not worried about getting my backside wet. I sit down and he joins me.

Remy stares at the sodden grass. "Must've been quite some storm that came through during the tournament."

"But this is summer, isn't it?"

He shrugs. "We have storms all year round. Bad ones. It's nothing unusual."

"Is that why all the buildings look like concrete bunkers?"

Remy frowns. "You say that like it's a bad thing."

"It makes the place look ugly. There's no greenery, no trees. Everything's gray."

"Those ugly, gray buildings are what keep us safe against the storms. Here, we don't need to worry. It's not like that back in The Ghettolands. Their houses are shacks compared to this. When a big storm comes through, a flood, a tornado, they're done for." He glances around. "These buildings have withstood everything nature has thrown at us."

Surely The Ghettolands must be better than this. The Primary feels like a prison. Primary. Prison. The words aren't that different.

Remy isn't like the guys I know back home.

"How did you get to be so level-headed?" I ask. "So mature."

Even in the dim light, his teeth shine white as he grins. "We're not that different, you and I. We're both smart. We both know where we came from and we don't want to go back. It all comes down to survival."

71

I haven't been so good at that back home. I struggled terribly. It had been as much as I could do just to get by, yet still I want to get back home.

Maybe it's time to tell Remy the truth, that I've somehow been thrown into Sasha Rodriguez's body, that I haven't lost my memory. Maybe he'll help me or maybe he'll have me thrown into a mental institution. It's a risk I have to take because I can't do this any more.

"Now the tournament's over, things can get back to normal," I say.

Whatever normal is.

"No," he says.

"I haven't been up front with you."

Remy's face turns scarily serious. "Neither have I. There's one more thing you have to do. It's not over yet."

He takes my hand into his. Though his skin is cool, his pulse is racing beneath his wrist.

"You have to prove nothing is more important to you than your country," he says.

"Why?"

"After that, our superior officers know they can trust you with anything. You have to kill for your country." The look on his face tells me he's not kidding. "Not just anyone. Someone very close to you. After that, you're a full member of The Primary. There's no turning back. It's just the way it is."

His words don't sink in. It feels like I'm floating in the air, looking down on the two of us from above. This isn't my life. I can't possibly be here.

"Who on earth am I supposed to kill?" I ask.

"Joey," he says.

"My little brother?"

Remy nods.

The words are a punch in my gut. I hunch over. Try to think. I tell myself I'm hallucinating, that this isn't real and my brother doesn't really exist.

But I'm real and I'm horrified.

I'm not going to be able to do something like that. No way. They might as well just shoot me now.

Somehow I have done this to myself. I know how I got here even if I don't want to face it. And now I have to get away, get back home.

No excuses.

CHAPTER SEVEN

Middleton

You're always scared, that's what my mother said.

I had reason to be.

My heart thudded in my chest – it had been doing that a lot lately – as I dropped down behind a bush in a neighbor's front yard and stayed still for a few moments. I couldn't hear anything, no footsteps, only the gentle rustle of the wind, and the smell of cigarette smoke seemed to be fading.

I stuck my head around the bush to take a look. The guy in the hoodie was still there. He must've finished his cigarette because his hands were in his pockets.

Was it safe? Would I ever be safe?

I slowly stood and walked backwards, grateful at how quiet my Chuck Taylors were. When Mr. Hoodie was out of view, I turned and sped up, heading for the house that backed onto ours. As soon as I hit the corner, I ran.

I slowed down to creep along the side path of my rear neighbor's house, feeling very much like a thief or a cat burglar. That was always the way. I felt bad or guilty while the people who pushed me around felt as if they were doing the world a favor.

I knew the people who lived in this house, knew they were decent people, that they'd help me. I also knew the guy in the hoodie would be gone by the time we did anything and then Mom would lose it big-time because I'd bothered the neighbors over nothing. Because that's what I was. Nothing.

Much better to take care of this myself.

At the back of the neighbor's garden, I got a footing on a low tree branch and hoisted myself over the fence. Though hardly a gymnast, I could do it. I used my key to get into the house, opening the back door as quietly as I could, then took off my shoes for extra stealth.

Ducking my head into the living room, I saw Mom had fallen asleep on the sofa, a cushion tucked under her head, her feet up on the coffee table. She looked so serene that I felt a pang for being so hard on her. Tiptoeing across, I placed a gentle kiss on her forehead. She smelt like soap and hand cream.

Mom was right. I was too soft. I was weak, all things I couldn't help.

I crept out of the room, something I was getting good at. In the kitchen, I searched for something resembling a proper meal and couldn't believe it when I saw a bowl of spaghetti that practically had my name on it in the fridge. Dinner was looking good after all.

I grabbed a fork to give the pasta a quick mix before popping it in the microwave, only for the cutlery to slip from my fingers and clatter onto the tiles. I flinched, waited a few moments, scared I might have woken Mom up.

"Darling, is that you?" she called out from the other

room.

Darling? When I had I become darling?

"Yes, Mom," I said. "Sorry about the noise."

"No problem." She appeared in the doorway. Her dark blond hair was mussed up and her glasses had slid down her nose.

I closed the door of the microwave and pressed the timer for two minutes. "I was just heating up dinner. Thanks for the pasta."

"You've been on your feet all night, Sasha." Mom put her hand on my shoulder and ushered me towards a seat at the kitchen table. "Sit down. You must be exhausted."

I was, though I'd long ago learnt that made no difference. Mom was always more tired, in more pain, had bigger problems. Whatever happened to me, she had something worse going on in her life.

I slid onto a chair, too nervous to make the most of her current good mood. One false move could set Mom off. I'd seen that happen many times before.

"Would you like some Italian bread with your spaghetti?" she asked, a lilt in her voice.

"Sure," I said. "I mean, yes please."

Mom busied herself in the kitchen. "How was work, darling?"

Darling again. Still, that didn't mean I could tell her about my stalker, or anything else.

After the principal had told her about the eraser with the suicide note wrapped around it, she'd been concerned and motherly. Briefly. Then she'd wanted to know how that could've happened and what I'd done to bring it upon myself. As if it'd been my fault. She couldn't see how making those accusations cancelled out her earlier concern or how it made me feel.

"Work was pretty boring as usual," I said.

"Unfortunately working in a supermarket is going to be dull, maybe more than a bit boring. It makes for very good life experience if only to show you what you don't want to do." She placed a plate and a glass of water in front of me. "Here's your bread, honey."

From darling to honey. What was going on?

I looked down at the plate in front of me. Mom had buttered my bread for me. She'd even cut it in half the way I used to like when I was a kid. Such a sweet touch yet it only made me sad.

The microwave pinged and I put my hands on the table ready to stand. Mom looked at me with brown eyes that were so familiar. We had the same eyes.

"Don't be silly," she said. "I'll get it for you."

Too scared to move in case I broke the spell, I stayed and waited to be served.

Mom sat down beside me, her elbows resting on the table. "How are things going at school? I've been so busy I've barely had a chance to ask."

If she thought it was time for the mother-daughter-deep-and-meaningful-discussion, she was mistaken. Not after all the times I'd tried before. I couldn't switch on the deep feelings and communication like a faucet. It didn't work that way.

"Do you still have those two new friends, Alec and Penny?" she asked.

"Yeah, we hang together every lunchtime." I shoved in another mouthful of spaghetti.

"I'm glad you've got friends."

So was I.

Mom leaned forward. "That boy, Alec Hooper, he's just a friend, isn't he?"

Always so suspicious. Would it be so bad if I had a boyfriend, if a guy was interested in me that way? Not Alec, obviously, but someone else.

"We're friends, Mom." I tried to hide the annoyance from my voice.

She shrugged. "Boys won't go for you anyway."

I stopped chewing, mid-mouthful. How could she say something like that to her own daughter? She couldn't help herself. Even when she was in a good mood like this evening, she had to drag me down.

Mom added, "After what happened with that boy at your old school, I thought you'd know better by now."

I'd had a boyfriend for all of about five minutes, until he announced in front of half a dozen people that he was dumping me. Adam hadn't done it in front of the whole school. It had only felt that way. I felt it now, the despair, the anguish, the embarrassment.

Spaghetti got stuck in my throat so I washed it down with a mouthful of water.

Mom pushed the bridge of her glasses up. "Surely you can find some other friends."

Like who? Had she forgotten the problems at my old school, the reason I'd left.

"There must be other kids other than that oversized stick insect," she added.

My jaw tight, I stopped eating and clenched my fist under the table. She always knew exactly how to get to me. I couldn't win – I knew that – and I also couldn't stop myself.

"Alec is a very good student," I said. "He wants to get

into law school. He got a scholarship too, you know. Gets top marks in all his classes."

Mom looked down her nose at me, a superior smile on her face. "Better than you?"

My shoulders tensed instantly. "Not better, just different. We both study, work hard, try our hardest."

Mom leaned back, her expression relaxed once again. I was off the hook. For now.

"You know you can talk to me about anything," she said.

I shrugged. "Sure."

"It's one thing to have friends but they won't look after you the way I do."

"Won't they?"

Mom got louder. "Sometimes you don't know anything. You're so naïve. Clueless. Other people care primarily about themselves. You can only trust friends to a point and then they'll let you down." Shouting now, she jabbed a finger at her chest. "I'm the only one you can trust. I'm your best friend. Your friends at school are just for company, you know that, don't you?"

"Y-yeah."

I couldn't disagree. That'd be asking for trouble. I grabbed my dirty dishes and placed them on the sink, couldn't wait to get out of there.

"Don't worry yourself with that, Sasha." Mom stood, quieter again. "I'll take care of the cleaning up. You can do your homework, or rest, or whatever you like. It's up to you."

I headed for the door. "Thanks, Mom."

The walk down the hallway to my bedroom was a long one. I closed the door behind me, dropped down onto the bed and hugged my arms around my waist.

Even when Mom was in a good mood, even when she was trying to help, she could turn. She never made things easier.

She was my best friend – was that for real? The only thing I could trust about my mother was that she could explode at any time. I wanted to kick something or scream or turn the stereo up loud.

I was screaming on the inside. Couldn't anybody hear me?

Brody. He'd listen. I rolled off the bed, sat at my desk and opened my laptop, hoping like hell he was online tonight, waiting for me, because he was the one thing in my life that kept me going.

I was in luck. He was on FacePlace and we could message each other which was far nicer than a long-winded email where I ended up complaining more than I should. Our communication was always better when he was online.

Somehow, I managed to get long-winded anyway. I told him about what had happened tonight with my stalker.

Brody wrote:

– *I'm a bit worried about this guy who's following you. This could get serious.*

I could type extremely quickly and shot back:

– *What am I supposed to do?*

– *You need to tell someone, someone who's not a teenager, someone who'll believe you.*

– *I can't do that. My mom will find out and that's the last thing I want. You know what she's like. And she didn't believe me when I told her he was lurking outside that morning. She's not going to believe me now either.*

— Then make her believe you. Maybe not tonight, but you need to keep a diary of what's going on. Write it down so you've got a formal record. Take photos on your phone if you can. Alert anyone who's nearby and use them as a witness.

— Like my boss, Russell, you mean?

— He sounds too sleazy for my liking but, yes, that's the sort of thing I mean. You should stay away from guys like him.

Brody was starting to sound like my mother and that was not a good thing. I shot back:

— I didn't have much choice. It's not as if I'd want to get it on with some older guy, especially not him.

A reply came back a few moments later:

— Sorry if I'm giving you a hard time about Russell. You're not the only one who finds it upsetting.

Sometimes Brody didn't sound like the other boys I knew. Even Alec was an airhead in comparison to Brody who always seemed to know the right thing to say and do.

I wrote:

— How do you know all this stuff about keeping records and witnesses?

— Maybe I watch too many crime shows on television. I've got enough time on my hands!

I didn't want to remind Brody of why he was home-schooled and stuck in his house all the time. I wanted to make him feel better, the way he did for me.

— I'm glad you're there to help me, Brody. I don't know what I'd do without you.

— Same here! You're my eyes and ears, my window into the world.

— You've got other friends though. You're not alone. You've probably got more friends than me.

I'd checked out his FacePlace page ages ago and Brody had friends at Morton as well as Southern Hills and plenty more too, even if he didn't have many face-to-face friends. He was the cousin of a girl at my old school, or at least I thought that was how I'd met him.

He wrote back:

— *My other friends aren't like you. You tell me about what you're doing and the other kids and what it's like at school. It means so much to me. You help me live…*

That dot, dot, dot at the end, that ellipsis, broke my heart. Brody had problems that made mine look like nothing. I had my health. I should remember how lucky I was.

He wrote:

— *Are you still there?*

— *Yes, I'd never run away from you.*

— *Phew! I can't let you go on such a negative note. We should always finish our conversations in a good way so we're both looking forward to the next time. Anything else going on at school?*

So I gave him the usual gossip, told him how Madison and Aisha had been bitchy and how Penny and Alec had argued.

I didn't mention anything about Domenic Simms, the kid who'd committed suicide though he'd kept coming to mind over the past few weeks.

Besides, I didn't want to drag Brody down. He deserved better and was always aching to hear about how things were going at school and home and with other kids. He loved it. All this everyday stuff, the boring details, Brody found it fascinating. Either that or he was exceptionally polite.

He wrote:

– *We've had a few warm days. Have you been swimming lately?*

– *No, I don't go very often.*

– *I used to love to swim.*

– *Do you still go swimming?*

– *No, I had a bad experience.*

– *Can I ask what happened?*

– *The scars on my chest are pretty unsightly and a couple of people freaked out when they saw me. I didn't want to go back again. To that swimming pool or any other. I don't really want to talk about it.*

Wow. And I thought my life was bad. Sometimes I could relate so well to the things Brody said.

I typed:

– *Sorry for being so pushy.*

– *You're not pushy. You're perfect.*

– *No, I'm not. That's silly.*

– *Sounds like you're modest too.*

– *Now you're the one being silly.*

At times like this, I felt close to Brody. I liked the gentle banter between us, the teasing, the ease with which we communicated. He understood me better than anyone else. He wasn't judgmental like Penny or immature like Alec.

It was a couple of minutes before Brody typed back. Maybe he was thinking the same thing as me.

– *Do you have any photos you can send me?*

– *Of what? I've already posted plenty of pics on FacePlace.*

– *Do you have any pictures of you at the beach or at a swimming pool? Maybe you've got some shots of you mucking around with your friends or posing by the poolside. I bet you look good.*

"What friends?" I said out loud.

But I did have some photos taken last summer. It was

after I'd left Southern Hills High and my life had been at an all-time low. Absolutely no chance of going to the pool or anywhere else with friends. I'd gone swimming on my own and there'd been a couple of Japanese tourists taking photos of each other. I'd offered to take a group shot of them and a young girl who spoke English had taken a few photos of me in my bikini.

Besides, I kind of liked that Brody was asking. It wasn't often I felt wanted.

— I have some pics taken by the pool on my phone.

— Fantastic!!

— Okay, hold on.

Damn it. A pang of sadness shot through me as I flicked through the images on my phone. I looked lovely in those pictures, certainly every bit as good as the other girls at school. I'm smiling and seem happy. On the outside at least.

I emailed them to Brody because I didn't want to post them on FacePlace for the world to see. Lots of girls did that, took selfies in their underwear or sometimes partially out of it, and put them up. The same girls thought I was a loser. At least I had a brain.

Brody wrote back:

— You look amazing! I knew you would.

— I haven't shown these photos to anyone. I left them on my computer. Besides, I don't like showing off.

— You know the old saying. If you've got it, flaunt it.

I wasn't sure what to say to that so I dithered over the keyboard.

Brody wrote:

— I hope I don't sound too much like a horny teenager. It's just that you look really nice in the photos and I can't go to the pool. I

don't go out much at all so it's good to see the sun shining and all the people in the background. It makes me feel like I'm part of something.

For once I knew exactly the right thing to say:

— *You are part of something. You're part of my life.*

— *It means a lot that you shared those photos with me. It makes them even more special. We'll talk again tomorrow.*

— *Definitely. I'm looking forward to it.*

Brody didn't need to worry about sounding horny. If I'd had the same conversation with Alec, his eyes would have gone wide and he'd have started salivating.

I flopped back onto my bed. I'd be able to sleep tonight. I could put the guy in the hoodie to the back of my mind.

Brody was so right.

Much better to finish on a high note.

CHAPTER EIGHT

The Primary

Maybe I'm in a coma.

That wouldn't be so weird. People have accidents; they end up in comas; doctors can't understand everything that goes on. Some things are a mystery even to medical experts.

Then I'd be alive in a hospital room in Middleton, waiting to be awoken and whisked away from this alternate universe, if that's what this place is.

Remy and I are on a train heading for The Ghettolands where we'll be staying with his family. After the stress of the tournament, he organized this short break partly so I can meet my little brother – though I don't know why – and partly to get me away from The Primary into safer surroundings.

I'm here and I'm not. Disconnected. Floating. I'm hovering below the ceiling of the train carriage, looking down on myself and Remy who has been kind and let me have the window seat.

Except that's not really me. With her black hair and striking blue eyes, she doesn't even look like me. Sasha Rodriguez is stronger, more confident and capable, more everything than me.

I look out of the window as the world spins by. We're already passing along the edge of the city which looks, well, like a city. Tall buildings, traffic-clogged streets, people with take-out coffee cups on the pavement, groups of kids on their way to school. Something resembling normal.

"Not long till we're out of here," Remy says.

I stand up and open the emergency escape window just a crack though signs warn against it. I listen to car horns honking, engines revving, the bustle, the white noise, the life of a city. It feels familiar, comforting.

Except for the sudden rain that pelts down along with winds that make the sheets fall at a forty-five degree angle. The first enormous drop splashes on my cheek. Cold and wet, it startles me, brings me back down to Earth or whatever this place is. More drops. It's good to feel something.

I press the window shut. I've seen rain before but not like this. It has a will of its own as it slams down onto the buildings outside and people take cover. Meanwhile Remy sits beside me, completely unfazed.

After a while, we're out of the city and he nudges me. "We're passing through one of the estates."

"Is that supposed to mean something to me?" I ask.

"It's where we'll end up living."

I screw up my face. "We'll end up living together?"

"I meant that people like you and me get to live here

or in another place that looks pretty much like this." He points out of the window. "This is luxury."

I stare at the concrete bunkers, some with shuttered windows, all with flat concrete roofs. They look like oversized public toilet blocks and that's the level of ambience they exude. This is not exactly material for lifestyles of the rich and famous.

I glance at Remy, then back out of the window. "What's so good about this place?"

"It's safe," he says. "Secure. These buildings will withstand anything nature throws at us, any storm, tornado or atmospheric turbulence."

"What about an earthquake?"

"That's how we lost LA."

His tone is so matter of fact it makes the hair on the back of my neck stand on end.

"What do you mean we lost LA?"

"The city was wiped out in a massive earthquake." He raises his eyebrows. "You can't remember?"

"What about San Francisco?"

"Seismic activity has settled down there and everywhere else since the big quake."

Another thing I don't know about. I bite my lip, not sure if I should ask about this big quake.

He sighs. "You seemed a bit freaked back at The Primary but it's the best place to be. Safer, more opportunities, a chance at a better life."

Even though I couldn't let on any weakness on my part? Even though I was forced to fight a monster?

"Didn't seem that way to me," I snap back.

"You don't get it. When you're a full member of The Primary, you can live in one of these houses and you get taken care of. You need to work, of course. We all do. But you don't have to worry about money or feeding your family or paying for schools and education. Everything is taken care of. This is the pinnacle of success. It's what most people strive for."

I stare out of the window and wonder why I'd need to worry about feeding my family. Besides, the view outside doesn't look like the pinnacle of anything, though at least they have more trees out here and most of the houses have small gardens. Surprising what a difference a little bit of greenery makes.

"It looks nicer than The Primary," I say.

After the train passes through the estate, our surroundings become more barren. Undulating hills are covered in patches of dried grass and dirt with the occasional copse of trees for light relief, the ground brown and dry and dusty. It looks as if the moisture and life has been sucked out of it. I don't see any animals. What creature would want to live here?

"The Desundra," Remy says.

I don't bother asking any questions, though I wonder how it can be so dry here when not far away the rains have been almost flood-like. I'll work it out in due course. Or not.

With each minute that passes, we're getting further away from The Primary and that's the only thing that matters. Getting out of there. Finding a better place because anywhere has to be better than The Primary.

Dread settles in my stomach. I won't be able to survive at The Primary. It's only a matter of time until someone works out I'm a fake and then I'll probably end up facing incarceration or some terrible punishment or a mental institution. Or perhaps elimination, as Remy fears.

But I'm fooling myself that finding a hiding place will help because I can't escape the locator tattoo and can't cut it out when it takes up my entire midriff.

The landscape changes again. Bit by bit, there are more trees, forests even, with lush undergrowth. The sun has come out, the sky a charming bright lavender color. The occasional rabbit hops along the ground.

I reach for Remy's arm. "Look, a deer. Did you see it?"

A smile on his face and warmth in his blue eyes. "Yeah, I caught a glimpse."

"Funny how seeing something like that can make you feel good."

"I didn't take you for a nature lover."

I nudge him in the ribs. "You liked seeing the deer too. You can't deny it, not with that look on your face."

"Okay, you got me. There's no need for anyone else to know about this. Anyway, we're nearly there."

Standing, he reaches for my backpack on the shelf above us and hands it to me.

"A gentleman, too," I say.

He slings his pack over one shoulder. "Yet another thing no one else needs to know."

As soon as we get off the train, the humidity hits me, air so thick it's like walking through soup. We make our way along the platform and people make way for us as if we're royalty. We're certainly not dressed like royalty. Both of us are wearing tee shirts, cargo pants and combat boots but, unlike the people around us, our clothes aren't rags.

This feels so different from The Primary, so different from anything I've seen before. Beggars line one wall, sitting on dirty blankets with hand-made cardboard signs beside them, shaking tin cans as they ask for money.

Someone bumps me in the hip and I look down to see an old man with no legs scooting along the concrete floor on a wooden cart with wheels beneath it. My gut tightens. I'm overcome by a desperate urge to help him but Remy reaches for my hand and pulls me along behind him.

In this place, his neat sandy hair and good looks stand out. He's a handsome specimen. Healthy too. That's the other thing that stands out. Compared to these other people, Remy is clearly a picture of health and good fortune. So am I, probably.

I have money with me, Sasha's money, and I wonder if I should give the beggars a few coins each or perhaps something more.

Remy ushers me forward toward the exit. "We can't help them."

He's right. Some coins might make their day easier but I don't have enough money to support them and make their lives better, not that this goes a long way to making me feel any better.

We didn't have to pay for the train and there are many other things we don't have to pay for too. Apparently that's how things work here. Others might beg but when you're a prime candidate at The Primary many things come free.

It's crowded outside. The sun shines through the clouds overhead and it's a relief to be away from the stale air thick with the sweat of human bodies inside the station. I glance down at a pool of stagnant water, mosquitos hovering over it, by my feet.

Looking up, I see a group of children playing a game using different colored rocks shaped into marbles. As soon as they see us, they jump to their feet and race toward us, their hands out as they crowd around. They're only kids. Yet desperate. My heart drops.

Remy digs into his pocket and hands out some coins. I do the same. The kids' faces light up. So does Remy's. My heart lifts a little.

I think about one little boy in particular and my gut clenches. Sasha's little brother Joey is probably like these kids. He's no doubt playing with his friends somewhere not far from here, oblivious to what's in store for him and how little his life will mean.

I still can't get it through my head that I'm supposed to sacrifice this little boy for The Primary. I wouldn't want to be in his shoes, not that I like being in Sasha's shoes either.

Remy and I turn to leave when a little girl tugs at his arm. Her clothes are dirty, brown eyes wide and clear against her olive skin. Wild curls have escaped from her dark ponytail.

"Sorry," Remy says. "I don't have any more change."

The girl's face falls. He tells her to hang on, then digs a chocolate bar out of his backpack and hands it to her.

"Thank you." Her voice is small but her smile is huge as she pulls two of her friends to the side to share the treat with them.

Remy strides ahead. "We've got to get out of here."

I rush to catch up. "I thought you said we couldn't help."

"We can't." He stops and turns to face me. "I couldn't walk past those kids. I used to be one of them. My parents are doing much better now but there was a time we were so poor there wasn't enough food to go round." The look on his face tells me he's not kidding. He starts walking and adds, "I'll show you something."

We head towards a small bus depot.

"Is this it?" I ask.

"No," Remy says. "Just a little further."

We're at the top of a ridge now, looking down a hill into a valley and across to another hillside. Roads wind their way up and across the hills. Houses cover every available square foot, except I've never seen houses like this before. They look like they've been pasted onto the hillside and could fall down at any minute. A few buildings appear to be brick. The rest are covered in sheets of pressed tin, wooden boards, other random materials.

The sun is about to set, the sky turning deep purple against the pale clouds, yet that's not enough to improve the scene in front of us.

Suddenly I can see the appeal of the concrete bunkers of The Primary and the estate we'd passed through.

Remy sweeps his arm across. "That's where we come from, you and I. That's what we're trying to get away from."

"You can't change where you come from," I say. "It's part of you."

I know that all too well. I'm a scholarship student from Middleton. I can never be brave and strong like Sasha Rodriguez.

"No," Remy says. "But you can see why we didn't want to stay."

I can.

I'm starting to understand what he means and where he's coming from. Starting to see things from Sasha's point of view too. Being in another person's body will do that to you.

The strangest feeling washes over me, one that's hard to explain, and staring at the sweeping townscape in front of me intensifies the emotion. It's not respect exactly. Perhaps it's closer to compassion. It's part-way between emotion and knowledge. A realization.

I have to take care of Sasha's body.

And do the best by her.

CHAPTER NINE

"From here, we can take the bus or we can walk," Remy says.

"Walk," I reply.

If I'm going to survive here, I need to get a feel for the place and better understand my surroundings. Besides, I'm starting to see there are people a lot worse off than me.

We make our way along a rutted path by the side of a road that winds along the hillside. The cars and trucks that pass are old and battered, however most of the traffic is bicycles, scooters and motorbikes. No helmets. Clearly they don't matter. No guardrails by the side of the road either, though the drop is abrupt.

On the other side of the valley, a steep area bereft of houses stands out like a bald patch on a head of thick hair. Further below, a pile of rubble sits near the bottom of the hill.

I open my mouth to ask about this but Remy gives a curt shake of his head. I can work out what has happened. One of the infamous storms must've come through and that wreckage is where houses have slid off the hillside. People had lived there. Probably died there.

We keep going. There are no street names, no signs,

and that doesn't stand in Remy's way. The temperature is falling slightly so the humidity is more bearable. I also have a feeling dusk is the best time to see this place. It's not going to look any better in broad daylight.

After a while, we reach a small house in an enclave where the buildings are made of masonry and seem more substantial than the rest of the ramshackle construction. I wonder if this is the upmarket part of The Ghettolands.

"This is it," Remy says.

He grins from ear to ear, the smile reaching his eyes – so happy I didn't know he could look this overjoyed. He has spent so much time helping me that it hasn't occurred to me he might have a life outside The Primary, a life of his own.

I smile right back at him. "You're happy to be seeing your family?"

"Of course." He grabs me by the shoulders. "We usually make separate trips back home so my family has never met you before and don't know what the old Sasha was like. I'll tell them you're exhausted after the tournament, that you need to rest, and that you won't be talking much. They'll understand."

I am glad they will even though I don't.

Remy knocks on the door and pushes it open. Stepping inside, he drags me along behind him. The smell of freshly baking bread and roast lamb fills the air, makes me think maybe this place isn't going to be so bad after all.

A fine-boned woman who can't be more than five feet tall, probably Remy's mother, throws herself at him. Several others are crowded into the room, all waiting, and they wrap their arms around Remy so there's a giant human ball of hugging in front of me. A pang of jealousy shoots through me and, at the same time, I'm pleased for Remy because he is loved and that must be a wonderful feeling.

Eventually the various layers of people are peeled away and Remy introduces me to his family. He gets his coloring, the sandy hair and blue eyes, from his mother though not his height. That comes from his father, along with the high cheekbones and chiseled features. The height has also been passed along to Remy's two brothers, Sam who is younger and his older brother Alistair. There's a young woman there too, Remy's sister-in-law, along with several cousins, uncles and aunts.

After a while, the extended family leave and Freya, Remy's mother, serves a meal at the cramped table while everyone chatters. For some reason, I feel comfortable here. In fact, cramped has never felt so good.

Though this is a house, it's the size of a small apartment. While the other relatives were here, it was standing room only and it's not much better now. There's barely space to walk between the kitchen bench and the table where we're seated. A sofa sits on the other side.

I nod with appreciation. "This is delicious. There's nothing like warm bread straight from the oven. Home-made, no less."

Freya frowns. "What other kind is there?"

I don't know if they can buy – or afford – bread from the store, and this isn't the time to ask.

"No one cooks better than you, Mama," Remy says quickly.

She hides a shy smile. "I'm sure you get better food at The Primary."

"Nope, not like this. No one can cook like my mama."

"Actually you're a bit behind the times," his father says.

Remy looks up.

His dad is grinning. "Your mother made the bread but I cooked the rest of the meal."

"Thanks, Pop. I should have guessed. Roast was always your specialty but you didn't have to buy meat just because I was here. I know how expensive it is."

"We can all enjoy it." Freya adds quietly, "You know we couldn't get by without the money you send."

And I realize they don't eat meat every day, probably not often at all, and that the table laid with roast lamb, potatoes, vegetables is truly a feast for them. And as I look at the slender faces around me, I realize there's a reason they are all so lean.

These people are poor. Many more are hungry. This is why Remy and Sasha tried to get away from here. There's nothing here for them, no future, because it's clear to me Remy wasn't running away from this family who adore him.

After dinner, I help Remy's parents with the dishes. They have running hot water and electricity, which I suspect is more than some people around here. I've already been told they share a bathroom with neighbors.

We sit around the table while the family tells jokes and stories designed to embarrass Remy in front of me. His dad opens a couple of bottles of beer, freshly home-brewed, he proudly announces.

It's celebration time and we all have a glass, me included though I'm not particularly fond of the stuff. It seems there's no legal drinking age in The Ghettolands. Remy's little brother, Sam, helps himself as he skims the frothy head from his father's beer.

According to Remy, his family is lucky to have this house with two small bedrooms. His parents have one room and his brother and wife another, while Sam sleeps on the sofa. For the next few nights, the boy is bunking down in his parents' room so Remy and I can have the sofa bed.

We wait until the others have left because there's not enough room to open out the sofa while people are sitting at the table. We're alone, the sudden quiet disconcerting.

I let my hair loose, take off my boots and pants, thinking I'll sleep in my underwear and tee shirt. Remy does the same. I can't help but notice his chest is strong and muscled, his stomach flat and rippled, and his legs long.

As I sit down on the edge of the bed, I wonder if Remy is looking at me too, at this strong body that doesn't belong to me. I'm also aware of the size of my breasts. Sasha's breasts.

He stands in front of me, not at all self-conscious. "You seem a bit put out. Like you're used to better."

I don't know where to start – the poverty, the squalor, the warmth of his family – I'm not used to any of this.

"No, it's not that."

"You can always stay in a hotel if you like," Remy says. "There are a few near the station. You won't have to pay either because you're from The Primary."

"That's not what I meant." Then I ask him one of the many things I've been wondering. "How come you got out of The Ghettolands and your older brother, Alistair, is still here?"

Remy sits down beside me. "I was lucky."

There's more to it, I'm sure. "This isn't the sort of place where you get by on luck."

He shrugs. "Initially, I'd missed out on getting in to The Primary. I was second tier among the thirteen-year-olds. Then some kid got sick and pulled out so I took his place. Scraped in by the skin of my teeth. I'm not better than Alistair. Just more fortunate. I've been working my ass off to prove myself ever since."

Remy hadn't made the grade? That surprises me.

"You're not second best any more though," I say.

"I'm also not as strong as you, Sasha. You're the strongest person I know."

I shake my head. "No way."

"Tomorrow, we're going to see your family."

"What family?" I'm desperate to get out of this. "There's only Joey. He won't know any better if I don't go and see him."

"Word will get out. Someone will see you and tell your aunt. The Ghettolands may look big but this is the sort of place where everyone knows everyone else. Joey will be devastated if he doesn't see you."

"How would you know?"

"I've met him a couple of times," Remy says. "And I know what it's like to be a ten-year-old boy."

Time for the truth. My mouth falls open but the words don't come out. My insides quiver at the thought of meeting this innocent kid and the magnitude of the task ahead. The heartlessness of it.

And why? To prove my allegiance to country.

"I can't face Joey," I splutter.

Remy holds my gaze. "You have to."

My body shaking, I feel something is going to explode

inside me, one way or another. I throw my arms around Remy. It's not like me, I know, but Remy's family is so affectionate that it's contagious. And it feels good to be held by someone. It eases the weight from my shoulders. Makes me feel warm inside.

After a while, I pull back and Remy pushes my hair back behind my shoulder, this beautiful long black hair that's not really mine. His hand lingers, sending a shiver up my spine, a pleasant one.

If this were another boy and different circumstances, I'd probably be longing for his touch but the intimacy doesn't feel right. I'd be leading him on. Lying to him.

Maybe Remy feels the same way because he gets up and stands next to the light switch. "We'd better get to sleep."

I say goodnight and slide across to the other side of the bed so Remy doesn't have to climb over me. He gets into bed without touching me, not that I thought he would. I can work out that much about him.

Also, part of me senses that a guy like him wouldn't be interested in a loser like me, though I can certainly see why he'd go for Sasha Rodriguez, star student at The Primary, with her stunning looks, killer body and the brains to go with it.

I can't help but wonder why he's helping me.

What's in it for him?

CHAPTER TEN

Middleton

Two months ago…

No altercations with my mother in the morning. Maybe things were looking up. Hopefully that meant it was going to be a good day, or better at least.

Then Madison and Aisha stepped onto the bus. I should never have let myself get lulled into believing my life was anything less than crap. At times like this, I wished I could drive myself to school but Mom wouldn't let me get my license yet and I hadn't saved up enough for a car anyway.

The two girls spotted me right away, giggling as they ambled down the aisle. I could feel them looking at me as I stared down at the book in my lap. Sure enough, they stopped.

Madison swung her bag in front of my face to grab my attention. I saw it coming through the corner of my eye and had my hands up.

"We've got something for you," she said.

Behind her, Aisha held a magazine folded in half. The smarmy grin on her face told me she wasn't going to be sharing the latest fashions from *Vogue*.

"Hey, Mads," someone yelled, Finn perhaps. "We're down here."

Madison looked down her nose at me. "You'll keep."

Aisha stretched out her slender, dark arm to tap my head with the magazine. "It'll be such a special treat."

Somehow I doubted that. The two girls headed down the aisle.

I glanced back to see Finn Masters waving at them. He must've been the one who called out and he probably had no idea how he'd saved me. Or maybe he did.

When we reached school, I pushed my way to the front of the bus and made sure I was one of the first off. I wasn't stupid enough to wait for Madison and Aisha to catch up with me.

"Hey." Suddenly Finn Masters was walking alongside me. I looked around to see if he was talking to someone else but I was the only one nearby.

He grinned, his green eyes sparkling. "You're really funny."

I hadn't meant to be.

"Hey, Finn," I said.

"How's your job at the supermarket going?" he asked.

I couldn't believe it. He wanted to have a conversation.

"Oh, you know, just the usual. It's pretty boring but it's a job."

"You must know Josh then?"

"Yeah."

After a short silence, Finn asked, "Did you hear about

Ella's party? It's less than two weeks away."

I was hardly likely to be asked to a party held by one of the most popular girls at school. Surely he must know that.

I had a horrible feeling he was making fun of me and leading me on. I even wondered if Madison and Aisha might have egged him on to speak to me as part of some nasty trick. Then, maybe he was just talking to me.

The look on my face must've given me away because Finn said, "You and your friends should come. You don't need an invitation. Anyone can turn up."

"I'll see."

"Loads of people will be there. No one'll notice a few extra. Look, I've got to go. See you later."

He did have to go. A group of his friends was passing by, so clearly he had more important people to talk to. No hard feelings. That was simply how things worked. I watched the back of his blond head as he left.

Penny bumped into me, literally, her eBook reader in one hand, Alec on the other side.

"Whassup everybody?" he said in his usual Alec style.

Penny's brown eyes widened. "Oh my gosh, you were talking to Finn Masters."

"Sure," I said as if this happened every day.

"What did he say?"

"Nothing much." That part was true. "He mentioned a party at Ella's house."

"Yeah." Penny pushed her light brown hair behind her ears. "I'm interested but Alec's not sure it's worth going."

They'd been invited and I hadn't. My heart sank a little. Petty, I know. Well, I'd been invited now or as good as.

"Maybe we should all go," I said.

Alec glanced in the direction in which Finn and his friends had disappeared. "You can't trust a guy like Finn."

"We were only talking, Alec," I said.

"He's good friends with Madison and Aisha, you know."

I knew. "It's no big deal."

The reason Alec wasn't popular was because he always said the wrong thing, and that was exactly what I liked about him. The more I got to know him and found out about him, the more I admired him.

Penny gave me a gentle nudge. "Yep, I'd definitely say it was no big deal if a hot guy had been talking to me."

I couldn't help but smile. Her gentle teasing made me feel wanted, as if I was part of something, and with my two friends I *was* part of something. And Penny wasn't like Molly from my old school who would've been jealous.

"What about me?" Alec threw his hands up. "Don't I count?"

Penny rolled her eyes.

"Hot!" I reached across and touched Alec's arm, then pulled away, pretending my hand had been burnt. He shrugged it off but I could tell he'd liked it. I turned to Penny. "You're in a good mood."

"I'm reading *To Kill a Mockingbird* and loving it," she said.

"For English?"

"No, just because I want to. It's full of great quotes. Like that one about how *you never really understand a person until you consider things from his point of view.*"

We'd studied the book at school so I knew the line: *Until you climb into his skin and walk around in it.*

It had made an impact on me too because I'd

wondered if people like Madison and Aisha ever considered what it felt like from my point of view when they were making fun of me. I knew the answer – not for one nanosecond.

"Atticus Finch is my ideal man," Penny said dreamily.

"He's a fictional character," I said.

Alec stuck his head between us. "And he's really old too."

"You've read the book?" Shock in Penny's voice.

"Don't tell anyone," he replied.

The rest of the school day passed without any major hitches. In the morning, we had to write an essay in English as part of our assessment. The other kids complained as if this was a great tragedy whereas I knew there were many worse things. After what had happened in English last month, I was always a bit edgy in class in case someone might bring up the theme of suicide or pass me another nasty note. In comparison an essay was a piece of cake.

We had a science test last period which was also fine by me. This was school. We were supposed to have tests and assessments and feel stressed. Even though this was a private school with a good reputation and a scholarship program, it wasn't the done thing among the kids to ace every test and be freakishly smart. Like I was. It certainly didn't help in the popularity stakes.

At the end of the day, I found a seat on the middle of the school bus. Seconds later an eighth grader sat beside me.

He looked like he might have had even less friends than I did. We all took our school ties off at the first possible opportunity or at the very least, loosened them, but this kid still had his firmly secured. His shirt was also still tucked into his pants, which was also completely the wrong thing to do. Maybe it was mean but it made me feel a little better to know there were nerdier people than I was.

Madison and Aisha were yelling out from the back of the bus. They must've been absolutely hilarious because the deep laughter of the boys mixed with the high-pitched giggles of the girls around them. I couldn't work out why everyone else seemed to think they were so witty.

After a while, the group settled down and it was quieter. I had a bad feeling about it. Like the quiet before the storm.

Silence was followed by more noise as Madison and Aisha pushed past the other kids who were standing in the aisle to stand beside my seat.

Aisha leaned across the eighth-grader and said to me, "Hey, we've got something to show you."

I glanced up from my book. "Thanks but I'm not interested."

"Of course, you're too busy reading your *book*," she said. Somehow she made it sound like a swear word.

Madison shoved me in the shoulder. Her blond hair was in the face of the eighth-grader who brushed it from his nose and leaned back further in his seat.

I glared at Madison, wishing I could come up with the right words that would send her away. She and Aisha had something planned. My stomach tightened.

Madison gave the eighth-grader a shove. "Hey, can you move out of the way. We want to sit next to our *friend*."

"No," I said too quickly. "He was there first."

But the boy was already moving away. My heart dropped. I couldn't blame him.

I shifted across, ready to do the same when Aisha dropped down on the seat beside me. Faster than me. I didn't have a chance against someone like her. Madison sat beside her so there were three of us on the seat and I was jammed between them and the side of the bus.

No room to move. Nowhere to go.

I swallowed. They weren't going to beat me up. They weren't the guy in the hoodie who'd been following me. They were smarter than that and knew there were lots of different ways to hurt people.

Aisha thrust a magazine in front of me. "We thought you'd like this."

Hard Core magazine. The cover had a picture of a ripped naked male torso.

Meanwhile Madison held a banana in her hand. I wanted to get out of there so I pushed Aisha but between her and Madison, they were stronger than me.

Aisha turned the pages, pretending to be interested. "Hmmm, look at this guy. What a hunk."

I finally managed to speak. "I'm not interested."

"But you should be." Aisha sounded so matter-of-fact. "That's the whole point."

Madison leaned across. "You think you're better than us because you're so smart, don't you?"

My heart jumped in my chest, my forehead suddenly sweaty "No."

She turned the page and pointed to a picture of an erect penis. "Do you know what this is?"

I hadn't seen a lot of erections in real life – none really – but I knew what they looked like. I wasn't that naïve.

"Of course I know what that is."

I was falling into their trap. I had to get away. But how? I glanced at the kids in the seats in font of me and behind. Some looking. All listening.

And no one would do a thing.

"You've never given head, have you?" Aisha asked as if it were the most normal question in the world. "I bet you don't know how."

"Leave me alone." My voice was small.

I was swamped, surrounded, drowning. Didn't matter what I said or did, nothing worked. I couldn't win. This was Southern Hills High all over again.

Madison passed the banana to Aisha who pushed her dark hair behind her shoulders, making a show of it. She peeled the skin off the fruit, slowly, sensuously, if such a thing were possible, then ran her tongue along the length of the banana.

"Mmm." She moaned, pretending to be enjoying it.

Someone behind me giggled. My heart thumped in my chest. Banged against the walls of my chest.

Aisha circled the top of the banana with her tongue and moaned more loudly. Around us, people cheered.

I wanted to scream, "Shut up, all of you. Go away." I didn't say anything. I couldn't, but I was screaming on the inside.

Aisha glanced my way, then opened her mouth wide, wrapped her lips around the banana and went down on it, making weird sex sounds.

Howls of laughter filled the air. A few rows back, someone thumped the seat, creating a drumroll. How could they find this funny? Couldn't they see what this was doing to me?

Louder now, Aisha's moans were more emphatic until she let out a sound emulating an orgasm.

She was done. I hoped.

Applause broke out along with a series of wolf whistles. A minute later, the show was over and the others seemed to have calmed down.

Not Madison and Aisha though, they were only getting started.

"Now you know how to give head." Aisha pointed to the pictures in the magazine. "Ooh, look at that big cock. I bet you've never had a bad boy like that one."

I turned away, looked out of the window. Aisha grabbed the back of my head with one hand and jammed the magazine up against my face. "Take a look at that guy."

I tried to push her away.

Madison leaned across. "Here, you should practice now you know how it's done."

Her blue eyes were wide, her expression so innocent as she shoved the banana against my lips. I pressed my mouth closed, turned my head. Too late. She rammed the fruit against my face, smearing banana across my cheek.

Nausea rose in my stomach, my mouth salivating as if I were going to throw up. This was never going to be over.

"You broke it," Madison said in mock surprise, a chunk of banana still in her hand. "You broke the penis."

Aisha laughed.

Anger rose to my throat, choking me. My chest was tight. I couldn't get enough air. My hands were trembling.

Aisha grabbed a hunk of banana and plastered it on the open page still in her hands. She lifted the magazine and rubbed my nose in it. More banana smeared across my face.

"That's how you do it," Aisha said between giggles. "That's how you give a blow job."

The final humiliation. Tears burned at the back of my eyes but I couldn't let them see me cry. Couldn't let them have that too.

The bus was slowing down and Madison and Aisha were in fits of hysterics. This was my chance. I pushed past them, smashing into Madison with my bag and knocking her to the floor.

"Vicious little thing," she yelled.

"Yeah, you owe her an apology," Aisha shouted and the two of them burst into another round of laughter.

There were no other kids standing in the aisle any more so I shot to the front, tears sliding down my cheeks.

I jumped off the bus and ran. Around a corner. Around another corner. Anywhere. I was sobbing so hard my chest and stomach hurt, my whole body in pain.

It was over. Except it wasn't over. A panic attack. No, no, no, not now. Not that too.

My heart was banging so hard in my chest it felt like I was going to have a coronary. I stopped, doubled over, my hands on my knees until I caught my breath. Except I couldn't catch my breath. Couldn't get enough air. I was suffocating.

Straightening, I looked around. Had no clue where I was. A suburban street like any other. Ordinary. Not ordinary. Exposed.

A stab of fear cut into my gut. This was too open. Not safe. They could find me. I had to find cover.

I saw a tree, a car parked under it. I ran toward the car and dropped alongside it, my back sliding down slowly along the passenger's door.

Fear gripped me, held me prisoner, didn't let me move. My heart was still racing, my chest so tight it hurt. I was never going to live this down. Everyone would know. It cut me to my core, my body wracked with painful sobs all over again, tears streaming down my face.

And all I could do was wait until it passed. The panic attack ran its course but that didn't mean this was over, nowhere near it.

I'd handled everything so badly. I should've stood up for myself. Come up with a cutting comment to put them in their place. Instead I was useless, just like my mom said.

My whole body flooded with despair. A bus full of kids and no one had stuck up for me. No, instead they'd egged Madison on because she was the star and I was a piece of shit.

My head dropped into my hands. What if someone had taken photos? I hadn't seen anyone take their phone out but that didn't mean they hadn't. God no, not that too.

Finn had been at the back of the bus. He'd seen. Everyone had seen. It was the same thing all over again. New school, different kids, same problem.

No point talking to the teachers. I'd tried that before and it got me nowhere. Sure, the principal had spoken to the ringleaders, then seemed to think my problems were over. Same as Mom. She wouldn't even have let me change schools if I hadn't earned a scholarship. To a better school. Supposedly. Now look where that had got me.

I tipped my head against the car door behind me. Thump, thump, thump.

A year ago, I'd been diagnosed with depression and was still on medication. It wasn't enough. It wasn't helping.

Everything was such a struggle. And for what? To go through the same crap again. That's what it was. Crap. That's what my life was.

Deep in my gut, I had the same feeling I'd had so many times before. I'd think things were getting better but they never did. It was the same thing over and over again.

Nothing stops.

CHAPTER ELEVEN

The Primary

"This isn't going to work."

I shove my hands into my pants pockets, my shoulders hunched as Remy and I walk down a Ghettolands street. He doesn't say anything. Above us, the sky hangs low like a dark violet ceiling threatening to collapse. Despite this, it hasn't rained for a while so at least one thing is working in my favor.

We're on our way to meet my so-called little brother at my aunt's house. This is wrong in so many ways I don't know where to start. I have no clue what street we're going to or where I am and that's the least of my problems because I don't know what I'm doing. The only thing I'm certain of is that none of this is going to fare well.

Getting away from The Primary seemed like a good idea but the thought of meeting Joey is killing me. Because that's exactly what I'm supposed to do – to him – though maybe not right now.

My heart rate rises, desperation coursing through my

veins. I can't do this, any of it. I have to get away.

Remy says, "You have to face the situation head on. There's no other way. You have to see Joey."

But there is another way. I can run. Hide. I shunt Remy hard in the shoulder, turn and race down an alley.

"Hey," he yells.

I weave between people, past makeshift stalls selling fruit and vegetables, and head around any corner I can find. At first, I hear Remy's footsteps behind me, then that particular sound disappears, leaving only the throng of the crowd. I've lost him so I slow down and try to catch my breath.

Out of nowhere, Remy appears. I stop in my tracks. He might know these streets better than me but I'm not done yet. I turn and leap to scale a fence. Fit and athletic, I'm not like that girl I left behind in Middleton.

Arms much stronger than mine wrap themselves around my legs as Remy pulls me down, pushes me against the fence. I don't fight back, though maybe I should. He's rough, anger glimmering in the slits of his eyes. This isn't the Remy I know. I've never seen him pissed before.

"Where the hell do you think you're going?" His voice is low, threatening.

"Away," I say.

"Are you crazy?"

I laugh. "I am completely crazy."

Much more than he can possibly know. I haven't slept, couldn't sleep, not when I knew who I was supposed to see today and what I'm supposed to do.

I'm also in denial. I want to close my eyes and wake up somewhere else and if that's not an option, then running away is the next best thing.

Remy pulls my shirt up, exposes my midriff and I wonder what on earth he's doing when it comes back to me. The electronic locator tattooed across my torso. I'm screwed. No point fighting it.

I laugh again because I truly am crazy.

"It's not funny, Sasha," Remy says. "They'll always be able to find you. You can't run away."

I haven't even done such a good job of getting away from Remy. Besides which, I'm not going to get very far on my own.

"You win." My shoulders slump. "I'll do this your way."

Remy places his hands gently on my arms. "I'm trying to help. We're on the same team."

"Except Joey. What team is he on?"

Silence.

Bridget Simpson is supposed to be my friend too, my best friend. I don't know what team she's on either.

Remy's eyes glimmer with sadness. "There's only so much I can do."

I've made him feel bad, worse than before, when there was no need for me to drag him down to my level.

"I won't run away," I say.

Remy's lips curl to a smile that doesn't quite reach his eyes. It's something. He takes my hand and leads me out of the alley back onto the street.

"It's not far now," he says. "Just around the corner and at the end of street."

As we slow down, his grip stays firm but there's warmth in it. And I like it. I like walking down the street holding hands with Remy. It makes me feel wanted. As if I'm part of something. As if someone cares.

116

We turn a corner onto a narrow street where a boy about ten years old is waiting at the other end. Even from this distance, his blue eyes are striking against his olive skin and short black hair, the family resemblance obvious. His resemblance to the girl who looks back at me in the mirror, that is.

Joey shoots past everyone who gets in his way, races toward me, then throws himself at me, nearly folds me in two. Wrapping his arms around my waist, he squeezes me tight, doesn't hold back, and it takes my breath away. Stunned, I stand there like a dummy, then drape my arms around him.

Now I know how Remy felt yesterday at his homecoming. Warmed throughout, because that's how I feel now.

I bite my lip to hold back the emotion simmering inside me. I'm Joey's big sister or at least that's who he thinks I am. I have to be Sasha and do the right thing by her. I have to hold back the tears because Sasha absolutely would not cry, I'm sure of it.

My arms trembling, I lay my hands on his little shoulders and crouch down to his level to give him another hug. "You've grown."

"Of course," he says proudly.

"Have you been good?"

He nods. "Most of the time."

I wonder what else a big sister would ask. "Have you been doing all your homework?"

"We hardly get any." He shrugs and I notice how thin his neck is, his head large. The rest of him is skinny too. "Anyway, I've been in training."

I stand, glancing at Remy. "Training?"

Joey nods. "Soccer and stickball and wrestling."

"The boys get together and form their own teams," Remy says. "It's non-stop."

Joey nods more vigorously, points at me first, then Remy. "When I grow up, I'm going to be just like you."

No, anything would be better than that. He couldn't possibly end up like me or like Sasha Rodriguez. The poor kid has no idea what he's up against, what's coming his way or how twisted this is.

That is, if he grows up.

My throat tight, I can't speak so I pull him in for another hug.

Remy places a hand on my shoulder. "You know what it's like, Sasha. All the kids want to join The Primary and only a few will make it."

"I'll make it," Joey shouts. "I'll be good enough."

I look at the kid with his threadbare tee shirt and faded jeans, then at the ramshackle buildings that surround us, the street that's filled with trash. They must have a problem with garbage disposal in this part of town because the pungent smell is lingering.

The longer I spend here the more I can see that The Primary is the only way out for these people.

"Okay, that's enough hugging," Joey says decisively. "Aunt Erin wants to see you."

He takes my hand and leads me and Remy down the street. Joey beams up at me as we walk. His hand is small in mine and he's so happy to see me that it's breaking my heart.

I've never had a little brother. I don't really have one now and I definitely don't want to let this kid down.

Half-way down the street, a middle-aged man with

salt-and-pepper hair approaches us, his eyes lighting up as soon as he sees me, but I don't have a clue who he is. I glance at Remy who shrugs. He doesn't know the guy either.

The gray-haired man bellows, "Sasha, how are you?"

He couldn't be louder if he was trying. Joey stops. His hand still in mine, I'm stuck so I put on a friendly smile.

"Fine, thanks," I say.

He whacks me on the shoulder. "Surely you haven't got so big for your boots at The Primary that you can't spare me a minute."

"N-no, that's not it." I try to sound confident. "It's just that we're on our way somewhere."

He grins. "You were my star student. It's no surprise you're doing so well for yourself. That was a spectacular win the other night." He looks down at Joey. "If you study and train hard, you could end up like your sister."

"Sure, Mr. Jones," Joey says.

We somehow manage to extricate ourselves from the conversation and head off.

Joey tugs at my arm as we walk. "You can't remember him, can you?"

"Sure I can. He's one of my old teachers." I've worked out that much from the gist of the conversation.

"What did he teach you?" Joey asks.

A pause.

"Everything," I say.

Joey squeezes my hand, looks up at me. "You don't know, do you?"

Remy slaps the kid on the back. "Sasha got knocked about a bit the other night at the tournament. She's not quite herself, but she's still a champion. We all know that.

She'll spring back soon. We don't want to mention it to your Aunt Erin, though. Don't want to upset her."

"Okay." Joey opens a door to a small house stuck between two larger ones, then shouts, "We're here, Aunty."

A dark-haired woman smiles and ruffles Joey's hair, affection in her eyes, then looks at me and there's something else in her eyes, something darker which makes the tiny hairs on the back of my neck stand on end.

Like Remy's parents' house, the room smells of freshly baked bread, the aroma a relief after the constant smell outside. Still, it isn't enough to make me feel at home.

Aunt Erin greets us and asks us to take a seat at the table while she pours coffee from a small enamel pot with a spout.

She sits beside Joey and points to a basket of bread on the table. "You must have something to eat."

I'm about to turn her down when Remy passes the basket to me, an expectant look in his face.

"Thanks," I say.

Apparently we have to eat. Luckily, the bread is every bit as good as the loaf we had last night.

"There's nothing like warm bread," I say.

"I'm sure you have plenty of bread at The Primary," Erin says. "Plenty of food. Everything you need taken care of."

I'm at a loss what to say.

Remy shrugs. "Life is certainly better there than in The Ghettolands. There's no comparison."

"How have you and Joey been doing, Erin?" I ask.

Her eyes are two daggers. I've slipped up. Maybe I should have called her 'aunt'. Something about her reminds me of my mother. You'd think I'd be used to being treated coldly by someone who was supposed to love me, but some things you never get used to.

"Is it okay if I call you Erin?" I ask.

She looks at me through hooded lids. "You always did."

Remy takes over the conversation, asking Joey about school and sport and his friends. Erin seems more at ease too.

Still, I jump on the chance to get out of there when Joey insists we have to go to the park. I haven't seen any parks nearby so I'll have to take his word on that. Stepping outside into the humidity is like a breath of fresh air compared to spending time with Aunt Erin.

I put my hand on Joey's shoulder. "Do you want to get in a bit of extra training?"

He nods earnestly. "Sure."

"See if you can run to the top of the hill non-stop and wait for us up there."

Just like that, he's off.

I turn to Remy. "Why doesn't my aunt like me?"

"I'm not sure, exactly. She's jealous because you made it out of here and she's still stuck. Greedy too. No matter how much money you send, it's never enough."

So even if you're at the top of social ladder and you're as popular and well respected as Sasha Rodriguez, it doesn't mean everyone loves you. She still has her problems.

I force myself to put one foot in front of the other as we head up the hill. "I'm never going to be able to hurt Joey. Regardless of whether I get my memory back or not."

"Some people have it harder than others," Remy says. "In your case, it's because you're the top student at The Primary that they gave you the most difficult mission. Remember, it's country above all else."

"So, everyone at The Primary has to kill? Wouldn't we run out of population to cull after a while?"

Remy steps aside to make way for an old lady coming the other way. "No, only the elite are given these missions."

Elite? That's too ridiculous for words. I'm not so *elite* that it gives me the right to kill.

"What?" I say. "And that's simply accepted?"

Remy grabs my arm, pulls me over to the side of the pavement and stops. "It's widely known. We just don't talk about it. At The Primary, we're being trained in close protection and you're likely to get the most prestigious job of all, bodyguard to the President and his family. When you're a full member of The Primary, you can make it in any career path you choose."

"I don't get why our country needs people like us. Why?"

"To protect against outside threats, invasion, things that endanger our way of life."

Anger curls in my stomach. "And I don't see why my country is so much more important than anything else."

"It's what our whole society is based on. You can't change the world, Sasha. It's just the way things are."

"Then the whole country is screwed."

That seems obvious to me. We're part of a privileged few, even though I don't feel particularly honored. Meanwhile the rest of the population lives in terrible poverty and they're telling us that crap about how it's country above all else.

Remy ambles up the hill. "I guarantee you'll be screwed if you don't do what you're supposed to."

"Why on earth should they eliminate me if I don't do as I'm told?"

"Someone else might get away with lesser punishment, but not you," he says. "You're too well known. They'd make an example of you. Above all, we have to be obedient."

I stop before we get to the top of the street. I wave at Joey and he waves back, grinning.

"What about you, Remy Christensen?" I ask.

He shrugs. "What about me?"

"Who is the target for your mission? Who do you have to dispose of?"

"It's done."

Remy speeds up but I'm not letting him off that easily.

I grab his shoulder and spin him around. "You've completed your mission?"

He nods.

"Who was it?" I ask.

A muscle in his jaw flinches. He looks down but not before I see a glimmer of grief in his eyes. Even Remy isn't that tough. No one can be.

"I got off easy compared to you," he says.

I'm insistent. "Who?"

"My grandfather."

A tremor runs through me. I try to imagine Remy doing the deed. He can't possibly have committed an act of cold-blooded murder simply to ensure his career at The Primary. He can't.

What kind of place is this? And what kind of person is

Remy?

CHAPTER TWELVE

I press my eyes shut and wish it were true that I was in a coma, unconscious in a hospital room in Middleton, because waiting for doctors to do their thing and bring me back would be easier than dealing with this.

It takes all my strength not to judge Remy when I haven't walked in his shoes, don't know the full story and don't have all the facts. He has done so much for me and needs my support though he'd never admit it. I open my eyes, reach for his hand, take it into both of mine and hold it tight.

Besides, I've made my mistakes. I'm no better than him.

Remy slaps his other hand over the top of mine and gives it a squeeze, then leads me up the hill. I'm glad I can show him warmth and human compassion because I know what it's like to live without it.

Joey waits at the top of the hill and leads us to a park that's not much more than a patch of green with a tree in it. The sky overhead is deepening to a shade of indigo but at least it hasn't rained for a while. This is the saddest looking park I've ever seen yet, in contrast, Joey is one of the happiest kids I could imagine. He stands on a bench and takes a flying leap, fighting off imaginary opponents, then turns to me.

His eyes narrow. "Time to wrestle."

An invitation I can't turn down.

"Hang on, Karate Boy," Remy says. "I have to go and help my uncle with some heavy lifting. It won't take long and I'll be back real soon. Can you take care of Sasha in the meantime?"

Suddenly nervous at the thought of being alone with the poor kid, nerves shoot through me. "Where will you be?"

Remy turns to Joey. "My uncle's house is next to Ricardo's Market. So stay here or wait outside the market. Nowhere else. Do you understand?"

Joey nods earnestly. "Got it."

Remy assures me he won't be long and leaves me in Joey's safe hands. I have a horrible feeling this is going to be a big mistake, except Joey takes my mind off my fears immediately. He pulls me forward in an arm drag. Catches me unaware.

I give him my best evil stare. "I won't let that happen again, kiddo."

He reaches up and puts his hands around the back of my head. We're neck wrestling, jostling for position and I've got to admit, Joey is good. He goes for a leg sweep and I let him take me to the ground where we roll around some more.

I obtain a superior position, then let him sweep me over again. I'm far from a pushover, though. I make him work for it until eventually he's sitting on my stomach in the mount position. It's a good position for Joey and a bad one for me, not that it matters because this is what training is for.

"What do you do when you've got the mount?" I ask.

"Bam, bam." He throws punches at my head while I cover to protect myself. The kid has been trained well, putting his whole body behind his strikes like a pro but without maiming me.

"Time!" I yell. "Joey Rodriguez is the winner."

He stops punching. His face drops. "When I fight, I'm not Joey. That's not my ring name."

I have to change the subject so I push him off. "Fight's over, kiddo."

He stares, his expression serious. "When we're training, you always call me by my ring name."

"My ring name is Sasha. I don't need a better name than that."

"What's *my* ring name, Sasha?" He sits on his knees beside me. "You don't know, do you?"

Silence. I've been caught out.

After a while he says, "When we're wrestling, I'm Rampage Rodriguez."

I raise my hand for a high-five. "Congratulations to the winner, Rampage."

Tightlipped, he won't lift his hand. "Can't you remember? Something's wrong, Sasha, and you won't tell me what."

I rest my hands on my knees in front of me. "It's like Remy said. I got knocked around at the tournament. I'll be fine in a while."

Innocent blue eyes stare back at me. "You can tell me. What's the big secret?"

My throat tightens. No, please don't tell me he's guessed that he's my target. Not that. This is already too hard.

"I'm your brother," he adds. "I'm ten. Old enough to know."

And I have to tell him something so I swear him to secrecy first, then come out with it. "I got hit over the head the other night and now I've lost my memory."

Joey nods thoughtfully. "So what can't you remember?"

"I can't remember anything."

Eyes wide. "Can you remember me?"

I shake my head. "I wish I could, Joey."

More emphatic now. "That's so terrible."

He reaches for my hand and asks a heap of questions which I answer as truthfully as I can. There's something truly pathetic about being comforted by a ten-year-old with tiny hands. I don't even mind that they're grubby.

Eventually Joey announces that wrestling is a dangerous activity for someone in my condition and that we should wait for Remy outside the market.

Since I have no idea where we are, I let Joey lead the way. The streets are crowded until we head onto a long narrow lane, a shortcut, apparently. Refuse spills out of an overflowing trashcan, the smell of rotting vegetables filling the air. The buildings to either side are brick, rising above us so this feels like a tunnel.

Something about this alley reminds of a dream I once had where I kept walking toward a light but could never reach it. The bustle of the city is still in the background but it's so quiet here that it's unsettling. I feel it in my gut. Something's not right. We should turn back.

"Joey," I say in a soft voice.

Suddenly, two men appear out of an open door and block our way, hands on their hips. Both men are scruffy despite their neatly shaved heads. And big, these guys are big.

I feel a twinge inside. Maybe I'm too suspicious. Maybe they're just two big guys who happen to be in the same place as us. Maybe I should give them the benefit of a doubt.

We stop. I grab Joey's hand. Behind me, boots scrape on concrete and I glance around to see a third guy with long brown hair. An ambush. We're surrounded.

My doubts dissolve.

I look one of the bald guys in the eye, then the other. "We want to pass. Let us through."

The two men step forward, still blocking our way.

There's no ring or cage, no referee, no rules, not on the street. I don't know who these guys are, if they've got weapons, or where they've been.

I know what they want, though. A victim.

CHAPTER THIRTEEN

Middleton

I didn't know what I'd do without Brody. Though the incident on the bus happened a week ago, I hadn't told him about it right away. It had hurt too much and I didn't have the heart for it. Or the guts.

Alec and Penny found out immediately of course and they'd tried to make me feel better but it wasn't the same. Penny seemed to think I should be able to get over things in an instant and Alec would always make some dopey comment and try to make me laugh.

It was sweet. It also wasn't much help.

On a Friday after school at the end of a long week, going online with Brody was absolutely the best thing to be doing. No one could see me while I was sitting at my desk looking like a slob and it was a chance to get things off my chest.

Brody was good at listening. Or the on-line version of listening. He'd ask questions, try to get me to talk about my feelings, and somehow I'd always end up a little happier. Like now.

– *You're better than those girls, you know that, don't you?*

He was referring to Madison and Aisha. I shot back:

– *It's not hard to be better than them. They're horrible.*

– *True. But you know what I mean. I could never have this sort of conversation with them. For a start, they'd never give me the time of day.*

– *I know the feeling.*

– *And I wouldn't want to talk to them anyway. You should forget about them, for a while anyway. Did you say you're going to a party next weekend?*

– *Yes, with Penny and Alec.*

– *You'll have to tell me all about it.*

I was happy to tell Brody about my life and share it with him. I only wished I had more good news to tell him.

He didn't get out much. Or at all. Years ago, he'd been burnt in a fire and disfigured. One side of his face was a mess. He refused to send me pictures of himself and I couldn't blame him.

After going through years of rehabilitation, he'd been put down a year at school with a bunch of kids who'd teased him mercilessly. I knew exactly what he'd been through. He described it so well. Something we had in common.

After that, Brody was homeschooled by his mom which was safer and much steadier for him. Also a lot lonelier. Thank goodness for the internet.

I wrote back:

– *It'll be my first party in ages.*

– *I've heard all kinds of stuff goes on at parties nowadays.*

– *Like drinking, you mean? I'm sure there'll be plenty of booze.*

– *Do you drink?*

– Not really.

I wasn't sure how to respond. I didn't think drinking was necessarily bad. I just wasn't particularly interested.

I'd heard about kids getting inebriated and falling unconscious, having their stomachs pumped, that sort of thing. I'd also heard stories about girls waking up in a stranger's bed the next day and not knowing where they were.

Having a couple of drinks was one thing. Getting completely plastered was another and I didn't believe a few sips of rum and coke would necessarily lead to disaster.

Brody wrote:

– What about drugs?

– Not my scene.

– Glad to hear it!

– I'm a nerd, Brody. Haven't you worked that out by now? Nerds don't drink and do drugs. We do homework. We study. We do well at school.

– That sounds like me! Except for the bit about the party, that is. What are you going to wear?

– I don't know.

– You've got a nice figure. You should wear something tight to show it off.

The conversation was getting a bit weird. I wrote back:

– All this talk about clothes makes you sound like a girl.

– I'm only asking. I can't go out and see people very often so it helps to get a mental picture of what's going on. That's why I ask all these dumb questions. Besides, you wear a uniform at your school, don't you? I assumed you'd want to dress up for a change. I thought all girls did.

– Dressing up is not my thing. You're right about the uniform, though. It's pretty bad. Have you seen it?

— No.

— How about if I take a couple of selfies and show you?

— Sure!!!

— Okay, back in a sec.

I used the camera in my laptop and took a couple of pictures to show how dowdy the uniform was, then sent the shots through to Brody.

He said:

— It might not be the best outfit but I've seen worse.

— I haven't shown you the school tie, yet. That's pretty bad. Hold on.

I grabbed the tie from my bag where I'd left it and placed it around my neck. I held one end up like a noose, pulled a goofy face with my tongue hanging out, and took a photo.

Brody wrote:

— I see what you mean about the tie. You'd look better without the uniform.

I paused, then shot back:

— Excuse me?!? What was that?!?

— I didn't mean it that way. Has anyone ever told you that you have a lovely smile?

Maybe I'd jumped the gun a bit and reacted too strongly. Brody probably wasn't suggesting anything at all. Just making a silly comment.

His last comment, however, wasn't dumb at all. No one had ever told me I had a lovely smile.

I wrote:

— Sometimes I wish I could talk to you on the phone. That'd be the next best thing to speaking to you in real life. It's easy to misinterpret things when you can't hear someone's tone of voice.

— I wish I could talk on the phone to you too. Sorry.

As if Brody didn't have enough problems, he was partially deaf as well. I wasn't sure if his deafness had been caused by the accident where he'd been burnt or if he was born deaf or how severe his disability was.

I'd asked lots of questions before and he'd explained it to me. After that, he hadn't wanted to talk about it.

There was always someone who was worse off than myself. I had to remember that. My problems didn't compare with Brody's.

That wasn't the only reason I liked him, though.

I liked him because he was Brody.

CHAPTER FOURTEEN

The Primary

In Middleton, I'd been scared.

I'm not in Middleton any more. I'm in an alley with Joey. Two big bald guys built for trouble are blocking our way. Another man is behind us.

My pulse races. Blood pumps to my muscles. If they lay a hand on Joey, I'll annihilate each of these men one by one and if it's the last thing I do, that's fine by me.

Something has taken hold inside of me. Something bigger than me. And primal.

I thank Sasha Rodriguez for this kick ass body and the years of training. I thank her for giving me the guts.

Because I am going to do this.

I step in front of Joey, sheltering him.

"Well, look at this," one of the men says. "She's from The Primary. She's got it easy. Not like us."

Of course he can spot I'm from The Primary, only unlike everyone else around here this man has no respect. His eyes are hooded and his upper lip is twitching in a sneer. He must've been practicing his mean face.

The other bald guy shakes his finger at me. "I know you. You were on television. I saw you in the tournament the other night." He whoops with laughter. "We got ourselves a live one."

"You can let us pass, or you can suck it up." I'm amazed at the words that come out of my mouth, the tough language to match my harsh personality.

The man sneers, stares at Joey and sends in a front kick toward the boy. A big mistake.

Anger rips through me. It's instant. Fury takes over my mind and muscles, every cell in my body.

"No-o-o!" I yell.

I shove Joey out of the way and take the blow instead. The shock is worse than the pain. Pain is temporary. It is nothing.

Making these thugs pay is everything.

And I will make them pay.

The guy looks smug as if he thinks I may crumple. His bald friend is grinning. All I see is teeth. Maybe back home people laughed at me, but not here, not any more.

There's another guy behind me. I can't fight three of them at once but I know exactly what to do.

No thought, only action.

I step in and slam in a round kick, then a second. The bald guy's leg shakes. He winces. I snap in a third, step in close and wrap my arms around the back of his neck. I yank him down and across so he's between me and his bald friend. That's the secret – I've got to keep him between me and my other opponent.

Then I finish him. Knees to the head. Blood splashes onto my pants. More knees. The crack of a broken nose.

Blood drips onto the ground. A long knee to his chest. He folds, falls to the ground.

The other bald guy isn't grinning any more. He turns and runs. He's seen enough.

Meanwhile, the long-haired dude trudges toward us, looking like a raging animal. He snorts.

I leap. A Superman punch that lands smack on the middle of his face. I don't even know where it has come from.

The guy staggers back, then charges like a bull. I push my legs back and sprawl. He's stronger than me but I'm smarter. He keeps coming forward at me so I step to the side and he loses his balance.

Crack. I send a kick across his stomach.

It only makes him angrier. He sends in a barrage of punches. I cover. Hit back. A fist slams against my jaw. Pain radiates across the side of my head. I'm dazed. My vision blurs.

Screw you.

I hit him back. Harder this time. Smash my fist on his cheekbone. I cop another one on my chin. I don't care about the pain. I only care about finishing this guy.

The Bull glances behind me, looks at Joey, bares his teeth. Evil glimmers in the man's eyes. It's only half a second and that's all I need. He's not getting anywhere near Joey.

No way.

I whip a round kick into the man's leg. It buckles. I slam another kick into his ribs. The crack of bone fills the air. He folds. On his way down. My leg is a baseball bat as my shin meets his jaw. The kick knocks his head back. Long hair flies across his face as he falls to the ground in a heap.

I turn and grab Joey's hand. Both guys are still down but I can't stand around and admire my handiwork.

"Which way?" I ask.

Joey points in the direction we'd been heading in the first place and we get the hell out of there as quickly as we can.

After a while, we're on another busy street. They all look the same to me. Joey yanks at my hand gripping his. "It's okay."

No, it's not. I just beat the crap out of two men and we weren't in a boxing ring. Is that assault? What have I done? What if one of the guys is permanently injured or maybe even dead?

"You're not listening," Joey shouts. "We're far enough away now. It's okay."

I look down and see tears in his eyes. It's not okay.

Stepping out of the way of the crowd, I pull Joey against the wall of a building and crouch down to his level. His face clouds over. His lower lip trembles. And he bursts into tears.

I was so concerned with taking care of myself that I missed what was going on right next to me. Poor Joey. I wrap my arms around his thin body and hold him tight. I press his head against my chest and stroke his silky black hair. I wait until his sobs subside.

Eventually, he says, "I was scared."

"So was I, Joey."

He wipes away his tears, his eyes wide. "No, you were brave."

I shake my head. "No one's that brave. Sometimes we just do what we have to do. Besides, I would've been stupid *not* to be scared in a situation like that. You never know what can happen."

He stares knowingly into my eyes in a way that makes me think he's a hundred years old, not ten.

"You're different, Sasha," he says.

"Me?"

"You don't talk like you used to. You didn't tell me how you kicked their asses and they got what they deserved. You didn't tell me toughen up or I'd never make it to The Primary. You're different."

He's right. Sasha would have had absolutely no doubts.

"Maybe I'm more mature now," I say, though even I'm not convinced.

Tears pool in Joey's eyes again. "I should've helped. I should've hit those guys. I was useless. I didn't do anything."

That word – useless. No, he is anything but that.

I grip his skinny shoulders. "You did the right thing. We're both safe and that's all that matters."

The frustration and despair, the feeling of being constantly under fire, I know exactly how he feels. And I don't want Joey to feel helpless.

"You're only ten, Joey, and already you're a scary dude," I say, bringing a smile to his face. "Your wrestling is awesome. When we were grappling, there were a few times you had *me* seriously worried."

"Really?"

"Just imagine what you'll be like when you're grown up. You'll be bigger than me, stronger, a hundred times scarier."

He looks up at me with those big blue eyes that are breaking my heart. "I've been training very hard."

"Listen," I say. "I think we need to go to the police now."

A frown forms in Joey's perfect brow. He looks at me as if I were an idiot. "Wow, you don't know *anything*. You really have lost your memory."

I lift my eyebrows. "No police?"

He shakes his head vehemently. "Definitely no police."

How on earth have I even made it this far in this place? I've been winging it but that's not going to last.

I've been lying to Remy, Joey and everyone else. The pressure of those lies weighs down on me. The strain of being Sasha Rodriguez is too much. I'm a fake and it's only a matter of time until I'm found out.

I stand. "We've got to get going. Remy will wonder where we are."

Joey seems happier now he has a mission on his hands as he leads me through the streets toward Ricardo's Market. Remy gets there at the same time we do. Perfect timing.

"What happened to your face?" he asks.

I lift my hand to my brow and push back some stray stands of hair. "It's not that bad, is it?"

"Your jaw is swollen along one side and your face is filthy." Remy glides his fingers along my jawline, my skin tender despite the gentleness of his touch.

Joey glides between us and looks up. "Three men attacked us and Sasha beat them all up."

Remy looks worried. "Three men?"

"Only two," I say modestly. "One of them ran away."

"Whoa, you better tell me exactly what happened."

I give Remy a blow by blow account. Joey interjects from time to time, then summarizes the situation by saying, "Sasha was a hero."

My heart swells. I've never been called that before and I like the idea even if it is an exaggeration. It beats the hell out of being a victim any day.

Back home, I'd never had an inkling what it felt like to be on the other side – to be the victor. I know the feeling now. It gives me something to aim for. Makes me believe I can achieve some small victory again one day.

"Are you sure you're okay?" Remy asks.

"Sure," I say. "Why wouldn't I be?"

That's the amazing thing about being in Sasha Rodriguez's body. The extraordinary becomes part of everyday life. Then again, maybe I'm still pumped after a big fight and when I calm down, I'll see just how dangerous the situation was.

Maybe it won't take long before I remember that I don't know what I'm doing. In the meantime, I'll make the most of every moment with Remy and Joey.

Right now, it's all I've got.

CHAPTER FIFTEEN

The next day Joey goes to school while Remy and I spend the day with his family before exploring The Ghettolands. It helps give me a feel for the place and how it fits into the bigger picture in this new world.

After school, Joey drags Remy and me to the street where he plays with his friends. There's something universal about the way a bunch of ten-year-olds look. They're poorly dressed, their hair uncombed, and they have the same mischievous expressions as boys that age in any part of the world.

They've set up large cardboard boxes as goals on the wet pavement at each end of the street and are playing a game. One boy has a football and is about to pass it by hand to another kid, except he's tackled to the ground. The ball falls from his hands and a hiss rises from the other boys. Another kid kicks the ball away. A small cheer.

I have no idea of the rules, no idea what they're doing, other than that this is a very physical game.

A murmur rises from the boys as we approach. They stop and stare at us. I look to either side, wondering if they're looking at someone else who's around. No, it's definitely the three of us. We're the big attraction.

Remy leans closer to me as we walk. "Don't forget, you're a star. These kids have probably all seen the tournament or at least heard about it."

A dozen kids gather in a half circle around us. It's drizzling so I do what everyone else does and ignore it. I'm not sure what to make of all the attention but as I glance down at Joey, he's beaming, enjoying every minute of this.

Joey points to a kid with curly black hair. "This is my best friend, Jeremy."

As we say hello, he leans across and touches Remy's hand. "Are you really from The Primary?"

Remy grins. "We sure are."

A murmur of approval runs through the crowd. These kids all hope to get where we are in life one day. It's sad and heartwarming at the same time.

A blond boy stares at me. "Joey told us you beat up three big men yesterday."

"Not exactly," I say.

Joey gives me a shove. "You have to tell them because they didn't believe me."

"Okay." I begin to tell the story.

"No, no." Joey's eyes widen, his whole face lighting up. "We'll show them."

Joey tells some of the kids to stand back and picks three boys to pretend to be the attackers. This becomes an impromptu re-enactment in the middle of the street as Joey directs the boys. He's playing the role of me of course, demonstrating each punch and blow in slow motion.

And I realize it's *me* he's playing. It's not Sasha

Rodriguez. She wasn't there. I was the one who beat off the men yesterday.

The boys ask the occasional question but mostly they look on in awe. It stops drizzling. For a while anyway.

Eventually the blond boy who'd been so doubtful of Joey's story earlier on asks, "And what did you do, Joey?"

He doesn't answer.

"Which of the men did you beat up?" the blond boy asks.

Joey's face reddens.

I step forward. "Joey did the smart thing. He stayed out of the way."

The blond boy screws up his face. "I would have beaten them all up."

"No," I say. "You would have got into more trouble. These were grown men."

The boy shrugs. "So what?"

"What's your number one tool in self-defense?" I ask, looking around at the group. "Can anyone tell me?"

Silence, then one kid offers up, "Hit 'em really hard."

I shake my head. "Good try, but it's not punching or hitting or choking your opponent. It's awareness. The most important thing you can do is to take note of your surroundings, notice the dangers and be aware."

The boys nod thoughtfully, making me feel like I'm some sort of oracle, the font of all knowledge. All the boys, that is, except for the blond kid.

"No way." He lifts his arms, flexes his muscles. "The most powerful man wins."

"Not true," I say. "Those three men were all bigger than me. I was more skilled and I was smarter. So was Joey. In fact, he saved us from getting into even more trouble. In a bad situation, I'd have Joey on my team any day."

He beams with pride, struggling to hold back a grin. The blond boy doesn't seem impressed but also doesn't argue.

My sense of awareness should have kicked in earlier yesterday. By the time I'd realized Joey and I were in a bad place, it was too late.

Also exhilarating. Empowering. Part of me had enjoyed it more than I should. Too much, perhaps.

I turn to Remy. "We should probably get going."

Joey grabs my hand. It's so cute that he's not embarrassed to do that in front of his friends.

"What about me?" he asks.

"You can come with us," I say. "I'd love it if you did. I'd also understand if you wanted to stay with your friends."

"Nope, I'm coming with you."

He says goodbye to his friends. He's only ten. If he was a few years older he'd have given a completely different answer. I know how important friends are when you get a bit older. I know because I have so few.

Joey thinks I'm a hero. I'm not. Not in Middleton.

We head for the park near Ricardo's Market because Joey insists he needs more training. On the way, we shelter in a doorway for ten minutes while it pours with rain. As soon as we arrive at the park, Joey sees two friends and rushes over. It's pretty obvious from his gestures that he's reliving yesterday's episode again.

I turn to Remy. "How come Sam doesn't want to hang with us the way Joey does?"

Since we've been here, Remy has spent a lot of time

with his little brother, talked to him, wrestled with him, chased him too, but the boy didn't want to tag along today.

"Sam is shy," Remy says. "Too shy for his own good. I think he's intimidated by the rough and tumble with other kids."

"He's okay when he's with you, though," I say.

"Because I'm gentle with him."

I'd noticed. "But he wants to get into The Primary?" A question, not a statement.

Remy's eyes fill with sadness and he lowers his voice. "He's nowhere near athletic or physical enough. He's got no chance, but I don't want to burst his bubble. I don't have it in me."

I wish there's something I could say to make Remy feel better. Instead Joey shoots across the park, heading straight for Remy who catches him and spins him around. It brings a smile to his face, one I'm grateful for.

Panting, Joey says, "Remy, don't you need to see your uncle again?"

"No, what gave you that idea?" Remy replies.

"I think you need to see your uncle." Joey is nothing if not insistent. "Sasha and I need to train together."

The boy wants to spend more time with me. He's such a sweet kid, heartbreakingly so. Joey practically pushes Remy along the pavement toward his uncle's house, waits until he's heading off, then motions toward Remy and says to me, "He likes you a lot."

"I like him too," I say. "We're a good team."

This is just an observation from a child, nothing more, yet I'm sure Joey is telling it like it is.

Joey looks me in the eye, punches the fist of one hand into the palm of the other, and says one word. Takedowns. Or maybe that's two words.

We stand a few feet apart on the grass, our legs parted, ready for action. Joey bends his legs and shoots in, trying to take me to the ground.

"Try again," I say. "Aim to get your shoulder at my waist and your hands around the back of my knees."

Joey shoots in for the take-down a few more times.

"Good work, I say. "This time, I want you to drive through with all your weight. Ram me and take me to the ground."

He nods eagerly and does exactly that. I'm flat on my back with Joey straddling me.

"Rampage does it again." I sit up, my back wet, my butt too, not that I care.

Grinning, Joey slides off and sits cross-legged beside me. He doesn't seem to care about getting wet either.

The sun is going down and it's getting cooler, reminding me how little time I have left with Joey. I feel a sense of urgency and want to get closer to him. I've never had a little brother. Never knew it could feel like this.

He looks me in the eye. "You said you lost your memory but something else has happened to you, Sasha."

"Whoa," I say. "Not so fast. I've got a lot to deal with at the moment."

"You just don't seem like yourself any more. You seem like a different person."

This is way too close to the bone. Surely he can't have guessed what's going on when even Remy hasn't worked it out. Joey's only a kid. He can't be that smart.

I clear my throat. "What do you mean?"

"I'm your brother. I know you."

"You'd never believe me," I say under my breath. I'm

leaning on one hand, my other arm resting on my knee, wondering what the hell to do.

"My sister would tell me the truth," Joey says.

I hold his gaze. "I'm not really your sister."

Realization dawning, Joey's gentle blue eyes narrow. He doesn't flinch. Doesn't give much away either.

Eventually, he says, "I knew it."

Maybe he'll believe me after all. Kids are honest and open-minded in ways that adults are not. Besides, Joey has already seen through me.

I tell him I'm from a different world and how I was thrown into Sasha's body. Eyes wide, Joey listens to my every word.

"So where's my sister?" he asks.

"I'm pretty sure Sasha is in my body back at my home."

Or what's left of my body. Because I'm not sure of the state of my body or my life and can't imagine what that must be like for a hard ass like her.

"Will she come back?" Joey asks.

"No doubt she's looking for a way back, just like I am."

After lying to Remy – and to everyone else for that matter – it feels good to get this off my chest, to be honest, to come out with the truth no matter how crazy it may sound. Despite my problems, I feel more at ease.

Joey sidles closer. "How will you get back?"

"Sasha went through some sort of traumatic experience that caused the body swap. At least, that's what I think anyway."

I've known this nearly from the start before I got carried away with other things. Joey has cut through the crap and reminded me what I need to do.

It was an extreme trauma that catapulted me here. There was a very specific set of circumstances at my end and no doubt at Sasha's too. Maybe this is a new cosmic phenomenon or maybe it has happened before. I wouldn't know. Maybe scientists wouldn't be able to explain it either.

Joeys' eyebrows go up in the middle. "Traumatic?"

"Like a shock or a blow to the head."

"Well, that kind of stuff would happen all the time at The Primary."

"You really are a smart kid," I say.

His lips curl to a smile that doesn't reach his eyes.

"You're worried about your sister, aren't you?" I ask.

"Yeah, I am."

"She'll come back to you, I know she will."

He nods, looking completely unconvinced.

I put my arm around him. "She loves you very much."

A faint blush washes across his cheeks. "You're just saying that."

"No, I'm not. I'm in her body and I can feel it in my heart."

"Are you sure?"

"Very sure. I've got Sasha's fighting skills and I've got some of her feelings too. She loves you, absolutely no doubt about it."

Though it's not the truth, it's not far from it. My heart feels like it's about to explode with overwhelming feeling for the poor kid. My love or Sasha's love? I don't know which.

I put my arm around his shoulder. "I'll take care of you. If Sasha's not here, I mean. I'll do my best, anyway."

Joey throws his arms around me. "Tell Sasha I love her."

Tears prick at my eyes for this beautiful boy with no idea what's ahead of him.

"Maybe next time, you can tell her yourself."

I struggle to keep the hitch from my voice. The poor kid deserves so much better. Safety, security, childhood, a life – surely that's not too much to ask.

And what was Sasha Rodriguez going to do when she was in my position? I can't fathom anyone would kill a loved one to prove their allegiance to country but it seems to be what people do. What Remy did.

I drop my head into my hands. I hope I can get back home. I hope Joey can stay safe and grow up.

I hope The Primary crumbles into a million pieces and falls apart.

CHAPTER SIXTEEN

Back on the train, back to The Primary, my new home.

Back to nothing. That's what it feels like.

Despite everything, I'd been on a high with Joey. On a high with Remy's family too, because they're so generous. We'd stay here longer if we could, but Remy insists that isn't possible. It's hardly surprising I'm on a low.

The train pulls out of The Ghettolands Station. Outside the window, beggars sit on dirty blankets asking for coins. Inside the carriage, Remy and I are cool and relaxed on padded vinyl seats.

I'm pissed off at leaving The Ghettolands, pissed off at coming here in the first place, pissed off at everything.

I lean back, put my feet on the seat next to my butt and wrap my arms around my ankles. Remy glances at my feet, then lifts his gaze to my face, a disapproving look in his eyes. What do I care? I'll put my feet up if I want to.

"Why did you bring me here, Remy?" I ask. "Why did you want me to meet Joey when I'm supposed to kill him?"

His mouth falls open and I wait for him to speak. It soon becomes clear I'll be waiting a while.

I prod him. "How can anything good possibly come of

this?"

He leans forward. "You've got amnesia, right?"

I'd almost forgotten. "Yes."

"You absolutely adore Joey. You only see him a few times a year but that doesn't make any difference. If anything, seeing him so rarely has intensified your feelings for him. You're a hard ass, Sasha, as hard as they come, except when it comes to Joey. Then you turn to mush."

"And?"

"I thought seeing him would bring back your memory. I thought it'd be like a blow to the head. You'd see him and your whole life would come tumbling back."

His words slam into me like a truck. That's never going to happen. I'm not that person, and Remy has no idea how far off track he is.

Eyes down, Remy shakes his head. "I gotta tell you, Sasha. If seeing Joey hasn't brought your memory back, I don't know what will."

"I don't know either." I shrug. "Maybe my memory will come back bit by bit. I think it'll work itself out slowly. It just needs time."

I'm not sure why I say these things when I know they're blatantly untrue. I want to make Remy feel better yet at the same time I'm not sure how much I can trust him.

With Joey, things were different. I felt it in my gut and knew he'd believe me.

Remy lifts his gaze. "You don't have that much time. It might take them a while but sooner or later Mason or someone else at The Primary is going to work out something is wrong."

"What about you? What happens to you if the

authorities find out I've lost my memory and you've been helping me?"

Remy shakes his head. "Not good."

"I won't let on." I drop my feet to the floor, straighten up and look down at my hands. "If things came to that, I'd tell them you didn't know, that I had you fooled."

"I know you'd never inform on me. It's not your style. You may have lost your memory but you're still the same Sasha underneath."

He might be surprised to learn how little of Sasha Rodriguez is in here. Still, that's okay because Sasha Pierce won't let him down in that way either.

A lot of things worry me. Going back to The Primary and trying to work out what the hell happened to Sasha worries me. The authorities want me to kill Joey to prove my allegiance to country and that worries me more than anything.

Just recently, Remy has started to worry me too.

"I'm supposed to eliminate Joey," I say.

I turn to Remy. Nothing.

"Your target was your grandfather."

He stares straight ahead. "I told you that already."

"How did you do it?" I lean closer because I have to know more. "How did you pull the trigger or push him off a cliff or do whatever you did? What could possibly have happened to make that all right?"

"He was old." Remy glares at me. "I don't want to talk about it."

His grandfather was old? Did that make it acceptable?

"Joey's not old," is all I say.

The train keeps moving and neither of us speaks, our silence a wall between us. It's a wall I can't leave in place

153

because Remy is all I've got even if I'm not sure where I stand with him.

I have another 'friend' too, Bridget Simpson, though I've only met her once and have no idea where I stand with her.

After a while, I ask, "Before I lost my memory, what did I say to you about my target?"

Remy grits his teeth. "The thought of completing your mission was killing you. I could see it in your face, but you refused to talk."

"Was I going to do it?"

"I honestly don't know what you were going to do, only that there's no way out of proving allegiance to country."

"Our country is a piece of shit," I say.

Remy grabs me by the shoulders, lifts me up and rams me against the closed carriage door. He's pressed up against me, the wall of his chest against mine, fire burning in his eyes.

I don't fight him or try to get away. I sense he's not going to hurt me despite his obvious anger.

He backs off, his chest heaving with big breaths. "Don't say anything like that ever again. It'll get you killed."

He's right.

"I'll be more careful from now on." Sasha Pierce would have apologized profusely but I can't bring myself to do so. I'm not that girl any more.

"Have you calmed down now?" he asks, apparently forgetting he's the one who rammed me against the wall.

"There must be a way out."

"Forget it, Sasha."

An idea comes to me. "Maybe I'll find someone who deserves it – a criminal or a serial killer – and kill them instead."

Though it's my voice, it doesn't feel like me talking. Sasha Pierce would never say anything like that.

Remy takes a seat. "It doesn't work that way."

"It does for me." I look down at him. "You don't get it. I've got nothing to lose."

I already died once.

Or at least I think I died in Middleton.

Maybe if I died again, that's what it would take to bring Sasha Rodriguez back here and make things right.

CHAPTER SEVENTEEN

Middleton

Six weeks ago…

By the time Penny's mom dropped us outside Ella's house, the street was jammed with cars and the party was in full swing. A few kids were hanging around on the porch. The front door was wide open and music was coming through loud and clear.

I closed the car door and Penny's mom drove off. Though she never said anything out of line, I always got the feeling she didn't approve of me.

Up ahead, a boy yelled, "This party's as boring as bat shit. See you at Dylan's."

On the other side of the road, a flash of messy dreadlocks under a streetlight grabbed my attention. I saw the side of the guy's face as he got into a car being driven by someone else.

I couldn't be sure…but the chill up my spine told me otherwise.

I grabbed Penny's arm. "Oh my god, that's him."

"Who?"

My heart raced. Ahead of us, a car door slammed and the vehicle sped off.

"Remember I told you about the guy who'd been following me," I said. "That was him."

Penny looked at me, then up the street, her mouth open. "Are you kidding? Your stalker? Are you certain?"

"Not a hundred percent."

This had to be a coincidence. He wasn't stalking me tonight, hadn't followed me here, so maybe I had this all wrong.

Penny shrugged. "He's left now. I don't suppose he'll be back since his friend said the party was boring."

That was true. And if he did come back, there'd be plenty of people around.

Besides, I couldn't bear to go home and explain to my mom why I'd left the party early, not when she'd keep questioning and nagging. She wouldn't understand even if I told her the truth and she'd find some way of twisting things to make it look like it was my fault.

"Are you okay?" Penny asked.

"I don't know. This is kind of weird."

For one thing, I wasn't sure that was the same guy. Wasn't sure why he'd been following me. Wasn't sure of anything.

The rest of the world, the other kids my age, everyone else I knew all seemed to be having a huge party. I'd finally made it to a party, finally had some friends. And now this.

Well, I was going to force myself to have a good time, no matter what it took. "One thing's for sure. I don't want to hang around out here any more. Let's go inside."

We walked up the steps to the front porch past a few guys smoking cigarettes. They glanced at us, then looked away. *Nerds*, that's what they were thinking. Penny and I weren't popular so it followed we barely registered as people with them. Fine by me. I wasn't going to hang around breathing second-hand cigarette smoke.

Penny walked ahead of me through the doorway and down a central hall leading to the rear of the house and the rest of the party.

She was wearing a navy dress, tight but not too short, because she didn't want to look cheap. I'd already told her she couldn't look slutty if she tried.

I had black pants, failsafe, and a red top with a deep V-neck that showed off my figure. If I had big boobs, they'd have been hanging out but since that wasn't the case, I had nothing to worry about.

The two of us had put a lot of effort into looking good for the party, despite the fact I'd played it down to Brody. It had taken a long time to get that natural look with our make-up and we'd both blow-dried our hair, leaving it hanging down around our shoulders.

Now all we had to do was find Alec. He'd sent us a text message a few minutes ago to say he was here already.

In the living room, helium balloons covered the ceiling, their colored ribbons hanging down. A punch bowl sat on the center of a dining table, the rest of which was covered in half-full bowls of popcorn and chips, a stack of clean red cups and many more used ones.

A couple of tall guys, basketball players, stood on the other side of the table, digging into the potato chips. Maybe they needed sustenance.

In the living room, a girl with long blond hair was

draped over the knee of a star football player and another couple was making out on the sofa. Everyone else was standing around with a drink in their hand, shouting to be heard over the music.

"Maybe Alec's outside," Penny said.

I followed her onto the rear patio.

Inside, the lights were dimmed whereas outside every effort had been made to illuminate the area. Garden lights shone in the yard, fairy lights hung from trees and rows of candles lined the path to a gazebo down the back.

Though quieter outside, it was no less crowded. Half a dozen kids sat around a table covered in empty shooter glasses having a drinking competition. I wondered how many of them would be able to stand. Several others seemed to be able to stand but were swaying.

It was only nine o'clock. We'd arrived late on purpose. It made me wonder what state these people would be in by midnight. I'd have to tell Brody all about it.

Penny looked around, her light brown hair brushing her shoulders. "Where do you think Alec could be?"

"He's tall enough," I said. "We should be able to find him."

We wandered through the yard and said hello to a few people. Still searching for Alec, we edged toward the side fence, only to hear some strange rustling sounds coming from the path that ran by the side of the house. It was probably the only part of the yard that wasn't lit up like a Christmas tree.

I stopped. My mouth fell open. That was not what I was expecting to see. Beside me, Penny grabbed my arm and we stood frozen to the spot.

Captain of the swim team, Jack Spencer stood with his

back to the fence, his shirt unbuttoned, jeans lowered. Madison Frost was her knees in front of him, her blond head bobbing up and down as she gave him a head job.

Jack moaned – that must've been the sound we'd heard – then looked our way, completely unfazed that we were watching. He closed his eyes and leaned his head back while Madison kept doing what she was doing, completely oblivious to our presence.

I felt a hand on my shoulder and turned to see Aisha Johnson glaring. She grabbed Penny and me by the arm and yanked us away toward the middle of the yard.

The scowl didn't leave her face. "What are you two perverts doing?"

"We're not the perverts," Penny said. "Did you see what they were doing?"

Aisha tossed her black hair behind her shoulders. "Of course I know what they were doing."

"Madison was giving Jack a blow job." Sometimes Penny was a master of stating the obvious.

"And what gives you two the right to stare like it's a freak show? It's nothing unusual. It's no big deal."

"We didn't know they'd be there."

With her smooth dark skin and exotic features, Aisha was a stunner but her upper lip curled to a condescending sneer, suddenly transforming her features into something ugly.

"Jack's not even her boyfriend," I said, the words slipping out.

"So what?" Aisha threw her hands up. "It's not like they were having sex."

Weren't they? Didn't oral sex count? It had looked pretty damned intimate to me, except for the fact they were doing it down the side path which was a bit crass.

Penny said, "But they were–"

Aisha cut her off. "You two really don't know anything about the ways of the world. It's just what you do. You should grow up." Still sneering, she turned to me. "I thought you'd know better after the little lesson we gave you. I'm surprised you even turned up tonight."

How could she remind me about that? How dare she? My face turned red but Aisha stormed off too quickly to see. Penny didn't notice either.

She grabbed my arm and led me away. "We've still got to find Alec."

Penny spotted him immediately. His head of black hair stood out, especially since he was a foot taller than the guys he was talking to. Compared to him, they looked like dwarves.

His eyes lit up as soon as he saw us. "Whassup everybody?"

"You won't believe what we just saw." Penny gave him the story.

Alec's eyes turned to saucers, the whites stark against the brown of his irises. "Where?"

Penny kept a grip on his shoulder. "At the side of the house but you're not going there."

He looked disappointed. "Aren't I?"

"Sometimes you're so uncouth," she said.

And sometimes Penny acted like a schoolteacher. I couldn't blame Alec for being curious. I also couldn't stick up for him right now.

My shoulders were stiff, my stomach in a knot from being reminded about that day on the bus. I just wanted one night where I could feel normal. Surely that wasn't too much to ask.

"I need another beer," Alec said.

Penny glared at him. I'd seen her give 'the look' often enough to recognize it. Alec came back with two beers and handed me one.

I stared at the bottle in my hand.

"It'll make you feel more relaxed," Alec said.

That didn't sound like such a bad idea. I'd been on edge ever since we walked through the door. Before we'd walked through the door, in fact. I didn't fit in. I never knew what to say to people. A drink certainly wasn't going to hurt.

Penny folded her arms. "Honestly, you don't need to drink to have a good time."

Alec took a swig of beer. "Yes, because clearly you're having a wonderful time."

I stepped between them. "Don't start, you two."

"We haven't even begun," Penny said.

I sipped my beer. This was worse than cough medicine though at least medicine wasn't usually bitter. The look on my face must've been a doozy because Alec laughed and even Penny smiled.

"You're doing it wrong," he said.

I raised my eyebrows. "How can you drink beer wrong?"

"You've got to knock it back and let it slide down the back of your throat. Tiny sips don't work."

I did as he instructed, knocked back a big mouthful and swallowed. "That doesn't taste any better."

"Trust me, it will."

"I'm nothing if not a good student." I took another swig.

"I don't know how you can stand the stuff," Penny said to Alec.

He shrugged. "It's easier this way. I have a few beers. I don't get drunk. People see me drinking so it gets the other guys off my back and then there's no pressure on me to have a drink. It's a win-win situation."

Penny screwed up her face. "Where do you get the booze from in the first place?"

"My big brother," Alec said.

Half-way through the beer, it still wasn't tasting any better but I could see what Alec meant about feeling relaxed. A pleasant sensation was settling in the pit of my stomach and even my knees felt relaxed. Better still, I didn't feel so stressed any more. I was thinking about Alec and Penny and how much I enjoyed their company.

Alec introduced us to his friends who, as it turned out, weren't dwarves. They were just a bunch of guys who were into computers and gaming. Maybe spending all that time indoors had stunted their growth.

"Damien is California state champion in Yu-Gi-Oh," one of them said.

I had a vague recollection of some sort of Japanese manga trading cards and maybe a video game. I didn't think anyone still did that sort of thing at our age. This took nerdiness to a new level.

Another kid, presumably Damien, blushed. "I don't want to brag."

I didn't have much in common with these guys so the conversation was stilted but I didn't mind. I had beer.

Alec leaned closer and handed me another long neck when my bottle was empty. "Lucky I brought extras."

"You read my mind," I said.

He shrugged. "I'm pretty clever like that."

Tonight I just wanted to forget. About every lousy thing that had happened to me at my old school, about my mother who never listened and could explode at any moment, about the guy with the dreadlocks who'd scared the daylights out of me, about Madison and Aisha and the other kids like them, and especially about the incident on the bus.

I had a lot to forget.

CHAPTER EIGHTEEN

Penny was arguing with Alec and I didn't even mind. I was in my own little world. Then Finn Masters walked past with a bunch of his friends, the sort who were way too cool to be seen talking to someone like me.

I smiled and waved. "Hey, Finn."

He stopped, his eyes lowered. "Hey."

"It's a good party."

Not the most scintillating line but it was a start. His friends wandered ahead, then stopped and looked our way. One of the guys said something and they all howled with laughter.

"I can't talk to you tonight." Finn walked off.

My heart dropped while I stood there like an idiot.

When he caught up with his friends, one of them glanced at me and pretended to wipe some sweat off his forehead as if to say Finn had got out of a sticky situation.

I knew those guys didn't want to hang with me. I wasn't stupid. I'd also worked out Finn couldn't talk to me tonight, not with so many people around, though it had taken me a while.

But there'd been no need for him to be so blunt. He didn't need to state it in so many words. Didn't need to make me feel so small.

Alec came closer, gently shaking his head. "I told you so."

He must've seen the whole thing and had indeed told me you couldn't trust Finn Masters but I hadn't thought I needed to trust the guy just to talk to him for a minute.

Alec put his hand on my arm. "I'll get you some punch."

"Good thinking," I said.

Seconds later he was back and I knocked back the sweet, fruity punch with ease.

"This is much nicer than beer," I said. "Why didn't you get me this stuff earlier?"

He spread his hands. "What's wrong with beer? It puts hair on your chest."

"And I really need some of that."

A cheeky expression on his face, he peered down my cleavage or what there was of it. I whacked him on the arm and he pretended to be offended. He could always make me laugh.

"You'll kill off your brain cells with all that drinking." Penny rolled her eyes at Alec. "Though sometimes I wonder where you got your brains from in the first place."

That was a mean thing to say. His mom was a hairdresser, his dad a plumber. They weren't professionals like Penny's parents but from what I could make out, they were a loving family.

"It's not just brains," Alec said. "A lot of hard work goes into my school results."

"Well, if you get drunk, you won't be able to study tomorrow," Penny said.

Alec glared at her. "Just because your mother nags you

into submission doesn't mean you can do the same with me."

Penny planted her hands on her hips. "I want to be a doctor like my mom so I can help people. Anything wrong with that?"

This was getting too heavy for me so I turned away.

Madison and Aisha were walking toward us, talking about Imani, a girl from Somalia or Namibia or somewhere in Africa.

"People often get the two of you mixed up because you're both so pretty," Madison said to her friend.

Aisha tossed her head back, her eyes narrowing. "How could they? She's so much darker than me."

They both laughed, though it didn't seem funny. Even in my hazy state, I wondered what was wrong with Aisha and if she was hung up about her skin color.

As they got closer, Aisha scowled at me. "Don't you have anything better to do than listen in to our conversation? Shouldn't you be at home studying? Or reading or cleaning?"

She definitely sounded hung up about something. If only I could work out what.

Madison leaned across to touch Penny's arm. "You know that dress goes really well with your glasses."

"Thanks." Penny's voice was small.

She knew it wasn't a compliment just as well as I did. She also didn't know what else to say.

Madison turned to me. "Your hair looks nice. What color do you call that? Dishwater blond?"

"At least it's natural," I said.

"Aren't we a bit sensitive this evening?" Madison feigned a posh voice and the two girls turned to leave.

"No wonder they call them the Ugly Sisters," Aisha said over her shoulder as they headed toward Finn and his friends to join the cool group where they belonged while we stayed where we belonged. Well away from them.

Maybe Aisha was right and I was sensitive this evening. Maybe I had every right to be. Maybe it'd be a relief if they just left me alone for once.

Aisha and Madison were Class A bitches. I knew that, yet that knowledge didn't help me.

"Perhaps now that Madison's mouth isn't full, she can speak again," I said under my breath.

Alec burst out laughing, one hand on his stomach as he doubled over. "Good one!"

Even Penny laughed. For once I'd come out with the sort of insult that could put Madison in her place. As usual, it had been too late, too little, and I probably wouldn't have been able to say it to her face anyway. I didn't have it in me.

I raised the red cup to my lips only to find it was empty.

"I've got just the thing." Alec lifted a bottle of tequila from behind his back.

My eyes lit up. "Where did you get that?"

"The guys having the drinking contest left it behind." Alec must've sensed my reluctance at drinking booze that wasn't ours because he added, "If you leave a bottle lying around, that makes it public property."

I held my cup out and he poured a shot. This was exactly what I wanted. I'd never felt the need for a drink before but I sure as hell did now.

The tequila burnt the back of my throat as I knocked back a second mouthful. I was starting to feel numb.

Madison and Aisha were nothing more than a blur in the distance. The same went for Finn. Why should I care if he didn't want to talk to me? Maybe I didn't want to talk to him either.

I held my cup out again. This was better than beer, better than punch. So much more direct.

Penny glared. It only made me want to drink more. So I did.

"You're getting good at this," Alec said.

The alcohol washed through me, a pleasant tingly feeling taking over. For once, I didn't feel out of place. I felt like I belonged. I was at a party. Having fun. This was what I was supposed to be doing.

I fumbled for Alec's arm. "It's so sweet of you to take care of me like this."

He shrugged. "I thought you needed to loosen up, that's all."

I lifted my hands over my head, then down along my waist, my hips swaying. In fact, all of me was swaying, a wide grin on my face.

"I've never been so loose in all my life," I said.

Penny slapped my arm. "Stop that, Sasha, you're making a spectacle of yourself."

Alec glared at her. "You need to loosen up too, Penny."

"Fine." She turned and walked away.

I noticed the music in the background, smooth, crooning, sophisticated. Tossing my arms around the back of Alec's neck, I hung there.

"Ooh, it's Michael Bublé," I said.

Alec gently placed his hands on my hips as if he wasn't sure what to do. "Do you like Michael Bublé?"

I giggled. "No, I hate Michael Bublé but what else are we supposed to do when they play this stuff?"

We stood and swayed together briefly before I stepped back. I may have been doing enough swaying for both of us.

The song finished and I pushed Alec away. "Another drink."

He reached for the bottle. "Sure."

"You're such a good friend, Alec."

"That's what I'm here for."

"You're fun." I lowered my voice. "Penny can be a poo-poo sometimes if you know what I mean."

"Glad I'm not a poo-poo." He looked sheepish. "Anything'd be better than that."

"You'll be a brilliant lawyer one day too."

"How do you know?"

"Because I do. You're smart and you'll learn all the laws and speak respectfully to the judge and help get innocent people off and throw guilty people in jail. You can start your own law firm, Hooper and Partners, and everyone will want to be your partner."

We went on like that for some time, drinking and talking, and standing beside each other, swaying. It felt good and I liked feeling good for a change.

Perhaps I liked the tequila a bit too much. One minute I was talking to Alec, the next minute my knees weakened and he was holding me up. Legless. I didn't know that was even a thing.

"You've had too much to drink," he said.

"But you kept bringing it to me," I said or at least that's what I thought I said.

His arm around me, Alec helped me over to a patch of

grass and sat me down. He was tentative about lifting his hand from my shoulder as if he thought I might fall down. It was so strange.

"Don't tell me," he said. "You don't feel so good any more."

"You're such a Silly Billy." I grinned back at him. "I feel fantastic."

"I'll get you a glass of water. Stay right there." He backed away, then left.

I nodded. I wasn't going anywhere. Vaguely aware of other people in the distance, I was alone but not lonely.

It was possible not to feel desperately lonely, not to feel like crap, not to feel like a loser. What a revelation.

Someone was approaching. It wasn't Alec. No, it looked like Finn's friends. Why would they be coming to talk to me? I couldn't be sure it was them. They were so blurry.

My head was suddenly heavy, lolling around on my shoulders, a huge weight. I couldn't hold it up any longer. Couldn't sit. Couldn't hold it together.

The back of my head hit the grass with a thump.

And that was the last thing I heard.

CHAPTER NINETEEN

So this was what a hangover felt like.

The pounding in my head had receded thanks to the Aspirin I'd taken earlier, however there was no cure for the nausea swelling in my stomach. I'd already thrown up twice this morning, after which I'd felt marginally better but unfortunately the relief had only been temporary and the nausea kept coming back in waves.

At least I hadn't vomited last night in front of my friends. Or I didn't think I had. That was some small consolation.

The rest of my body was in a pretty sad state too. My knees which had felt relaxed last night now felt like the rest of my joints – stiff and heavy.

I could get out of bed. I'd had to get out of bed, in fact, so my mother wouldn't notice what was wrong. If she found out I'd been drunk, she'd rant and yell for hours – probably longer – so I was doing everything in my power to make sure she didn't find out.

Still, I didn't care about the pain and the nausea.

It had been worth it.

I packed my laptop and a few other things into a backpack and headed for the living room where Mom was sitting with her feet up on the coffee table watching a movie. She was wearing faded jeans and an old tee shirt, her hair scraped back into a ponytail.

"I'm off to the library," I said from the doorway.

"What?" She looked at me, an angry glint in her dark eyes. "What are you talking about? Why do you want to go there?"

"Mom, I've got a lot of school work and I need to do some research for one of my projects."

She dropped her feet to the floor, sat up straight. "You're pathetic. Always such a mess. So weak that's what you are."

Where the hell had that come from? It was nothing I hadn't heard before and shouldn't have surprised me, but it did. Every time, it felt like a punch to the gut, and that only made me more desperate to get out of the house.

"If you were better organized, you wouldn't need to rush off like this," she said. "Who else is going to be there?"

"No one." I cleared my throat to stop my voice from cracking. "I'm going to study. I don't know who else will be there."

She stood up, pointing her finger at me. "I know what goes on. I'm not stupid, which is more than I can say for you. God, you're so naïve."

That was pretty much what Madison and Aisha had said, that I didn't know what went on around me. It felt like the whole world was ganging up on me.

Mom was always worried I was going out to meet boys, just like she'd been concerned there'd be members

173

of the opposite sex at the party last night. I didn't know why she should be so worried when she'd told me often enough that boys were never going to be interested in me and she wasn't that far from the truth.

Anyway, I wasn't really meeting a boy at the library. I was meeting Alec which was completely different.

"Fine, I'll drive you," Mom said, a growl in her voice.

She had an ulterior motive. She wanted to make sure I was actually going to the library and not somewhere else. I opened my mouth to argue, then thought better of it. I wasn't sure I could make it all the way there on foot anyway given the state I was in.

"Thanks," I said.

She swept the car keys from the coffee table. "It's not as though I don't have anything better to do than drive you around all day. I knew you'd be too lazy to walk."

I'd only said 'thanks'. How could that have been the wrong thing to say? What else had I done wrong?

"Would it be better if I walked?" I asked. "Just let me know what's easiest for you, Mom."

She shoved me against the doorframe on her way out of the room. "It'd be easier for me if you shut up and got in the car."

"Don't push me," I said, my voice small.

"What?" Mom kept walking. "You're the one who's always pushing me."

Things always seemed so different to her. From where she stood, she was a loving mother giving her daughter a lift. In her mind, she was doing her best to get by while I was being difficult.

She was always like this. She'd swear, call me names, and rant for hours – then wouldn't remember a thing or at least she'd pretend she'd forgotten.

I didn't care about the pain in my arm from being shoved. That was nothing compared to the frustration simmering inside me. As if I needed this on top of the hangover. How much more was I supposed to take?

I just wanted to get away. From her. From everything.

As a kid, I used to dream my father would mysteriously turn up in a white Cadillac and save me, but I worked out a long time ago he could've found me if he wanted to. And Mom was already enough to deal with.

In the car, Mom took the corners too quickly for someone in my delicate state but I could hardly tell her that. I glanced at the speedometer as she headed down the main road. She was driving over the limit. Then I realized she had a better view of the dial than I did and probably wasn't speeding. It all depended on the position of the observer. Parallax error.

Eventually, I arrived and that was all that mattered.

Dropping down onto one of the sofas inside the door of the library, I waited for Alec. He'd sent me a text earlier so I knew he wouldn't be long. A few minutes later, the automatic glass doors slid open and he walked in, all six feet three of him.

"Let's go outside." I stood.

He sniggered. "You need the fresh air, do you?"

Truth was I needed a lot more than fresh air. We settled on a bench under a maple tree in the garden next to the library. I unzipped my backpack and pulled out a bottle of water.

"Good thinking," Alec said. "You've got to keep hydrated."

"Bit late for that now, unfortunately."

Alec looked down at his hands. "I'm sorry about last night."

I turned to face him. "No, *I'm* sorry. That's why I asked you here, so I could apologize for getting so drunk."

Reluctantly, he looked across at me, his black hair in his eyes. "It's my fault, Sasha. I shouldn't have plied you with alcohol. I should've known better."

"No, you didn't force me to do anything. It was all my stupid fault. Hope I didn't embarrass you too much."

He waved his hand as if it were nothing. "Nah, I've done plenty of stuff more embarrassing than that."

"Can I be honest with you?"

Alec nodded. "Sure."

I straightened. "Part of me isn't sorry at all. I had a really good time last night. Until the end, that is."

Alec got that cheeky grin he was so good at. "It was kind of fun."

"I've got an ulterior motive, too."

"What's that?"

"There are a few things I can't quite remember and I was hoping you could fill them in for me."

"What kind of things?" he asked.

"Like how I got home."

If I didn't sound particularly confident, there was a reason for it. Getting home was one of many things I couldn't remember about last night.

"Penny's mom was supposed to take you," Alec said. "We decided that wasn't such a good idea, so I asked my brother to give us a lift home."

Now I was getting worried. "My mom was already asleep, wasn't she?"

"Yep. I unlocked your front door, put the keys in your

hand, pushed you inside and hoped for the best."

I covered my mouth with one hand. This was worse than I thought. I had no recollection of this whatsoever.

"Thanks, Alec," I said, wondering how I was ever going to repay him.

"Honestly, it was no problem and my brother didn't mind at all. He's seen it all before."

"Seen what before?"

Snatches of memory came to me. I remembered leaning over some bushes and throwing up. I thought I hadn't but I had.

My stomach was still swirling with nausea and now it twisted into a knot. How embarrassing. Humiliating even. And there was no changing it.

"Would you please apologize to your brother for me?" I said in a small voice.

"Sure, but there's no need. He was cool with it." Alec held my gaze, his expression more earnest. "I was a bit worried when I came back with a glass of water and you'd passed out on the grass."

"What? Like, properly passed out?"

I hunched forward, the knot in my stomach tightening. What had I done? What had I been thinking?

"That's not all," Alec said. "They'd pulled your top up over your head."

I went from worried to horrified. "Who?"

Alec put a hand on my shoulder. "Don't panic, your tee shirt wasn't completely off and you still had your bra on."

"Great, I feel much better."

Alec dropped his hand, looked down at the ground. "Finn wasn't with them but it was the guys he hangs out

177

with who did it. They'd pulled your top up and were standing around, gawking. I told them to fuck off and got rid of them."

I raised my eyebrows. "You told them to fuck off."

"Well, I said 'leave her alone'."

"And they left?"

"Yeah. I pulled your tee shirt down of course. I didn't just leave you there like that."

I dropped my head in my hands. Shame flooded through me. And gratitude.

"Thanks for looking after me, Alec," I said. "For being such a good friend. I can't thank you enough."

"Honestly, it wasn't such a big deal. I've been drunk and blacked out before too. I know what it's like. I also know you'll get over it." He nudged me, a grin on his face. "You looked cute in your bra. Black is very sexy, you know."

"Alec, please don't," I said.

"That butterfly shaped birthmark is cute too."

That was when it hit me. He wasn't joking or mucking around or teasing me. There was no other way Alec could've known about the birthmark on my ribs under my left breast.

And I had done this to myself.

With all the other incidents in my life, the bullying and the taunting, I could honestly say I didn't know why those things happened to me or why I was picked on. This was different.

Alec was very sweet. We talked and he tried to make me feel better. Maybe for a while, he did.

Then he left and I called Penny to apologize. That was the aim of the phone call. I apologized over and over again and every time I said the word 'sorry' I meant it. For all the good it was going to do.

"I warned you," Penny said. "You shouldn't have had the first drink. That's where it all starts. And you weren't even enjoying the beer. I don't know why you were drinking in the first place."

I knew why. To forget and to feel good. It had backfired. I didn't feel so good now.

Penny was pissed and she wasn't hiding it. I only had two friends at school and now I was losing one of them.

"I was way out of line," I said. "I know that."

"Do you? Do you know how you ruined the whole evening for me?"

"I'm sorry," I said. Again.

"With you and Alec out of action, there was hardly anyone for me to talk to so I called my mom to pick me up early. I was so embarrassed by the whole thing."

"So am I."

Suddenly Penny reminded me of my past friend Molly at my old school and what she'd said when I told her I was leaving Southern Hills High. One word. Goodbye.

Sometimes I thought the only reason I'd chosen Penny as a friend was because she'd have me. Maybe that sounded unkind but I had so few friends to choose from that I'd learned to look for the good in the people who were there.

"This is only going to get more humiliating," Penny said. "Have you checked FacePlace?"

I covered my mouth. "Oh no, you're not going to tell me they took photos?"

"You can't remember, can you?"

No, but I could have regrets. I had plenty of those.

"I've got to go."

Grabbing my bag, I headed into the library, found a spot in the back corner and opened my laptop to find I'd become a FacePlace sensation among my so-called friends.

Considering the photo was probably taken on a phone in the dark, it was crisp and clear. The flash had been working just fine. There I was, sprawled out on the grass, clearly drunk, with my midriff and birthmark on display. The only good thing about the picture was that my tee shirt was pulled partly over my face, though that did nothing to diminish my embarrassment.

What had I done?

The photo wasn't the thing that hurt the most, though. The comments were coming in thick and fast from people at my old school, my new school, from all around.

— *Academically gifted and extremely retarded!*

— *Pissed as a newt!?!*

— *Thank Christ she left the rest of her clothes on.*

— *This is what happens when a slut like her gets drunk.*

The last comment was from Madison. *She'd* given some guy a blow job yet I was the one who was a slut. How did that work?

I deleted the photo from my page and hoped my mother didn't cotton on. She wasn't big on social networking anyway. But the picture was already on plenty of other pages and there was nothing I could do about that.

A huge weight pressed down on my shoulders. My chest felt crushed, the air sucked right out of me. I was never going to live this down. I'd get taunted at school too. This was more ammunition for the bullies.

I could see where this was going.

PARALLAX ERROR

It wasn't going to stop.

CHAPTER TWENTY

The Primary

Back at The Primary. Back to the real world, as Remy said after the train pulled in.

The vacation is over, if that's what you can call our time in The Ghettolands. The tournament is over too. Not training, though. That's never over and neither is my nightmare.

Remy is at my side as we stride down the wide corridor toward Mason's office where we've been asked to wait. I'm the one who has been summoned here, not Remy, but still he sticks to me like an overbearing parent. I've got one of those back home and don't need another.

He has been helpful and seems genuine yet I don't think he's the right person to help me with the next steps. I have to get out of here before anyone else works out what's wrong with me and to do that, I need to discover what else was going on in Sasha Rodriguez's life, what she was up against and what propelled her into my universe. If that's where she went.

I can ask Remy about what happened to Sasha one more time. It can't hurt. Actually I'm not sure I've asked him outright before.

"Why did you go looking for me in Mason's office that day?" I ask.

Remy slows down, looks at me. "Why so suspicious?"

"Because something happened just before that to make me lose my memory."

He stops, pulls over closer to the wall of the corridor. "I'd looked for you everywhere else. That was the only place left."

I stand by the wall beside him. "Why were you looking for me?"

"We were supposed to meet up that day."

"Were we?"

"We're friends, Sasha. Friends do that sort of thing all the time."

"What about Bridget? She's supposed to be my friend too."

Bridget Simpson and I have both been summoned today. All I know about her is what Remy has told me: that she's my best friend and we've had a disagreement, a serious one by the sound of it.

"I'm not going through that again," Remy says. "You've got to be careful not to give yourself away. Keep your wits about you."

I stare at him, thinking that of course my wits are with me. Where else would they be? Then, I shouldn't blame my irritability – or my situation – on him.

"You don't trust Bridget, do you?" I ask.

A pause. "I trust her. Just not where your life is concerned."

We head toward Mason's office. Something about it reminds me of the alley I walked down with Joey before we were attacked. There's a twinge in my gut, the feeling that something's not right, which is ridiculous because nothing is right while I'm in this place.

Mason's office door is open so Remy knocks and we enter. The General sits behind his big desk while Bridget stands on the other side, her blond ponytail immaculate, spine rigid, hands behind her back.

"What are you doing here, Christenson?" Mason asks.

"I'm aware my presence wasn't requested." Remy sounds very sure of himself for someone who's not obeying official orders.

Mason stares. "Is there something going on I should know about?"

"Not that I know of."

I'm glad Remy's the one answering the questions because my stomach is churning.

Mason stands. "Take a seat. No need to be so formal."

He comes around to the other side of the desk, pushes some papers to one side and perches on the edge. His military haircut and the lines on his face give him authority. The three of us sit on the available chairs, not quite as relaxed as Mason.

"I've got a job for you two." Mason looks at me first, then Bridget. "We've got some promotional talks scheduled at a couple of schools in the estates and you two would be perfect." He shrugs and adds, "It'll be a breeze. Just the standard presentation you've made before will be fine, Sasha."

I wonder what 'standard presentation' that would be. How am I supposed to stand up in front of a group of people and speak authoritatively about The Primary when I've only been here a few days?

My expression remains even. I do my best not to give myself away.

Remy must be thinking the same thing because he says, "With all due respect, Mason, surely this task is beneath someone with Sasha's experience. She hasn't done that sort of promotional work for a long time."

"I didn't ask you." Mason shifts his gaze to Bridget, a smug look on his face. "It's not beneath Bridget Simpson. I'm having trouble finding tasks lowly enough to suit her skill level."

Redness spreads across Bridget's face to the roots of her blond hair, the blue of her eyes stark against her flushing skin.

I'd stick up for her if I knew how. I glance at Remy and see he can't make out what's going on either.

"I'll get someone else to do the promotional work." Mason smiles as if he's completely forgotten the insult. "I've got another idea. A training exercise. It's something you'll have to go through anyway so maybe you should both do this now."

"Let's…get it out of the way then." I hide the hitch in my voice.

I've got a much better chance with this than with a public speaking engagement. At least with training, I might be able to wing it.

"You're well on your way to success, Sasha," Mason says. "The Primary has given me so much. I only hope you get as much out of this."

Doesn't he have anything else in his life other than The Primary and his career? Friends? Family?

"I haven't heard anything about this exercise, Mason," Remy says.

"You can report to the facilities office and help with the set-up." Mason waves a hand toward the door.

Remy stands reluctantly but doesn't leave yet. "So this exercise will be at the training facility, the one that's set up to look like a regular street only with fake buildings and a fake gas station?"

"Where else would it be? What's with you today?" Mason shoos him away. "Off you go."

Remy was giving me all the hints he could to help me get by. I'd look like an idiot if I didn't know what the facility was used for. When Mason suggested a training exercise, I thought he was referring to the sort of martial arts I'd done with Remy. That wasn't what he meant at all.

Only one way to find out what I was in for.

*   *   *

Bridget and I stare at the street ahead of us, the fake street. The buildings on either side of us are real though they're only used for training, one marked 'general store' another 'post office'. This is where students at The Primary come to act out real life scenarios. I've seen this sort of thing on a documentary I watched about a police academy where they'd stage a fake robbery and then police officers would test what they'd do in real life.

I figure we'll have to do the same sort of tactical exercise.

Earlier it had poured with rain but now the sun is out, a pleasant change. It doesn't smell fresh, however. It never does in this place.

"It's only a matter of time," Bridget says.

"Until what?" I ask.

"Until I get sent back to The Ghettolands."

"Why are you going back there?"

She frowns. "As if you don't know."

Which makes me wonder what I've done wrong now.

Perhaps today's exercise is a test for Bridget to see if she's good enough to stay at The Primary. So far, I've been making the grade whereas her skills seem to be under question.

It's quiet here. Unsettling. Once again, a vision of the alley where Joey and I were attacked flashes before me. I've got to get those thoughts out of my head and focus on what's in store today.

Footsteps behind us. Mason is striding toward us, an impressive figure in black tee shirt, cargo pants and combat boots.

He stops in front of me. Holds my gaze.

"What's the drill?" I ask.

Mason points down the street. "You go into the burning building. The rest you'll work out when you get there."

I raise my eyebrows. "The burning building?"

"Smoke bombs are being set off to simulate a real fire," he says.

"And what's the aim of this exercise?"

"You'll know when you get there."

"When do we start?" Bridget asks.

Mason looks ahead. Smoke curls out of the open windows of one of the buildings.

"Now," he says.

Bridget heads toward the building. I stay frozen to the spot. Bars cover the windows of both the ground and first floors. A shiver shoots up my spine.

My powers of perception don't extend to reading Mason's mind. I don't know what on earth we're supposed to do inside this building with its simulated fire.

Is the aim to save some people who're inside? Do we put out this fake fire? Do we simulate choking to death?

"Are you going to tell me what we're supposed to do in there?" I ask.

"We're the same, you and I." Emotion glimmers in Mason's hazel eyes. "My parents didn't believe in me as a kid either. I got pushed around. It made me stronger. You're so much like me, only sharper, quicker, younger."

I am nothing like him. "You haven't answered my question."

Mason steps closer. "Aim high. Look to the top."

He stares at me as if it's obvious. This is all way too mysterious for my liking.

Bridget stops, turns and shouts, "Sasha!"

"Go," Mason says.

I run to join Bridget and we jog to the door of the building. When I glance down the street, Mason has gone. I'm ready to kick down the door. Instead Bridget tries the handle, then throws the door open which is a much more sensible idea. Smoke billows out so we stand on either side of the open doorway and wait a moment.

Smoke catches in my throat. "What are we supposed to do in there?"

"I don't know." Bridget coughs. "We'll work it out inside. We do as we're told, remember. For as long as we're here."

For as long as we're here? I wonder whether she expects to remain at The Primary and what the alternative is.

"This is crazy," I say.

She glares. "You should be used to it by now."

Bridget steps inside and I follow. She hunches over, her head at waist height, and I do the same. Smoke rises so there's more oxygen closer to the floor, and this is the safest approach. Not as safe as breathing apparatus. Not as safe as staying out of here but that's not an option.

I can't work out what's going on. Noise is being piped into the house or at least I think that's what's happening. One minute it sounds like a wounded animal is roaring, the next as if the building might fall down. The noises are discordant, disorienting.

They also take away one of our senses. We won't hear what's coming. Anxiety settles in my stomach.

Bridget and I check the rooms on the ground floor. Nothing. The place is set up with a few pieces of furniture to make it look like a house. It's definitely not a home. No one would want to live in this dump.

There's no fire and it's not even that hot. Still, I'm sweating and we're both coughing and spluttering. The smoke we're swallowing is very real, the acrid taste stuck at the back of my throat.

I point up the stairs. "This way?"

Bridget nods. We trudge up the stairs to find there's more air up there than below. The smoke bombs must've been let off on the lower level.

We hear it at the same time, the high-pitched wail of a baby crying. Bridget nods to indicate this must be what we're looking for, but surely they couldn't leave a baby in a smoke-filled building.

We're standing by the stair well. The building has only two floors however the stairs also go up to another level, perhaps a terrace. Several doors, all of them open, line the corridor. Behind us, a ladder rests against the wall, and there's a hatch in the ceiling above it that probably leads to an attic.

I open a door to my right. We walk inside and check behind a large bed and in the corner behind a bureau. I could've sworn the crying sound was coming from here but the creaking and roaring sounds that surround us are making it hard to tell.

Bridget and I don't talk. Her throat is probably as raw with smoke as mine. We leave the room and she heads down the hall.

"Wait," I say.

I hold a finger to my lips while we try to work out where the sound is coming from. Bridget is listening too as the shrill wail of a baby cuts through the rest of the noise.

She points to her left. That seems to be where the sound is coming from.

I go in first. The room is hazy. I make out a closet and a single bed. The wailing gets louder. I see a crib in the corner and step toward it. A crib, but no baby, only a small recorder. I switch it off, relieved because that must've been the aim of this exercise.

I turn, ready to tell Bridget we're done here only to find she's gone, the door closed. Something is wrong. I was sure she'd followed me into the room. No way would she have closed that door.

In the distance, close or far, I can't tell, I hear smashing sounds. A painful roar rips through the air. A human roar of pain.

My heart thumps inside my chest. Because that wasn't a recording.

It was Bridget's voice.

CHAPTER TWENTY-ONE

We've been set up. This is a test. Of what, I don't know.

And Bridget is in pain.

I rush to the door. Locked. I ram it with my shoulder but it doesn't budge. Taking a couple of steps back, I send in a push kick. The first one does nothing. The second knocks the handle off. The third sends the door flying open.

I look around the hall. Which way now?

A pained scream cuts through the other strange noises that are being piped into the building. I head toward the sound, hoping this is the right direction. Hoping there's no ambush. I don't know what's right or wrong any more, only that I have to follow my gut.

The sound becomes more of a groan. Peeking through an open doorway, I see Bridget sitting on the floor in the middle of an empty room. I scan the room first, then rush toward her. She has rolled up one leg of her pants, her shin exposed. She's clutching one knee, rocking back and forth, moaning.

I drop to the ground in front of her, my eyes on her

SUSANNA ROGERS

leg. It's bent, clearly broken. A splinter of something white has broken through the skin. Must be bone. A shudder shoots through me at the pain she must be in.

Shocked, I ask. "Who did this to you?"

"There were two of them," she says between gasps. "With baseball bats."

There's no way uninvited guests could've got in, not with security at The Primary, also no way intruders can have known exactly who to target unless they'd been informed. No, there is nothing 'uninvited' about their presence. It's all part of the exercise.

Except this isn't training. It's torture. Aimed squarely at Bridget. Anger surges through my veins, my breaths coming short and fast.

She reaches for my arm, tears in her eyes. "You stayed."

"We've got to get out of here."

She squeezes my arm, her grasp so desperate I think she might not let go.

"Both of us," I add. "Come on."

I help her up onto her good leg. She leans on me and hobbles to the door, groaning and gasping but she can do it and that's the main thing. Her body is probably in shock, adrenaline running through her system. The pain will hit her harder after that wears off.

I stop. The hair on the back of my neck stands on end despite the sweat I'm covered in. The air around us feels electric, the smell of smoke thicker than before.

"Listen," I say.

The air is still filled with the same strange discordant sounds as if a building is collapsing but there's something else in the background, something constant, a crackling sound more sinister than any loud noises.

I hope that's not what I think it is. I don't even want to think it.

"Wait here," I say.

Bridget nods, leans against the doorframe.

I pull up the neck of my tee shirt to cover my mouth and rush down the stairs. Searing heat hits me right away, nearly knocks me back. I don't make it to the bottom. The foot of the stairs, the hallway below me, the entire ground floor is engulfed in flames. Orange flames lick the bannister below.

I rush back to the top.

"Fire," I yell. "Real fire."

Bars cover the windows on both levels, so the only way is up.

I put my arm around Bridget, lead her to the stairs heading up and tell her to wait. I scoot up the steps, ready to break down the door at the top but there's no need. It's not locked. I hesitate.

Aim high. Look to the top. That was what Mason had said. I'm not sure this is such a good way to go. It's also our only choice.

I fling the door open. Fresh air floods in. I can breathe again but that same air will probably be fuel for the fire. I've got to move fast.

At the bottom of the stairs, I get into position. "Piggy back."

Bridget doesn't argue. She slides up onto my back, her arms around my neck. I try to be gentle but it's impossible when going up the stairs, each step up causing Bridget immense pain. She holds back muffled moans. She's braver than I am. I'd be crumbling under that sort of agony.

We're outside on a small concrete terrace which seems to be a dumping place for old furniture and other assorted crap, all of it flammable. Beside us, there's a pitched roof with skylights that the fire could easily make its way through.

I drop Bridget carefully to the ground where she can sit.

At the other end of the terrace I see our target. Mason had said we'd recognize it when we saw it. The one thing he hadn't lied about. A large round wooden plaque with a red mark in the center sits on an easel.

That's it? That's what this stupid, futile, deadly exercise is about. I can't believe it. Anger burns in my stomach.

"They'll send someone to help us," I say.

Bridget looks at me, fear in her eyes. "No, they won't. That's not what this is about."

"Then what's it about?" No answer. "Shit!" I stamp my foot like a child.

I'm not giving up. I'm not taking no for an answer. I haven't come all this way to burn at the top of a building because this is some demented person's idea of a challenge.

Looking around, I survey the surrounding area to see if anyone is coming to help. No such luck. The next building is only eight feet from this one. I can jump and make it across to the other roof safely. That is, Sasha Rodriguez can do it.

I turn to Bridget with her broken leg. She won't have a chance.

"It's okay." She puts on a brave face. "It's best if you leave me. Save yourself."

In that moment, I know exactly what Sasha sees in Bridget. She's selfless, a quality that probably doesn't rate a mention at The Primary.

I stride past her towards the stupid goddamn plaque. "It's not over yet."

Fury courses through me. I've been angry many times in The Primary – angry when they threw me in the octagonal cage with The Monster, horrified when Remy told me what I was supposed to do to Joey, and furious when the men in the alley surrounded us.

But not like this.

This supposed training exercise was planned. Orchestrated. And Bridget and me? We are pawns. We are nothing.

I've been nothing before. Not any more. Thanks to Sasha Rodriguez I'm someone now. And I'm not going down without a fight.

I lift the plaque from the easel and sling it across to the rooftop of the next building. I kick the easel over. Then realize I'm wasting time.

In an instant, I'm back down those stairs again. The fire has made its way onto the second floor but hasn't reached its peak yet. I hold my breath and run to the other end of the corridor where a ladder is leaning up against the wall. It must lead to an attic that's under the pitched roof. I want that ladder.

I yank it from the clips that secure it at the top and turn. Flames lick at the carpet that lines the hall. I slide the top portion of the ladder down so it takes up half the space and tuck it under my arm.

The thought flashes in my mind. *This is too hard*. I can give up. I can stay and let the fire consume me.

I have another thought.

Screw that for a joke.

I sprint. I'm at the top of the stairs before I know it. I dump the ladder and hunch over trying to catch my breath.

Bridget points at me. "Sasha!"

My pants are on fire. Shit. I roll on the concrete trying to suffocate the small flames, hoping like hell they don't become big flames. I find puddles of water in the uneven concrete surface and for once, I'm grateful for the storms they have here.

"Sasha, Sasha." Bridget is calling my name. "Are you okay?"

Lying on my stomach, I look up at her. "I'm here."

"Are you okay?" she asks again.

"I'm fabulous," I say through gritted teeth.

Getting to my feet, I brush myself off and check I haven't missed anything obvious like more flames or some broken bones. No, I'm good.

I rush to the door I've just come through and close it to help keep the fire at bay. I glance at the skylights in the pitched roof beside me that are lit up orange. It's only a matter of time.

I pick up the ladder, extend it into its full length and notice what I didn't see before. The ladder is a rickety piece of crap that's not good for anything except being a prop. It's also all we've got.

I lay it across the space between this building and the adjacent one. It reaches – just – and that's the best I can say about it.

Suddenly there's an explosion. The roof beneath our feet shakes. What the hell is going on? Buildings don't just explode on their own.

There must've been a petrol bomb planted in the building to up the stakes, to spur us on, perhaps to char Bridget's body to a cinder.

That's what the authorities want. It's what Mason wants. He's teaching Bridget a lesson and I'm along for the ride.

Soon there won't be any building left. And who knows what they have planned for us next?

This isn't over yet.

CHAPTER TWENTY-TWO

Middleton

Four weeks before...

Alec was right. It had been a couple of weeks since the party and I felt better. Not good, just better, and that was as much as I could ask for.

In some ways, nothing had changed. It was back to school and study and tonight it was back to work.

Ten minutes until knock-off time, the best time of the evening. At work, I was appreciated and the people seemed to like me well enough but it was still work. Still boring.

The automatic doors at the other end of the supermarket opened and Finn Masters walked in. My heart jumped, not in a good way. It was a nervous, not-knowing-what's-going-to-happen kind of way.

A couple of minutes later, he was headed toward my register. There were no other customers around, no one else waiting to be served, nothing else I could pretend to be doing. Avoiding him wasn't an option.

He placed a Coke and a bag of chips on the counter, apparently his staple foodstuff.

"Hey," he said.

I scanned the items. "Hi, Finn."

Naturally I'd seen him at school over the past weeks and he often smiled or gave me a small wave. If his friends weren't looking. I understood. It was no big deal.

He held the scrunched up bills in his hand tightly. "I'm really sorry about what happened at Ella's party."

I shrugged. "I'd rather forget about it."

"The things people said on FacePlace were really mean."

Finn hadn't posted any comments, something I'd noticed. He hadn't stuck up for me either, not that I'd have expected him to.

"I wasn't with my friends when they took that photo," he said.

I looked down at his hand. "It's okay."

Finn handed over the money and I gave him back some change.

"I just wanted you to know I didn't have anything to do with it," he said. "You know, in case you thought I'd been in on it."

I shook my head. "I didn't think that."

He smiled and I had to admit he looked cute, his blond hair hanging over his green eyes.

"So we're good then?" he said.

"Sure."

"Maybe next time I see you, we can talk or something."

I smiled right back at him. Hoped I looked half as cute

as he did. "We're talking now, aren't we?"

"Yep, see you around."

Finn gave me a quick wave and left.

What had that been all about? Maybe my life wasn't completely crap after all. Maybe I had a chance of making more than two friends at school.

My heart dropped again. And maybe I was kidding myself. Still, I'd take whatever came my way.

My boss, Russell, walked past and told me it was time to close off my register. He didn't need to ask me twice. I couldn't wait to get out of there.

As I was heading along the walkway that led out of the store, he came up to me, jingling the car keys in his hand. He made a clicking sound with his tongue which I assumed was supposed to impress me. He was *so* not cool. It would've been better if he tried to act natural but that seemed to be beyond him.

He nudged my arm. "Can I offer you a ride home?"

"No thanks. My mom is picking me up." A small lie.

Leaning closer, he raised one eyebrow. "Is there anything else I can offer you?"

I stepped outside, stopped and pretended to look for my mom's car. "No, I'm fine, thanks."

While Russell headed toward his truck, the sound of raised voices and arguing made me turn. Two blond women stood under a light in the parking lot, their hair illuminated, only one of them wasn't a woman. It was Madison and the other was probably her mother.

"Give it to me!" The woman snatched a carry bag from her. "You can be a nasty little bitch sometimes."

Madison put her hands on her hips. "That's rich coming from you."

"You can't talk to me that way." The woman looked up, saw me and added, "Get in the car!"

Car doors slammed and they left using the rear exit. Madison Frost had an overbearing mother. Who'd have thought? Maybe her life wasn't so rosy either.

Russell pulled out. I looked around expectantly, waited until he'd driven off, then started walking home.

I wasn't going to let him or Madison ruin the one pleasant thing that happened to me today. Sometimes the little things in life could make me feel like it was all worth it. Like talking to Finn tonight. He'd gone to all the trouble of popping in to see me and that meant something. Not much perhaps, but something.

I waited until the traffic cleared, then crossed the road and walked around the corner. The soft shuffle of footsteps cut through the air so I stopped and turned. The street was empty. Must be my imagination. Still, the hair on the back of my neck stood on end.

Upping my pace, I passed a small park that wasn't far from home, the smell of mulch and freshly cut grass wafting through the air. The streetlight was broken, no lights in the park.

This time I didn't hear it coming.

Didn't see it either.

Someone grabbed me, a hand over my mouth. Dragged me backwards into the darkest part of the park. A scream caught in my throat. I tried to kick, tried to get away, but this guy was stronger than me.

Suddenly I was thrown to the ground, landing hard on my back. It winded me. The air left my body and I couldn't move.

I looked up. The guy had the hood of his jacket pulled

over his head. He wasn't stupid enough to leave his short dreadlocks on view for anyone to recognize.

I opened my mouth to scream but he landed on my chest with a thump, his knees on either side of me, one hand smothering my face.

In shock, I couldn't breathe. Couldn't do a damn thing. I was useless, always useless.

"Scream and you're dead," he said. "Understand?"

I nodded, my heart going a hundred miles an hour.

He sat on top of me breathing heavily and scowling. "No one likes you. You know that, don't you?"

I nodded again.

"Can't say I blame 'em."

I was too scared to speak, too scared to do anything.

He was heavy on my chest. "They've told me all about you."

"Who?" I asked.

He pressed my cheek onto the grass. Playing with me. Letting me know he could do what he wanted.

I thought about screaming, thought about trying to fight him off, but those ideas were in my head. They didn't mean anything when my whole body was gripped with fear. I didn't have the guts to scream and I had absolutely no doubt he could beat the crap out of me if he wanted to. Maybe we could get this over quickly if I did what he said.

"Must be a crappy life when you've got no friends." He sneered. "When everyone hates you. When you're a piece-of-shit-loser."

I didn't move. Didn't say anything.

He knew me. Probably knew the kids from school. This guy wasn't much older than me, probably only a year or two out of school himself.

"Did someone pay you to do this?" I asked between ragged breaths.

He laughed. "You think I need to get paid to have fun like this? I'm just helping out some friends."

And I knew.

Someone had asked him to follow me, give me a hard time, scare me, maybe even beat me up.

Was it Madison and Aisha? Or Finn's friends? Desperation tugged deep in my gut. Why would they do something like that? Why would anyone?

The guy in the hoodie leaned over me, the smell of stale cigarettes in my face. "I know you. I know all about you, where you live, where you work, where you go to school. And if you try, anything, I will find you and I'll make sure you're sorry. Next time, I won't be nice."

I nodded.

"Tonight I'm gonna sing you a little song instead."

So he did. He hummed, then sang the first couple of lines of the theme music from the film we'd seen in English.

Suicide is painless.

He grinned, his teeth glimmering in the faint light. "Maybe you should try it. Put us all out of our misery."

I didn't speak. I couldn't. I sure as hell couldn't scream.

The guy stood. I didn't dare move until he'd left, then I brushed myself off, but my legs were shaking so much I couldn't stand. Instead I leaned against a tree and stood there, too scared to cry, too scared to do anything.

My body seized up with pain, actual physical pain. How could it hurt like I'd just been in a crash? How could people hate me that much?

That guy wasn't kidding when he said he knew all about me. He knew the kids from school.

And they despised me enough to do this to me. The knife twisted deeper into my heart. Couldn't they use a real knife and get this over with? Because I didn't know how much more I could take.

The joke wasn't funny any more. And it had never been a joke.

Meanwhile, I was…nothing.

CHAPTER TWENTY-THREE

Three weeks before...

I wanted to forget. For everything to go away.

It had been a week since I'd been roughed up by the guy in the hoodie. I'd told Mom about it and she'd taken me to the police, not that she believed me. I wasn't sure the police had either. I didn't have a scratch on me and there was no evidence, nothing to back me up, not even the word of my mother. The police probably thought I was some ranting lunatic. And maybe they were right.

Mom was asleep. Earlier this evening, she'd told me I was weak, but I wasn't. Couldn't she see how strong I was to have put up with so much? Couldn't she see my pain?

I'd fallen asleep, then had woken with a start at midnight, eyes wide, my heart racing, my forehead on fire. I couldn't remember the dream but that damn song was in my head. *Suicide is painless.* At night that stupid song would run through my mind over and over again, that melancholy tune dripping with sadness, and I couldn't get rid of it.

Sitting up in bed, I dropped my head in my hands,

waiting until my heart rate slowed. I went to the bathroom for obvious reasons, came back to my room and slumped onto my bed in my flimsy pajamas, a little top and blue checkered shorts.

I leaned forward resting my hands on my knees. It wasn't good enough. Nothing I did was good enough. My head was pounding, filled with horrible thoughts, ready to explode.

I was like a little puppy dog that'd get kicked and would then come back panting, ready for more, only to get kicked again. And again.

I picked up the phone. Penny had barely been speaking to me since the night of the party. Still, I needed to talk to someone. She answered on the second ring.

"It's after midnight." Her tone was terse.

"But you're still up."

"I was reading *To Kill a Mockingbird.*"

"Still?" I asked.

"I was half-way through before when I had to stop and read a bunch of stuff for English. Now I'm right near the end and you've interrupted me. What do you want, Sasha?"

I wasn't sure what I wanted or how to put it into words.

"Are you drunk again?" Penny asked, disdain in her voice. "Is that it?"

No, loneliness was very different from drunkenness. So was desperation.

I swallowed, looked up at the dark ceiling. "I thought maybe we could talk."

I miss you. The words I couldn't say. *I need a friend.*

"You should have thought about that before you got

off your face," she said.

"Can't we leave that behind us?"

Penny wanted to be a doctor so she could help people. Here I was, one of her best friends, screaming for help and she couldn't see it. Between my panic attacks and depression, I was a textbook of problems waiting to be fixed.

But Penny had no idea how to be warm or caring. I think she knew it too and maybe that was part of the problem.

"I'm going to bed now," she said. "You should too. Goodnight, Sasha."

I stared at the phone in my hand. Penny was the one who'd quoted the line from *To Kill a Mockingbird* about how you need to consider things from a person's point of view to understand them. Yet she couldn't do that. Couldn't see what life was like for me.

All I wanted was some relief, was that too much to ask? I needed something to take the edge off so I could keep going. Some breathing space.

My heart thumped in my chest. A panic attack perhaps. I'd had a few of those lately. I took slow, deep breaths. Thought about the razor I kept in my top drawer. It gave me confidence and, amazingly enough, my heart rate slowed.

Getting up from the bed, I sat at my desk, switched on my desk lamp and dug out the razor blade from the drawer. I'd looked at it many times. Thought about cutting. Imagined it. Wondered what it would be like. I was done thinking.

I slashed the skin on the inside of my arm and watched the blood flow. The cut wasn't deep. It wasn't meant to be.

My pulse raced. In a good way. I felt alive. Blood flowed to my muscles, hormones and chemicals cascading through my body. There may have been pain. If there was, I didn't notice.

It felt like freedom.

I sat there for a while until the feeling faded. Once wasn't enough. I wanted to cut myself again, to feel that same rush. Not on my arm, though. Someone would notice.

So I held the razor between my fingers and slashed my inside thigh. It sizzled. I felt pain this time, sharp and immediate. I gasped. I didn't care.

My face went rosy. My whole body flushed. Blood rushed through my veins, my heart beating faster.

I felt I could take on the world. *I'm alive. I can do this. I can keep going for as long as it takes.*

The sensation faded. Nothing good could last.

Maybe it was bad to cut yourself like this. Still, it made me feel better for a while and that was more than I'd had in a long time.

Sleep was useless so I opened my laptop and switched it on. I was in luck. Brody was online. My life wasn't complete crap after all.

He said:

– *You're up late.*

– *Couldn't sleep.*

– *Me neither. You're still upset about what happened last week, aren't you?*

He meant the guy with the dreadlocks. Brody had convinced me the guy wouldn't be back and that he'd only wanted to scare me, which was probably right. It didn't make it less shit, though. Didn't make me less scared either.

I wrote:

— *Sometimes I wonder if I'm ever going to be able to sleep properly. That's always been the one thing I've had going for me. I've always been able to sleep even when things were bad. Not any more.*

— *You have to believe things will get better.*

I shot back quickly:

— *They can't get any worse.*

— *Don't be like that. What if you had something to look forward to?*

— *Like a trip to Paris? As if that's going to happen.*

Brody wrote:

— *There's something I've been wondering for a while. About whether you're ready to meet me.*

Excitement coursed through me. Genuine excitement. Brody finally wanted to meet me, despite his scars and his appearance.

— *Of course I'm ready to meet you!! I've wanted to see you for ages.*

— *It's not that easy, Sasha, and it won't be like you think. You might think you're prepared for seeing me but you won't be. You'll probably think I'm a monster.*

— *I'd never think that.*

— *Do you promise?*

— *Of course I promise.*

— *Because you'll have to be mature about it. That's one of the reasons I've been waiting.*

How wonderful. After all this time, who would've thought this was finally happening?

I wrote back:

— *Just name the time and place.*

— *We can work that out later. You're very special to me. You're really pretty too. In the pictures you sent me, you look stunning.*

— *Thanks. It's nice of you to say that. I don't get many compliments.*

— *Maybe you could send me some pictures that are special, some pictures that are just for me.*

I had a feeling I knew what kind of pictures he meant. Lots of girls took selfies and sexy shots of themselves and posted them on FacePlace. And I mean *lots*. I'd heard stories about girls taking nudes of themselves too to send to their boyfriends. And now I knew for a fact that at least some girls performed oral sex on random guys for the hell of it. I'd seen that for myself.

The rest of the world was out there having fun, having a huge party, having the time of their lives. Was it so wrong to want to be part of it?

Brody wrote:

— *Are you still there?*

— *Still here. I'm thinking about what you said. You mean shots that are more…artistic?*

— *That's exactly what I mean. You've put it much better than I ever could. I can't tell you how much this would mean to me.*

— *Hang on.*

A sly smile crept to my lips. I couldn't believe I was going to do this. A sultry sizzle shot up my spine, my whole body tingling.

Most of all, I felt desired. Someone cared. Brody cared. I wanted to feel good for a change. Surely that wasn't too much to ask.

I stepped over to the full-length mirror in the corner of my room, pulled my top off over my head and tossed it onto the bed. My breasts were small but they were still shapely. I had a lovely figure with a gentle curve to my waist and below that, my pajama shorts were hanging off my hips.

I looked good. Just as good as the next girl, damn it.

Strutting across to my desk, I got the laptop into place for some snaps.

I knew exactly how I wanted to do this. Almost as if I'd planned it.

The first shot was coy. I covered my breasts with my hands so you still couldn't see anything. For the final shots, I had my boobs fully on show, or what there was of them. I still had my shorts on of course but I was showing off my boobs, looking sexy, feeling sultry. I could be me, just for a while.

I put my top back on and zipped through the photos, taking out any where you could see my face. In one shot the fresh cut on my arm was visible. I froze but only for a moment, then pressed the delete button. No point editing out the birthmark on my ribs. That wasn't possible. It was part of me and, besides, Alec had said it looked cute.

I was still tingling all over when I sent the shots to Brody.

For the first time since I could remember, I felt truly special.

CHAPTER TWENTY-FOUR

The Primary

"We have to go." I half-help, half-drag Bridget to the edge of the building by the ladder I've placed across the void between the two buildings.

My ears are still ringing from the explosion, my throat raw from the smoke, and I'm the lucky one. My leg's not broken.

Bridget stops. Shudders. "Are we using that to get across?"

"No, *you're* using it," I say. "I'm going to jump."

She stares at the ladder, then looks up at me. "You've got to be kidding."

Clearly, it hasn't escaped her attention that the ladder is a piece of crap.

The sound of breaking glass shatters the air. The skylights go up in flames. Shards of glass land on an old sofa on the rooftop. Flammable. Instant bonfire. Dust and smoke fill the air.

"Sasha, I can't do this." Bridget's voice cracks. "I want

to get out of here but not like this."

Get out of here. Does she mean the burning building or The Primary? I'm wasting time. I have to do something.

"I'm not as strong as you." Bridget yells the words at me like an insult.

"You don't have a choice."

I stare at the building on the other side, my stomach gripped with sudden fear. I take a step backwards, then another. I can't do it. Can't jump that eight feet. It might as well be eight miles.

No, but Sasha Rodriguez can do it.

Before I can think, before I change my mind, I run-up and leap across, rolling as I land on the adjacent roof.

And somehow I know…it's not only Sasha's body that did that. It was her mind too, her inner strength, and maybe some of that is seeping through to me.

Bridget has positioned herself at the end of the ladder, still on the other building. She looks across at me, fear radiating from her every feature.

Behind her, orange flames are taking over. I can feel the fire's heat even from this distance.

"I can't, Sasha," she says. "Not with this leg."

"Just do it," I say.

Maybe I should come up with something with more warmth and encouragement, but there's more 'warmth' behind Bridget than she'll be able to cope with.

I'd go and get her and drag her across the ladder if I could, but there's no way that thing will take the weight of us both. We'll be lucky if it takes hers.

"Don't worry about me," she says.

"Too late," I yell. "I'm already worried."

"Sasha…" Her voice fades.

I press my eyes shut. *Don't do this now, Bridget.*

Eyes springing open, I shake my finger at her. "Climb onto the damn ladder or I'm coming over there and I'll break your other leg."

Sasha Rodriguez's words or mine, I don't know which.

Bridget reaches forward, grabs the sides of the ladder and pulls herself forward. I'm on edge, nerves simmering in my stomach, because I desperately want this girl I barely know to make it.

A few more yanks forward and she has cleared the building behind her. Her broken leg hangs over the edge of the ladder so she's leaning to her left for balance.

"You're doing a great job," I say. "Now use your good leg to push yourself along. Don't use your arms so much."

Which is easy for me to say from my position of safety. Less obvious when you've got a broken leg and you're dangling from a dangerous height on a shaky ladder.

Warm and encouraging, I tell myself.

"Good work, Bridget," I yell. "You're nearly there."

She grunts, keeps going. The ladder groans and shifts under her weight. It wasn't designed to be used horizontally.

"Just a little bit more," I say.

My heart swells with pride for Bridget. Despite the pain and the pressure she's doing her best. She pushes off using her good leg and reaches forward with her arms, close enough now for me to grab one of her arms and pull her closer.

No more warning. The ladder buckles, snaps in half behind Bridget. Slips from the wall on the other side.

Bridget's eyes are wide with fear. My heart races. A picture of her falling flashes in my head. *No.*

I grab her other arm. I've got her now. The ladder crashes to the ground. Bridget's body slams against the wall below me. She screams in pain.

"I won't let you go," I yell.

Doesn't matter that we're both hanging over the edge of a building. I'm going to do this. If I were stronger, one big heave would do it but I'm not quite that powerful so I keep pulling her up slowly. I grunt with the exertion of each yank. Bridget moans in pain.

She's nearly there. Her stomach pressed into the edge of the building, her feet still dangling down.

"I'm going to give you one big yank," I say. "I want you to roll onto the roof."

I heave her over. Bridget rolls. She screams in pain. Understandable under the circumstances.

Sitting with my hands on my knees, I try to catch my breath. Bridget is splayed on her back, breathless too. She lifts her hand and I wonder what she's doing until it hits me. I give her a high five.

She stares at me. I'm not sure what she's looking at.

"Do I have dirt on my face?" I ask.

"That's not it," she says. "Behind you."

I get to my feet. The rooftop we've come from is covered in flames, smoke thickening. I cough.

We've still got to get back to the ground, a task that should be relatively easy in a building that's not burning down.

A fire truck appears in the distance. Better late than never. A lone figure is ahead of the vehicle, running towards the burning building. I shout out and wave from the rooftop.

The person gets closer. It's Remy.

He stands at the bottom, cups his hands over his mouth. "Are you okay?"

Fabulous, I think.

"Bridget's leg is broken," I shout. "She needs medical attention."

He nods.

This mess is Mason's doing, I'm sure of that, but I wonder how much Remy had to do with it.

Remy, who didn't think the school visits were a good idea. Remy, who agreed a training exercise would be more up my alley. Remy, who looks so healthy and clean, while I'm covered in dirt and sweat and stink of smoke.

I look down at him. Nothing about him says he's surprised. Because he knows the drill, just like he knew exactly what Bridget and I were in for.

I grab the stupid plaque and fling it down at the ground next to Remy. Screw Mason. Screw The Primary. Screw everything.

CHAPTER TWENTY-FIVE

Middleton

Ten days before…

I couldn't believe I was finally meeting Brody after all this time.

He thought I might be shocked by his appearance and maybe I would, but he trusted me and I couldn't let him down. We'd been through too much together. I was mature enough and this was the time to show it.

I jumped off the bus and looked around to get my bearings. Brody's house wasn't very far from Morton College, but I didn't know the area well and had checked it out on Google maps. That was me. Always prepared.

This neighborhood was prettier than mine, the houses a little bigger, the front yards greener and the streets were lined with trees. I tried to avoid their shade so I could enjoy the sun on my back. I was taking my time, looking around, enjoying the sense of anticipation.

Spotting a garden lined with enormous rose bushes, I

leaned over the front fence, cupped a red rose in my hand and brought it to my face. It must have been bred for beauty, not fragrance because it didn't smell like much, not that it mattered. The flowers brought a smile to my face.

Ms. Dyson had come up with a quote in English class the other day. *A rose by any other name would smell as sweet.* I knew what Shakespeare was saying: that it didn't matter what name you gave things. Maybe Shakespeare had missed something too. Roses were beautiful and that's why we were attracted to them.

Appearances were important. I wasn't naïve enough to think the way you looked didn't matter. Madison and Aisha got away with so much because they were both good looking and popular. Though I didn't want to admit it, maybe the same went for Finn.

At the opposite end of the spectrum, I had a flat chest, ordinary face, dirty blond hair, and always got taken advantage of and pushed around. Still, it was a hundred times worse for Brody. Whatever other problems I had, at least I wasn't disfigured.

I'd been thinking about him when I got dressed this morning and had come up with the most average outfit of all – jeans, a white tee shirt and a pair of red Chuck Taylors. I loved my sneakers and didn't care that other kids had brands that were trendier and more expensive. If only I could be as confident about everything else in my life.

Brody's house was easy enough to find. It looked pretty much like the other houses on the street with its picket fence, green lawn and white weatherboard front. A motor bike sat in the driveway.

As I walked up the front path, I remembered that Brody was deaf or perhaps it was only deaf in one ear. He hadn't mentioned anything about that recently, almost as if he'd forgotten. Strange. Still, we'd get around it somehow.

My fingers tingled with anticipation as I raised my hand to knock on the door. I figured that was normal under the circumstances which were anything but average.

A man opened the door and smiled. Recognition flickered in his eyes so I figured Brody had told him about me, maybe even shown him a photo.

"You must be Sasha." He swept his hand aside for me to enter.

"Hi," I said. "Is Brody home?"

"Yes, come in."

The hair on the back of my neck stood on end as I stepped over the threshold. I'd come to the house of a person I'd never met in a neighborhood I didn't know and, what's more, no one knew I was here. I'd mentioned where I was going to Alec but he barely knew Brody.

And the thought occurred to me... Maybe I didn't know him either. Then again, that was probably just nerves on my part.

"Take a seat." The man ushered me into the living room.

He stood in the doorway while I perched on the edge of the sofa. He was slim with short light brown hair, brown eyes and a friendly face, not the sort of person who'd stand out in a crowd.

I wondered if Brody had got his looks from him. Then, this man didn't look old enough to be Brody's father. And if he was an older brother, there must be a huge age gap between them.

"Where's Brody?" I asked.

"Wait here and I'll get some Cokes."

Something wasn't right and it had nothing to do with Brody's disfigurement. My chest tightened, my throat constricting.

I could leave. I *should* leave, but that'd be rude.

Before I had a chance to move, the man was back, two cans of Coke in his hand. He'd done exactly as he said he would. Maybe I was overreacting.

He looked ordinary. The room looked ordinary too. Lacy drapes framed a window that looked out onto the front yard. There was a flat screen television, coffee table and a couple of other chairs other than the sofa I was sitting on.

The man placed the drinks on a coffee table in front of the sofa. "Sasha, I know this is going to come as a shock to you—"

"Where's Brody?"

"That's what I'm trying to tell you." He sat on a chair opposite me. "*I'm* Brody. I'm the guy you've been messaging and emailing all this time. And I'm pleased to finally meet you."

I froze. That's what I always did. I couldn't move, couldn't speak, couldn't do much of anything.

My eyes darted toward the door. I thought about running. My pulse skyrocketed. My muscles seized up. I wasn't going anywhere.

"It's not what you think." His voice was calm and even. "I'm not some weirdo pedophile trying to take advantage of you. I'm like you. I was lonely. I didn't have anyone. No one listened. Then I found you. And your company made my life a little easier."

I opened my mouth to speak but nothing came out. My heart rose to my throat. I was choking.

He put up his hand, palm out. "Take your time. I won't rush you. I'm sure this is a lot for you to take in."

"Yes," I said finally.

"I never meant to mislead you, though I'm sure that's how it looks to you now."

My eyes widened. If only they'd been open earlier. "Yeah, it does."

"I don't make friends easily either," he said. "But we've known each other for a while now. Our friendship doesn't have to change. We don't have to let a little thing like the age difference stand in the way."

I gritted my teeth. "You lied to me."

He lowered his gaze. "I'm sorry for that. Sorry you have to go through this difficulty now too. But I didn't know how much I was going to like you or how well we'd get on until after I'd got to know you. By then, it was too late."

"You haven't been burnt," I said. "You're not disfigured. You're not deaf."

"I'm not deaf to your feelings either." He rested his arms on his knees, steepling his fingers. "I've hurt you. I can only imagine what you're feeling at the moment. I hope I haven't let you down too much. Also that the friendship we've built up is strong enough for us to get through this because it'd be a shame to lose that. I don't know about you but I don't have so many friends I can afford to lose any."

Brody always knew the right thing to say. That was what I'd always thought. And he was just as eloquent in real life as he'd been when we were sending each other messages.

Of course he knew the right thing to say because he was older and more experienced and probably knew he could walk all over me. Which is exactly what he'd done. He was a monster, he truly was.

Fear skittered along my nerve endings. I had to find a way out of here.

"What's your name?" I asked.

"Brody."

"What's your real name?"

I edged toward the arm of the sofa at the end closest to the door.

"You can leave," he said. "I'm not stopping you but you don't need to worry. I'm not going to hurt you."

He wasn't going to hurt me.

Why would he even say that?

My throat tight, I swallowed.

Cooler than I imagined anyone could ever be, he added, "I'm also not going to go away, so you might as well hear me out."

What was he saying?

He stood slowly, probably so I wouldn't get scared. "I'll show you. My laptop is in the next room on the dining table."

I stood too. He'd said the magic word. Laptop. That computer probably had every message I'd ever sent him, every email, every attachment.

And every photo.

God, no. The topless photos. What had I done? How could I have been so stupid?

I tried to stay calm, tried to think this through, but my head was pounding and my heart was thumping and my whole world was being turned upside down. He could smell my fear. I was dripping in desperation.

No point heading for the door. That wasn't going to

make any of this go away.

"You can come and see if you like," he said.

So I followed him. I'd come this far.

Unlike the tidy living area, the dining table was covered in mess. Two dirty plates and glasses, probably left over from lunch, sat at the other end. A leather biker jacket, a helmet and a black canvas bag with a phone and other bits and pieces spilling out of it had been slung onto the table.

I took a deep breath and waited, my legs shaking. Brody – for want of a better name – reached under the canvas bag for a padded laptop bag and unzipped it.

Through the corner of my eye, I saw something, tried not to stare so I didn't give myself away. Brody's wallet was sitting on the table.

He flipped open the lid of the computer and booted it up. "Hang on, and I'll get the Cokes."

He left. I reached for the wallet, opened it. His driver's license sat behind a clear plastic window. Footsteps behind me. I slid the wallet under the jacket and turned to take the can from Brody. I repeated his name and address in my head over and over.

He handed me a Coke, took a drink from the can in his hand and turned the laptop to face me.

Thumbnails of the shots of my boobs stood out loud and clear. My heart stopped, just for a moment, then kept right on banging in my chest. I wished my pulse would cease, that I could disappear between the cracks in the floorboards, slide into oblivion.

I couldn't do this.

I wasn't strong enough.

I wanted everything to go away.

The man's fingers hovered over the keyboard. I

couldn't bear it.

"Please don't," I said.

Too late. A photo of my naked breasts opened up onto the screen. My boobs. I gasped. Took a step back.

"It's okay," he said. "I'll trash the photos later if you like. You can watch me do it but first I want to talk to you."

So stupid of me to have let this happen, but I wasn't that stupid. Electronic photos didn't go away that easily. People made copies, sent pictures to their friends, posted them on FacePlace.

No, no, not this. Sick to my stomach, I shuddered. This couldn't be happening. Dear god, how was I ever going to get rid of those photos?

"We've got to know each other so well." Brody's voice was even. "I'll remove all trace of those images if you do me one little favor."

His words were so calm. They didn't give even a hint of the evil glimmering in his dark eyes.

"You're very special to me," he said. "And there's a way you can show me how special I am to you too. If you do me this one little favor, this problem will go away completely and it'll be as if those photos never existed."

I shook my head slowly. This was never going to go away. *He* was never going to go away.

"I won't touch you," he said. "I won't grab you. I won't force you into anything. I'm going to pull my jeans down and I'd like you to give me a special kiss. That's all."

Disgust curdled in my stomach. No, no. My mouth dry, I couldn't speak. Couldn't even bring the Coke can in my hand to my mouth. I stood there swaying, unable to get a word out.

He held my horrified gaze. "If you don't do this, I'll put those photos on FacePlace and everyone will see them. Aisha, Finn, Penny, Alec, I'm friends with everyone at your new school and your old school. I know them all."

It was true.

He had all the power and I had nothing.

I was nothing.

It didn't matter that this wasn't fair, that he was an adult, that I'd made a mistake. All that mattered was that my boobs would be out there for the world to see and I'd never hear the end of it. Never. They'd never stop.

My body shaking, I clenched my fists at my side. I hated this man. Despised him. And he was feeding off my fear.

"This is all up to you," he said. "No one has to see those photos."

Liar.

I threw the Coke can at his face, turned and ran.

"You won't even see it coming," he yelled.

He laughed. Didn't chase me. He didn't need to.

CHAPTER TWENTY-SIX

The Primary

I'm holding Bridget's hand in a hospital room. We both stink of smoke though at least she's wearing clean clothes, an extremely unattractive blue hospital gown. Her previously immaculate blond hair is a mess. Mine's probably not much better. The bed Bridget is lying on has been tilted up and I'm on a chair beside her.

The medical staff said they don't allow visitors immediately before a patient is prepped for surgery but Bridget was insistent to say the least.

I even used the words, "Don't you know who I am?" The funniest thing was that they did know. I can be insistent when I want to, too.

There's a clock ticking inside me. My time is running out. Life is cheap at The Primary. Life is something to be toyed with during reckless training exercises or used to prove your allegiance to country.

I got out alive this time. For what it's worth. If anyone else finds out I've lost my memory, my life won't be so valuable any more, and it'll be worse if they find out the truth.

Sasha Rodriguez went through a traumatic experience in Mason's office that caused the body swap, of that I'm sure. Before that, she had an altercation with Bridget and, surgery or no surgery, I'm going to find out what happened.

Bridget's hand in mine, I hold her gaze. "I want to talk to you about the big argument we had."

She looks away. "It wasn't exactly an argument."

"We still need to talk."

"No, we don't." Bridget's warm brown eyes glimmer with gratitude. "You saved my life back there, Sasha. It's probably the only thing you could've done to make it up to me and you did it."

"I couldn't leave you there," I say.

"Yes, you could."

I can't believe she thinks I'd betray her, think only of myself, abandon her in a burning building. If anyone has the skills to save Bridget's life, that person is Sasha.

So what's the rift between them? Why would Bridget doubt her?

"What did I do that was so wrong?" I ask.

Bridget pulls her hand away from mine.

"I'm sorry," I say. "Whatever I did I'm very sorry."

She glares at me. 'Sorry' isn't going to cut it.

I clear my throat and try again. "I've got to get a few things straight in my head. I need to see it from your point of view and hear it from you. Pretend I don't know anything and that you're telling the story to someone else. Start from the beginning. Just humor me."

"This isn't very humorous."

"I saved your life, didn't I?" I say, sounding very much like Sasha Rodriguez. "One small favor is not too much to ask. Close your eyes and give it to me in your own words."

Bridget sighs deeply, closes her eyes. "I don't know exactly when it started. You were the star student, the one who excelled, the one who always had people hovering over you wanting to be your friend."

If only that had been my life. "Go on."

"Mason was always singing your praises. You embodied everything a prime candidate should be whereas I was average at best. He was always picking on me and you could never see it. Then, by the time you noticed, it was too late."

What had I seen? Why won't she come out with it? I'm silent. I wait.

Bridget's eyes spring open. "How could you do that to me? Mason wanted to teach me a lesson. I could take it from him. I couldn't take it from you." A sob catches in her throat. "He'd chained me to a cell in the punishment quarters. He put a collar around my neck, forced me to get down on all fours. Told me to bark like the dog that I was, then he led me around on a leash."

A piece of my heart crumbles. Just when I think there are no new ways left to humiliate someone, I hear this. A tear trickles down Bridget's cheek.

I can work out why Mason picked on her. He sensed her weakness, her lack of resolve.

"What next?" I ask.

"You know what next."

"Just tell me."

Bridget's lips go thin. "Then Mason asked you to get a tin of dog food. He told you if you didn't do it, he'd do the same thing to you. Or worse. So you got the dog food and tipped it into a bowl. I don't need to tell you what happened after that. I'm not stupid, Sasha. I saw the look on your face. I knew you weren't enjoying it. But you did it. You took care of business."

Nausea rises in my stomach. I feel sick. I thought Sasha Rodriguez was a hero, a hard ass, invincible. Now this.

She wouldn't have left it at that though. She must've known how badly she let Bridget down, how cruel she'd been. That weakness would've eaten away at Sasha. She'd have taken action and told Mason what she thought.

Maybe she did. Maybe that was how Sasha ended up in Mason's office that day. I was walking around in Sasha's skin. I could work out that much about her.

"I'm sorry," I say in a small voice.

I truly am. Unfortunately I know exactly how Bridget feels, the pain, the humiliation, the feeling of being let down by everyone around you. I know it all.

"You watched the whole thing and said nothing," Bridget says between sobs. "Not a word. I've told you now. Are you happy hearing it from my mouth in my own words?"

"No, Bridget, I'm not happy."

"After a week, I thought about it, decided I'd be better off in The Ghettolands. I could also see you'd done the only thing you could do, that you didn't have much choice either. So at the tournament, I told you I forgave you."

I look down at my hands. "What will happen to you now? They'll take care of your leg. What about after that?"

"The broken leg might be a godsend. I was probably going to be sent to one of the labor camps for a couple of years. Thanks to the leg, they might let me go straight back to The Ghettolands."

"Back to your family, you mean?"

She nods. "I need to face up to my failures at The Primary and go back to where I belong."

"Do you have someone special there?"

A glimmer in her eyes. "You know I do."

She might be surprised at how little I know. "I'm glad you have someone."

Bridget's lips curl to a shy smile. "After I told Callum what happened, he came straight here. He borrowed the money for the train fare because he wanted to be with me. That kind of sealed it for me."

I squeeze her hand. I might not know him, but I'm glad this Callum is there for my friend and cares for her.

I've spoken to Bridget. That makes it one down, two to go.

Remy is next.

Then it's straight to the top.

CHAPTER TWENTY-SEVEN

Middleton

Five days before…

Alec stared at me as we walked to science class together. "You haven't been yourself lately."

Things were never going to get better. I was never going to be myself again. I felt sick when I thought about Brody. Sick when I didn't. Sick all the time.

"I know you're still upset about being grabbed by the guy with the dreads," he said. "But at least you didn't get physically hurt."

I'm not sure Alec believed me about that. Besides, he had no idea what else had happened. How could he when I hadn't told him about meeting Brody? I hadn't told anyone.

I shuffle along beside my friend. "I've got some other stuff going on in my life."

"Is your mom giving you a hard time again?"

Alec came from a loving family and didn't really

understand about my home life, but he tried, which was more than I could say for Penny.

"Home's not a problem. It's not that."

I hadn't heard from Brody since I'd been to his place. At first, I'd wondered what he was waiting for, then I worked it out. He was biding his time, waiting for the right moment, then he'd go in for the kill. He'd been grooming me for long enough and wouldn't simply disappear.

Meanwhile, I was one of those people who looked normal from the outside, except there was something eating me up on the inside – a parasite was living inside me, eating my intestines, defecating inside me, slowly killing me.

Brody's face would come back to me in flashes while I was reading a book or listening to the math teacher or serving a customer at the supermarket. Other times it played on a loop in my head, over and over.

Couldn't anyone else see I was dying on the inside?

I had to talk to someone. Now. Before I changed my mind.

"You know Brody, my online friend?" I asked Alec.

"No."

"You should. He's one of your FacePlace friends too."

Alec swatted his hand. "That doesn't mean anything."

I was going to have to start from the beginning. "He's the one who'd been burnt as a child so he was communicating via the internet. I told you about him, only he wasn't what I thought. He'd made up lots of stuff about himself, stuff that wasn't true."

"Lot's of people do that. You can't believe half of what's on the net."

I knew that *now*. First-hand experience was different

from being told about what had happened to other people.

We stopped outside the science room. The bell rang so we had to wait until the shrill sound was over until we could speak. This was typical. I was desperate to talk and the damn bell had gone.

I said, "The situation is really complicated and I'm not sure where to start."

"This probably isn't the best time," Alec said.

Finn Masters came up beside us and looked at me. "Sasha, can I talk to you?"

I turned to face him. "Sorry but we're in the middle of something."

"Then I'll be in touch," Finn said. "About coffee on the weekend."

Where the hell had *that* come from? Stunned, I stood there with my mouth open and watched him leave.

Alec stepped in front of me on his way into class. "Maybe you should talk to Finn about this really complicated thing instead. Come on, we're late."

The moment was gone. I still wanted to talk to Alec. I wanted to talk to someone. Anyone.

*   *   *

Four days before…

I'd never been asked out for coffee by a boy before. When I'd gone out with Adam a while back, it hadn't been much of a relationship and we'd barely even gone on a proper date.

Not that this was a date. Anyway, Finn Masters would be the last person I'd think would want to meet me for coffee. Mostly likely he wanted me to help him with some school assignment, which was fine by me.

It was such a relief having something like this to look

forward to. Some breathing space. That was all I needed, a little space so I could breathe again.

As it was, I spent nearly every waking hour thinking about Brody, waiting for what I knew would come. It was killing me slowly, eating me up, because he wasn't finished with me.

The café was Finn's choice, a small dark place with red brick walls that was well hidden from the main street. I didn't imagine they'd get much passing traffic and there was certainly no chance of him being seen here with me.

I was sitting in a corner booth at the back when Finn walked in, his wavy blond hair mussed up, jeans hanging off his hips, a black tee shirt with a skate motif stretched across his shoulders. He looked cool without trying. Couldn't look any other way.

He spotted me right away and swaggered closer. "Hi Sasha."

It felt good to hear him say my name. "Hi."

"I'll get you something. What would you like?"

"A cappuccino would be lovely." I dug my hand into my jeans pocket but he said, "No, this is on me."

That confirmed it. He probably did want me to do his homework for him, not that I was complaining. This was the best thing that had happened to me since...I didn't want to think about since when. And maybe that was the saddest thing of all.

Finn came back a few minutes later with my cappuccino and a black coffee for himself. To my surprise, he put both cups on the same side of the table and sidled across the booth to sit beside me.

"So." He shrugged. "What's up?"

I skimmed the froth from my cappuccino onto my

spoon. "I should probably be asking you the same thing."

Finn sipped his coffee. "Sometimes it's nice to see people away from school. You know, it's more relaxing. Life's not all about school."

"That's true. I've got work as well!"

He laughed, though my joke hadn't been particularly funny. "I thought you'd have a sense of humor."

"If you think school is boring, you should try working at the supermarket."

"No thanks." He smiled, the corners of his eyes crinkling and, damn, he looked cute. "I'd rather be out skating."

"Skateboarding? Sounds like fun."

"Not good on a day like today, though."

He nodded toward the window. It had poured last night and wasn't much better now. Finn had probably made sure to arrange this meeting on a day when it was raining, but there was no reason to let that get me down. I asked him about skateboarding and we had a real conversation.

I sipped my coffee. "You know, I thought you'd asked me here because you wanted help with your history assignment or something."

"Nope," he said. "I've got that one under control. You've got Mr. Camberwell for history as well, haven't you?"

We were having a regular conversation. And it felt good. It felt normal. *I* felt normal. It beat the hell out of feeling like crap all the time.

"I'm sorry about what happened to you at Ella's party," Finn said.

I looked down at my empty cup. "I'd rather not talk

about that."

He raised his eyebrows. "I heard you caught a little action down the side path of Ella's house. Saw more than you were supposed to see."

It wasn't every day I saw someone performing oral sex on a boy. I was hardly going to forget that in a hurry.

I lifted my gaze. "How did you know about that?"

"Jack told me."

Eyes wide, I couldn't believe it. "Jack told you?"

"Yeah, he was pretty pleased with the, uh, service he got that night."

"Whoa." It seemed there was a whole big world out there I knew very little about.

Finn nodded. "Yep, whoa."

Pushing his coffee cup back, he leaned closer and tilted his head. His eyes were closed as he pressed his mouth against mine and kissed me. This was the last thing I was expecting.

Finn's lips curled to a nervous smile. I smiled too, probably equally nervously.

He looked down at the table. "Not so bad, eh."

This was far from bad. Still, it didn't feel the way it should.

"My parents are out for the afternoon." Eyes still down, he added, "There's no one else home. I thought you might want to come back to my place. You saw Madison. You've seen how it's done."

Shock rocketed through me, disgust burning at the back of my throat.

He didn't like me, not in that way. He was using me. For a blow job. Which wasn't even something to brag about, not with me – no, that'd be something to hide –

unless he had some other humiliation planned for me.

"We'll have plenty of time." He glanced across. "We can do whatever you want."

"I don't think so," I said.

He nodded toward the door. "You can think about it on the way back to my place." Before I could get another word in, Finn sidled closer. "We can have something a little stronger to drink if you like. Take a little time to get to know each other better if that makes you more comfortable."

"No."

There, I said it.

Finn sneered. "What? You can't possibly be turning me down. A guy like me."

Just like that, he'd turned. He wasn't the same boy I'd been talking to only minutes earlier. I'd been on completely the wrong track.

He backed away, edging his bottom off the seat of the booth. "Oh man, what a mistake."

He left the café. Left me sitting in that booth in shock, my head in my hands, with no clue as to what had happened or why.

Brody's face flashed before my eyes. The horror I'd felt that afternoon gripped me again, nausea swelling in my stomach.

If only I didn't feel this way.

If only I could make it go away.

CHAPTER TWENTY-EIGHT

One foot in front of the other, that was how I walked onto the school grounds the following Monday.

Mom had given me a lift to school, not a common occurrence. Her timing couldn't have been better because there was no way I could have stepped onto that school bus, not that morning.

My head down, I glanced up to see Aisha and Madison standing in their rightful places with the cool crowd while I shuffled along the front path alone.

"I'm surprised that slut can show her face at school," Aisha said over her shoulder.

"Must've been her lucky day on Saturday," said someone else.

It was all over FacePlace.

The lies were everywhere.

I strode past the group, hoping they couldn't see the hurt in my eyes, and found Alec and Penny. I'd text messaged the two of them earlier so they were sitting on a bench in a small courtyard where they said they'd be. Not exactly private but this was the closest we could get to it at school.

"It's not true," I blurted out.

I dropped my bag to the ground and sat beside Alec. Penny stood up, presumably so she could get away if she needed to. I still wasn't sure if she was speaking to me. She'd found other friends, safer ones who wouldn't embarrass her by getting drunk and throwing up. Easy for her. I didn't have other friends.

"What happened with Finn?" Alec asked. "I know you were meeting him for coffee."

"That's all it was." My voice cracked. "Coffee."

Word had got out on FacePlace that I'd had sex with Finn on the weekend. There were various versions but the gist of the story was always the same. That I was a bitch, slut, whore. *A lucky slut*, Madison had said, to have been with Finn.

I hadn't even done anything.

In response, I posted one message saying I'd never had sex with Finn. The hate messages poured in even faster after that. Why did people despise me? How could they say those things?

Despite all the trash that was coming out on FacePlace, Finn hadn't said a word. He'd stayed clean throughout. I'd sent him messages asking him to tell people it wasn't true. For all the good it did.

"Okay," Alec said. "Let's have the full story."

So I told him and Penny everything, tears streaming down my face as I spoke. Alec leaned forward, his arms resting on his thighs as he listened to every word. Penny stayed, shifting uncomfortably on her feet.

"So you didn't have any sort of sex with him?" Penny asked, though it was clear from my explanation that I absolutely hadn't.

"No," I said.

She looked down her nose at me. "I don't know why you went out for coffee with him at all. As if a guy like him would be interested in you in the first place."

Alec glared at her. "Turns out he was a little *too* interested."

"You know what I mean," she said. "Guys like him don't go out with geeks. That's not how it works."

Still, I'd thought Finn had liked me in some small way, not as a girlfriend but as a human being. I could work out what had happened after he left the café. He'd told someone, got it off his chest, and that person had a field day on FacePlace.

It was also possible Finn had been in on this from the start, maybe with Madison and Aisha. But I didn't want to think that.

I wiped the tears from my cheeks, tried to be strong. "It was only coffee. I didn't go asking for trouble."

"No, but you seem to attract it," Penny said.

Alec stood up, towering over Penny. "That's not fair and you know it."

I could've kissed him for sticking up for me.

Instead I stood. "I'm sorry, Penny, but I didn't do anything and I sure as hell didn't know this was coming."

She took a small step back. "Fine."

From the way she said it, it was clear nothing was fine.

The bell rang. That seemed to be the story of my life. Alec gave me an encouraging pat on the back and headed one way while Penny and I ambled towards the science block.

Talk about an uncomfortable silence. Meanwhile, other

kids were pushing past, rushing to class, calling out to each other.

Penny stopped outside the classroom and adjusted her glasses. "This is a huge debacle."

I rolled my eyes. "Tell me about it."

"I can't do this any more."

"Do what?"

"I can't hang out with you any more. I need to concentrate on other things, study, for one."

"I'm sorry," I said. "I can't tell you how sorry I am about everything."

She walked through the doorway and waved to a girl on the other side of the room.

"Penny," I called out.

She didn't turn around.

I couldn't bear to lose her too, the loneliness a huge hole in my gut. Desperation clawed away inside me because I needed her. I needed someone.

But I couldn't give up.

*   *   *

There was only one person who could help clear up this mess.

"Finn," I yelled across the hallway.

Everyone turned. That's what it felt like with all those faces looking at me. Butterflies fluttered in my stomach and I wanted to disappear and be swallowed up by the earth. I couldn't change my mind now. No turning back.

I stepped forward. The people on either side of me parted like the Red Sea, only I didn't feel like a savior. I felt like I was drowning.

Finn was standing by his locker, surrounded by his friends, the coolest of the cool. Madison and Aisha pushed their way to the front of the crowd.

I sucked in a deep breath, steeled myself. "Finn, would you please tell these people nothing happened between us on the weekend."

He looked down at the floor.

"Finn, you've got to tell them," I said.

Still, nothing.

Couldn't he sense my pain? Didn't he know how bad this was for me?

He shrugged, averting his gaze. "I barely know her."

"Finn, that's not enough," I said. "My life is hell at the moment."

"Fine." He spat the word out. "I don't know who started the rumor. I didn't have sex with Sasha. She didn't blow me."

Silence.

It didn't last.

"Ooh," someone called out from the back.

A few kids laughed. Others turned to go on their way. The tension eased.

One of Finn's friends slapped him on the back and said loudly, "You wouldn't have sex with her if someone paid you!"

Howls of laughter rang through the air. This was truly hilarious.

Still in shock, I remained fixed to the spot like a concrete pillar while around me everyone went on their way.

Finn had finally come out with the truth but it hadn't helped. Somehow I still looked like the guilty party. My name had been slurred and it was sticking.

Aisha stepped closer and looked me in the eye.

"Maybe you brought this on yourself by being such a stuck-up frigid bitch."

Madison added, "Yeah, maybe if you'd given Finn a blow job instead of making all this fuss, none of this would've happened."

Now, it was my fault because I hadn't done what he suggested. It was always my fault. I was a slut. I was a frigid bitch. Always in the wrong.

This wasn't going to go away. I was never going to be good enough. Never going to fit in.

It didn't matter what I did.

Nothing stopped.

CHAPTER TWENTY-NINE

The Primary

I've just left Bridget in the hospital where she's about to have surgery. I'm in my room, which is Sasha Rodriguez's room, writing her a letter because she's the only one who can understand, the only one in the same position, and I have to believe she'll be here one day to read it because we'll have swapped places again.

A knock at the door. I hide the letter and open the door.

Remy strides in like he owns the place. "Mason wants to see you, but I had to catch you first."

I don't say anything.

He puts his hands on my shoulders and pulls me closer. Looks me up and down as if inspecting me. I stare right back at the short sandy hair and the face that's familiar and strange at the same time.

"Are you okay?" he asks.

"Fine."

Remy's shoulders drop and if I'm not mistaken, he seems relieved.

"Bridget's the one with a broken leg," I add.

"I know."

I drop down onto the edge of the bed and motion for Remy to sit on the chair at my desk. Instead he slides onto the bed beside me. He has probably been in this room many times and seems comfortable here, much more so than me.

My heart rate is rising. I hate being confrontational but sometimes there's no other way.

I'm not sure I can trust someone who killed his grandfather to prove his allegiance to country, and who may have been involved in sending me and Bridget into a burning building.

One thing at a time.

I clear my throat. "You never told me how you finished off your grandfather."

He scowls. "What's that got to do with anything?"

"Just tell me."

"No, why don't you tell me about some of the most difficult things in your life instead?"

"B-because I can't."

"Damn it, Sasha, what do you want me to tell you? That I couldn't do it? That I'm soft?"

My breath catches in my throat. Not what I was expecting.

"If you didn't do it, then how did your grandfather die?" I ask.

"He knew about my mission. He guessed. And he made it easy for me. He jumped off a cliff. Sacrificed himself for me."

Though dry, Remy's pale eyes are filled with grief and disappointment. On top of everything else, I'm flooded with sadness for Remy and his grandfather and what they've been through.

"He must've loved you a lot," I say. "And you loved him."

"You were the only person I could tell. Believe me, it was hard for me to admit my weakness."

"You're not weak, Remy."

"I'm also not as strong as you. You said I should accept this one sliver of good fortune that came my way. Just like I should accept you in my life." The hint of a smile plays on Remy's lips. "I didn't have a problem with the second bit."

Maybe that's why he has been helping me – to prove himself to Sasha, to earn her love.

"Sorry, Remy, but I have more questions." I have to keep going. "Why were you so insistent that Bridget and I *not* do those promotional talks?"

"Because you couldn't do it. You'd give yourself away."

"So the training exercise we did was so much safer?"

"I didn't say that." His face clouds over. "I only worked out what Mason had in mind when it was too late. A test for Bridget."

"Dangerous for both of us, not just her," I add.

Remy slides his hand across my knee, not something one friend would normally do to another, especially not after my accusing tone with him. I stare at his hand and he pulls it back.

"Later Mason told me he knew you'd get out of there," Remy says. "Whereas he thought Bridget wouldn't. I'm so glad you're okay."

I stand and walk to the desk, unsure what to think any more. Remy sounds sincere and I want to believe him. I'm desperate for this one thing in my life to be good.

He gets up, reaches for me, ready to take me into his arms. My heart races. I have to stop this. I need a clear mind to work out if Remy is sincere or if he helped orchestrate today's test. If he comes any closer I won't be able to think straight.

If I was Sasha Rodriguez, I'd make him keep his distance. I wouldn't let him get one over me.

My eyes narrow. "Stay back."

He doesn't. I give him a sharp shunt, a jolt to his chest. He stops in his tracks, stares back at me. Where I expect to see fire in his pale eyes, there is only softness.

"I can't do this any more, Sasha," he says.

"Then don't!"

"I want you so much it's killing me."

My mouth falls open. "What?"

"Isn't it obvious?" He reaches out to me. "I'm in love with you."

My pulse rockets. Where the hell has that come from? I know the answer. I don't even need to think about it because it's clear the words have come from Remy's heart.

Suddenly, the pieces tumble into place. Remy doesn't have ulterior motives. He doesn't know exactly what happened between me and Bridget and Mason. Remy wants to help.

Joey has already told me as much: *Remy likes you a lot.* I hadn't realized how much. I've been doubting Remy, thinking things through too much, then jumping to conclusions. It's time to start trusting my gut.

Remy is close, so close. I breathe him in. No aftershave, no hair gel, nothing. Just Remy.

I've showered but must still smell like smoke. Then, why am I even thinking this? What has that got to do with anything?

"I've loved you since I first laid eyes on you when I was thirteen," Remy says. "I just didn't know it back then."

"I'm in trouble, Remy." My voice cracks.

"Is there some small part of you that can remember what things were like between us?" His eyes are dry but they brim with emotion. "Do you remember how it felt when I held you?"

He wraps his arms around my waist and I can't help it. I slide my hands up his muscular chest and lace them around his neck. I'm putty in his hands. I'm pathetic. Human.

"I can't remember," I say.

Remy pulls me closer. "What about my kisses? Can you remember them?"

My lips part, my eyelids lowered, head tilted upward. My body language, every part of my body and being is saying yes.

Remy covers my mouth with his. His lips are soft and warm. A sizzle shoots up my spine. This feels right. It feels wrong too. And I don't care.

He pulls back, stares into my eyes and waits a moment. Another kiss follows, more passionate than the last. Our lips part and he rolls his tongue against mine. Heat sizzles deep in my belly and I feel alive.

Remy pulls me closer. I stand on tiptoe and snake my hands behind his neck. I want him. I want this. I want everything to be right.

And it can never be.

Breathless, Remy pulls away slightly. "You have no idea how hard it has been for me to hold back. When we were sleeping on the sofa at my folks' place, I wanted you so bad. More than that, I wanted you to want me like you did before."

He really was in love with Sasha Rodriguez. Perhaps they'd made love too by the sound of it.

But I can't do that. In a hundred years, I can't make love to Remy. It'd be the biggest lie of my life because I'm not the girl he loves. I can never be that girl.

He pulls back, grips my arms. "Can you remember, Sasha? Please tell me you remember."

"Did other people know about us?" I ask.

"It was no secret."

"I always put you second, didn't I? I always put career and success ahead of you."

I'm not sure how I know this. Perhaps from Remy's desperation. Perhaps I can feel a little of Sasha Rodriguez inside. And maybe I've learnt something about her in my time here too.

Remy nods. My heart aches for this loyal young man who gave so much more than he got. He is still giving, reaching out to Sasha, doing everything he can.

"That kiss was real," I say. "There was nothing fake about that. I'll remember it. Always."

There's a glimmer in Remy's eye, lust or love or something else.

"I can't do more than kiss you," I say. "Remy, I'm not who you think I am."

An understatement.

I can't tell him the truth, that I've swapped bodies with

Sasha Rodriguez. I told Joey but that was different. Joey believed me whereas there's no way Remy would. Hell, sometimes I don't believe it myself.

Remy deserves more than this. He has deserved better all along.

"Listen to me." I hold his gaze. "One day I'll tell you a weird story about this time of my life, something completely crazy, something so far out that no reasonable person could possibly believe it. And when I tell you, I want you to think about it, to listen with an open mind, and try to believe."

He raises his eyebrows. "What story is that?"

"You'll have to wait."

"Is this your way of saying you don't want to kiss me again?"

I smile and place my index finger over his lips. "But I do. I do want to kiss you."

Sasha will come back to you one day. That's what I want to say. Then I remember not to talk about myself in the third person.

"I loved you before, didn't I?" I ask and he nods. "I'll love you again, maybe more than before. You've got to believe that."

"I do."

I press a gentle kiss to his lips.

How can Sasha Rodriguez have put her career ahead of this? I know deep in my heart that if she comes back — *when* she comes back — she'll know this relationship is more important than anything else in this godforsaken place.

Remy is what matters. Joey too. And Bridget. People matter. Sasha has friends, people who care for her, and these are the things that give her life meaning.

Maybe I have friends back in Middleton too. Maybe if I go back people will listen to me now. Maybe things will be different.

My big chance is coming. I'm close. I feel it.

I'm going to stand up to Mason, face up to whatever it was that flung Sasha out of here, and that will propel me back home. Hopefully.

I'm suddenly once again aware of Remy with his arms wrapped around me. This time when he kisses me there's nothing gentle about it. I kiss him right back.

Because life is for living.

CHAPTER THIRTY

Middleton

Three days before…

I stared at the computer.

My boobs were on the screen.

My boobs were everywhere.

Sitting at my desk, I dropped my head into my hands and thumped a fist against my temple.

What had I done?

I pulled open the top drawer and picked up the razor I kept hidden under a book. Stared at it. Thought about cutting myself. Thought about a lot of things.

"Fuck," I said under my breath.

I threw the razor back in the drawer and slammed it shut. Not too hard. No, I wouldn't want to wake my mother. Anything would be better than that.

If only I hadn't taken those pictures of myself. And sent them to Brody. If only he hadn't posted them on FacePlace for everyone to see. If only I hadn't been so fucking stupid.

Tears streamed down my face. They were my boobs on the screen and there was no denying it. Everyone had seen the picture of me drunk at the party with my top pulled up. Everyone had seen the butterfly-shaped birthmark on my ribs. It was every bit as distinctive as a tattoo. That's what it was. It marked me. It proved that the boobs in the pictures that were plastered all over FacePlace were mine.

My birthmark, my breasts.

The comments were coming in thick and fast on FacePlace.

— *Nice tits, shame about the face.*

— *Maybe next time she'll flash her vagina.*

— *Don't gross me out. The boobs are revolting enough as it is.*

— *Slut*

— *Porn star*

— *Prostitute*

They went on. They were never going to stop. This was even more ammunition for people looking for someone to pick on. And that person was me.

Brody had also posted the photo I'd taken ages ago where I'd put on a goofy face and held my school tie up like a noose.

The comment:

— *Sometimes suicide is a good idea.*

And that was from a kid I didn't even know.

Tears turned to full-blown sobs. I couldn't help myself. I just sat there on my own, hunched over my computer, crying my guts out.

Brody had said I wouldn't see it coming. He'd been wrong about that. I'd known it was coming. I just hadn't known when.

He'd made me sweat, waited until the scandal with Finn had broken out on FacePlace and I was at my lowest point, then gone in for the kill.

And that's what the other kids at school would do now.

Go in for the kill.

I'd known Brody would misuse the photos, but I'd still hoped for the best. Hoped this might all go away. No hope of that now.

I checked the screen again. Alec was online. My chest heaved with a combination of relief and desperation. I had to see him, had to talk to someone, and he was the only friend I had left.

What's more, he didn't need to think twice about sneaking out at midnight to meet in the garden outside the library. Neither did I.

It didn't take me long to get to the library. I ran, then sat on the bench, waiting for him. I was wearing a windbreaker and thought I'd be dressed warmly enough. I zipped up the jacket, folded my arms to keep warm and jiggled my knees.

As soon as I saw Alec, my lower lip trembled and the tears started again. I jumped up and threw my arms around his neck. He hugged me back which is exactly what I needed.

"Hey, hey," he said, rubbing my back. "Let's take a seat."

We sat close beside each other, our thighs touching. It felt good to be next to someone, to feel his warmth, his kindness.

"The photos are real," Alec said. "They really are your

boobs?"

It was a question, not a statement, though he knew the answer.

I nodded. "I should never have taken those pictures."

"Who put them up? It wasn't Finn, was it?"

"No," I said. "This is nothing to do with Finn. Not really. It was Brody."

"Who's Brody?"

I had to explain it to Alec over again. That was the problem when you had 800 FacePlace 'friends'. It was impossible to keep track.

"He's not a teenager, though," I said. "He's a grown man."

"How do you know that?"

I held Alec's gaze in the dim light. "Because I met him."

Guilt flooded through me at what I'd done, at the things I hadn't done, the precautions I hadn't taken.

"I tried to tell you the other day at school," I said. "But then Finn came along."

"You liked him, didn't you?"

"Who?"

"Finn," Alec said.

"This isn't about him. It's about something else, something he tried to force me to do. I didn't want to do it, you've got to believe me."

"Sasha, you're not making sense. What *didn't* you want to do?"

My heart was in my throat. I didn't know if I could say it.

"Perform oral sex," I said in a quiet voice.

Alec didn't say anything. I hadn't explained myself

properly. He didn't know about all the events leading up to the situation or how Brody had threatened to put the pictures on FacePlace if I didn't do what he wanted.

"It was horrible," I said.

"I knew you were having coffee with Finn that day. I heard him ask you about it. You went back to his place that day, didn't you?" Accusation in his voice.

"No," I said.

"You really did give Finn a blow job." Alec shook his head, accusation turning to disbelief. "That's what this is all about, isn't it?"

"This has nothing to do with him. He wasn't the one who posted the topless pictures on FacePlace."

"I thought I knew you."

"You do know me."

I had to make Alec listen. I hadn't made myself clear. He'd misunderstood and now this was even more of a mess. If only I could work out what was going on, maybe I could clear things up between us.

He stood. "Of course you'd choose Finn over a guy like me any day."

Realization flooded through me. The way Alec had taken care of me when I'd been drunk at the party came back to me. Even tonight, he'd snuck out of the house simply because I'd asked him to. Then there were Alec's little comments about Finn. He wasn't warning me about Finn. It had been jealousy

Alec liked me. He more than liked me. That's what this was about.

And now I'd let him down though I'd never meant to hurt him.

I rose, reached for his arm. "I didn't choose Finn.

You've got it all wrong. It wasn't Finn. It was Brody."

"Actually, for the first time I think I've got it all straight." Alec shook me off, took a step back. "I don't need to put up with this. Goodbye, Sasha."

No, not goodbye, anything but that.

"Please don't go," I called out. "I care about you."

I couldn't say the words he wanted to hear, that I loved him, because that wasn't true. Besides, this had gone way beyond that, beyond anything I could do, beyond repair.

I stared at Alec's back as he walked away, shoulders hunched, his hands shoved in his pockets.

You're my friend...

First I'd lost Brody, then Penny, now Alec. Everyone needed friends. I had no one.

CHAPTER THIRTY-ONE

Two days before…

I hadn't said a word since I'd left home that morning.

Not a word to anyone on the bus to school. I'd simply sat there and listened to the insults, pretended it wasn't happening. Not a word in the classroom. It was as though the teachers must've been able to sense something and didn't bother me on this particular day. Not a word to anyone at lunchtime when I went to the library. Not a word to any of the kids at school. What was the point when I didn't have any friends left?

I hadn't said a word and no one had noticed.

I was nothing.

The day had passed. The bell had rung to mark the end of the day. And not a word.

I saw Penny heading home and couldn't bear it any longer.

"Penny," I called out and ran toward her.

"This isn't a good time, Sasha," she said.

"I just wanted to ask how you were doing."

Her lip curled in disgust. "How could you do that to Alec? How could you treat him so badly?"

"No, I didn't mean it."

"You know how he feels about you."

"What?" I shook my head. "Honestly, I didn't have a clue, not until last night."

"Well, you know now. He deserves better than that."

I spread my arms. "How was I supposed to know if he never said anything about it?"

She scowled. "Of course he didn't say anything. He was afraid of being rejected."

"I'm sorry I hurt him," I said. "But with the photos and what people have been saying, I've had so much going on in my life."

"The photos…" She looked at me if I was the scum of the earth. "I have to go."

She turned and left.

I stared at the school bus on the side of the road. The bus again. This was too hard. I couldn't do it.

I'd endured the taunts on the way to school this morning by burying my head in a book, not that I'd actually been reading. I'd been grateful there hadn't been another banana incident, grateful for small mercies.

But the other kids hadn't bothered with mercy. They were having too much fun for that. It was one insult after another wherever I turned up during the day. I'd only got through it by morphing to a strange zombie-like state. I was getting by. Only just.

"Porn star, porn star," yelled a girl brushing past me.

A boy I didn't even know grabbed his crotch. "Suck my fat one."

The same girl shoved him in the shoulder and laughed.

"Good one. As if."

I was still staring ahead as Madison and Aisha walked past the bus and headed toward a car parked on the road. They waved at a guy leaning on the car and he waved back. It was the guy in the hoodie, I was sure of it, only he'd had a hair cut and chopped off the dreads.

So he was a friend of Madison and Aisha's. They must've been the ones who'd asked him to threaten me. For fun. For the pleasure of it. Anger coursed through me. I was sick of having all this crap thrown my way.

I ran towards his car and yelled, "Hey you! I know you."

Mr. Hoodie signaled to Madison and Aisha to hurry, got in the car and started the engine. As soon as the girls were in the car, he took off.

I slowed and stopped. I was never going to catch them, so I decided to walk home instead. It'd probably take me over an hour but that beat the hell out of taking the bus.

Not far from me, a woman approached a group of kids. She had long dark hair and wore a tight tee shirt that made her huge boobs look even bigger. The only other thing about her that was vaguely remarkable was the mole by the corner of her mouth.

She was asking the kids something. They motioned toward me. I looked around, wondering what they were pointing at. Clearly it was me, but I didn't know this woman and had no clue what was going on.

Then I saw it, trouble heading my way. The woman turned, fire in her eyes, and stormed toward me.

I walked away, hoped I had this all wrong, hoped she'd go away.

She shoved me in the shoulder. "You're Sasha. Sasha Pierce?"

"Who are you?"

She stepped forward and I stepped back, trying to get away from her. She was taller and bigger than me. Another shove in the shoulder sent me stumbling back further.

We were still on school property near the side of a building. Kids were slowing down, gathering around. In the distance, some were hopping off the bus to see what was going on.

"I don't know you," I said. "What do you want?"

She sneered. "I should be asking you that, you little whore."

What was she talking about? What was going on?

I looked around. Kids had stopped to watch. A murmur went through the crowd. No one was yelling names at me any more. They all wanted to see what would happen next.

I swallowed. "You've made a mistake."

"No, you're Sasha Pierce. You're the slut who was with my fella."

Slut…fella…None of this made sense.

I frowned, took another step back. "Is this about Brody?"

She kept pressing forward. Pointed her finger at me. "I know what he was doing, what he called himself. I know what you did too, you skanky whore, how you wanted him for yourself, how you sent him those photos. Well, he's mine."

What? She must be Brody's girlfriend. That had to be it. I didn't know how she'd found me or how it had come to this. She had it all wrong.

I shook my head. "It wasn't like that…I didn't…"

The woman slapped me. My cheek burnt with shame more than pain. I kept walking backwards, trying to keep my distance yet somehow it felt like she was closing in on me. The whole world was closing in.

More kids gathered. All around me was a sea of blue and gray uniforms. And eyes watching.

The woman slapped my other cheek. "How does it feel now, bitch?"

More shame. More pain.

I looked around at the faces waiting expectantly. At the back, more people joined the crowd. They weren't going to help. They weren't going to do anything.

Somehow we ended up at the side of the administration building or at least that's where I thought we were.

My pulse raced, heart thumping wildly in my chest. I had to get out of there.

I pushed the woman in the chest, tried to get past.

She put her hand over my face, shoved me into the wall behind. Pain shattered the back of my skull.

Murmurs rose from the crowd. Excitement, not disgust.

I tried to push past her but the woman punched me in the face. I even tried to hit her back. For all the good it did. She kept punching until I lost my balance and got knocked to the ground. Powerless, I curled into the fetal position, the smell of dirt in my nostrils. She kicked me while I was down. Over and over.

My ribs were bruised. My face was battered. Pain shot through every limb and bone and nerve in my body. Pain was part of me, layered on top of the pain on the inside.

The woman pressed her shoe on the side of my face and rolled my head on the ground as if it was a Coke can on the side of the road. She could kick me, she could crush me. She could do whatever she wanted.

"Stop that right now!" A man's voice sailed over the crowd.

Let her finish me...

I didn't say the words. I couldn't. But it was what I felt inside. I wanted everything to be over.

The scuffle of feet running away. A murmur through the crowd. More shuffling. More noise from the crowd.

A hand on my shoulder. "Are you okay? Oh my god, what happened?"

"What?" I said through my fat lip.

"She's gone now. It's okay. You're safe."

She's gone. I tried to let that register. *You're safe.* No, I wasn't. I was never going to be safe.

I didn't want to stay curled in the fetal position so I leaned against the man who was now crouched beside me. It was a teacher, Mr. Foss. He'd come to help me and scared off the woman who was beating me up.

Somehow levering myself up, I sat with my arms on my knees, my head hanging down. Mr. Foss helped me. Finally someone was helping me.

"We'll have to call an ambulance," he said quietly then yelled at someone, "Hey you, have you got a phone?"

Through the corner of my eye, I saw a backpack drop to ground as some kid unzipped it and handed his phone across.

"You three, stay here," the teacher said. "I'll need a hand. The rest of you, get out of here. Out of my sight."

"No ambulance," I mumbled.

I was in pain all over but didn't think anything was broken and I didn't care. Besides, there was nothing the doctors could do. They wouldn't be able to help me.

"Call my mom," I said. "Call her and she'll come and get me."

Mr. Foss put his arm around me. "Okay, that'll do for a start."

Call my mom. The words I thought I'd never say. Poor Mom, I actually felt sorry for her. And she was all I had.

Mr. Foss was on the phone, then he was issuing instructions to the few kids who remained. A couple more teachers turned up. They were sympathetic. They were outraged. Couldn't believe what had happened.

Soon, Mom would turn up too and there'd be no way around it. We'd have to go to the police.

Yet even after recent events, after what Finn had said about me, what Brody had tried to do, the pictures on the internet, the bullying. Even after being beaten up by some feral woman. Even after the pain that was still throbbing in my head, my face, my ribs, my everywhere. Even after those things, there was still one thought I couldn't get out of my head.

All those kids had watched.

They'd gathered around for the spectacle with their eyes open and their minds closed. They'd stood there. And done nothing.

Because I wasn't worth it.

I was nothing.

CHAPTER THIRTY-TWO

The day before...

Mom and I had already spent most of last night with the police. Time wasted.

There may have been dozens of witnesses to my beating yesterday but they were all useless. They'd be no more use to the police than they'd been to me when I'd needed them.

Not that I was much use to the police either. I didn't tell them the whole truth. I couldn't.

I told them I didn't know the woman who'd attacked me or why she'd done that. I didn't mention the photos of my boobs on the internet though the police could easily find them on FacePlace – if they looked and maybe they would eventually.

Most of all, I didn't tell them about Brody and what he'd done. I was drowning in shame and my own stupidity. I'd trusted him, sent him photos, gone to his house. And I couldn't tell them any of this in front of Mom.

Only that hadn't been his house. It was someone else's

place, perhaps his horrible girlfriend's. I'd seen his real name and address in his wallet. I had one up on him and didn't want to use it. Didn't want revenge or justice.

I just wanted this to be over. And it would be soon.

Mom walked back into the living room where I was sitting on the sofa, my knees tucked under me. Now that I didn't have any friends left, it was Mom and me. The two of us. It wasn't so bad. That's what I told myself.

"I'm glad you took the day off work," I said.

She placed a bowl of popcorn on the coffee table between two glasses of orange juice, her version of being healthy while having a junk food afternoon.

I shoved a couple of kernels into my mouth. "Yum."

"Smells good too," Mom said.

It sure did. The aroma of popcorn made me feel lighter.

"Which movie should we watch first?" I asked.

"You choose."

Mom felt bad about the beating I'd copped yesterday and maybe about other things as well. She was acting happy and pretending everything was fine though we both knew that wasn't the case. That was okay. I could pretend too.

"You want to watch the old Audrey Hepburn movie, don't you?" I stood and popped *Roman Holiday* into the DVD player, then slid back onto the sofa. "This means you have to sit with me through two movies of my choice."

"Fine by me," she said. "I'm sure I'll like the romantic comedies you've chosen. Anyway, I thought that was the plan. That we have a movie afternoon and eat chocolate later."

"Or sooner. You can't have too much chocolate."

Besides, staying home beat the hell out of going to school. The doctor had said I should have at least a few days off and perhaps think about going back to school next week. As if that was going to happen.

I felt strangely calm today. It might seem weird considering I'd been beaten and was stiff all over. My ribs hurt when I sneezed or laughed. My face was a mess so I refused to look in any mirrors.

But my calmness didn't seem strange to me at all.

The promos on the screen were for other classic black and white movies. The next trailer was for some lame '80s movie with big hair and shoulder pads. There was nothing classic about those fashions.

I pressed the pause button as the movie was about to start.

Just like that I said, "You've never told me about my father."

Mom's eyes widened. "What brought that on?"

"I've always wanted to know and you've never said much."

She shrugged. "Because there's not much to say. I'm ashamed to admit he wasn't a proper boyfriend, just a guy I'd been with a few times. That's why I'd rather not talk about it. Then when I told Darryl I was pregnant, he moved to another town. I shouldn't have been surprised, really."

Mom had shown me pictures of the two of them when they'd been together. There were only a couple of shots, all taken before I was born.

"Big mistake, was it?" I asked.

Her eyes glistened. "The mistake was all his. He's the

one who missed out on having a wonderful daughter, not me. You see, I know what he missed out on and I'm absolutely certain that if he'd ever laid eyes on you, he wouldn't have been able to leave. It would have been love at first sight."

"You think?"

"Definitely." Mom nodded, her expression growing more serious. "Do you want to track him down after all this time? Is that what this is about?"

"No."

Maybe I should, but I didn't. Not now. I had more questions.

"Why do you get so hung up about it if you think I'm hanging around with boys? You're always making little comments about how guys don't go for a girl like me. Always being so negative. Always putting me down. I'm not so horrible that no boy is ever going to be interested."

Her eyes glimmered with surprise as if this was news to her. "I never said that."

No, she never remembered shouting at me or the mean things she came out with.

"Why?" I insisted.

Her lower lip quivered. "I worry too much. I want you to do better than me."

As if I was doing so much better than her. Hadn't she looked around? Seen the writing on the wall?

"I'm afraid you'll end up like me," she added. "On your own."

"But you're not on your own. You've got me."

With those words, guilt gnawed away at me. It felt as if a huge chunk had been ripped from my insides.

I had to move on from that subject. "You could look

for a boyfriend. Other women your age do it and you're still nice looking."

Her smile didn't reach her eyes. "It's not that easy. I've seen a few men on and off. Mostly off. It took me years to find a guy I liked. Do you remember Steve?"

I nodded. I'd only met him a few times because Mom kept her private life away from me.

She sucked in a big breath. "I didn't like the way he looked at you."

"What?" I said, incredulous. "You mean…?"

I knew what she meant, that Steve had found me attractive or fancied me or whatever the term was for it. The thought made my stomach churn.

"That was years ago." I was freaked. "I was probably only twelve at the time."

"That's right. And I wasn't going to let him get anywhere near you. Maybe in a few years when you're older, I might find someone but not now. I'm not interested."

Talk about an enlightening discussion. I'd probably learned more about my mom in the past ten minutes than I had in the past ten years.

Mom sounded matter-of-fact and for once, she wasn't complaining or shouting or taking it out on me. Now I could see through to the unhappiness that underpinned everything she did. She was biding her time, getting by, and not much more. She also didn't seem to know how to appreciate the good things in her life, if indeed I was one of them.

She looked me in the eye. "I can read you like a book and I know what you're thinking, that I'm a cranky old cow. But I'm trying my best, honey. Honestly, I am."

"I'm trying my hardest too."

"Are we going to watch the movie now? Because you need to relax and take your mind off things."

Mom thought we could spend a day together and watch movies and everything would be better. But that wasn't true. Things would never get better.

I forced a smile. "Okay, movie first, popcorn now and chocolate later."

That was pretty much the order of things. Two more movies and a lot of junk food later, it was dusk outside and I suggested we might need some proper food, so the two of us headed for the kitchen.

I opened the fridge looking for the right ingredients. "How about a bacon and tomato pasta sauce?"

My cooking repertoire was fairly limited so there weren't a lot of options.

"Sounds great." Mom fumbled in the cupboard for a large pot.

"It's okay, Mom. I know my way around the kitchen."

"Really?"

"Yes, really."

She tapped her fingertips on the bench top. "Because I'd like to take a quick shower."

But she was afraid to leave me alone. She didn't need to say it.

"Then go," I said.

I had an ulterior motive, something else I wanted to do and it wouldn't take long.

"A nice warm shower will do me good," Mom said but didn't move away. Just as well because there was one more important thing I had to say to her.

"Mom." I held my arms out. "I love you."

"Love you too, honey."

She threw her arms around me and held me against her chest. I couldn't remember the last time she'd given me a hug, which was kind of sad.

Pressing her away, I said, "Take your time in the shower."

"Okay."

Mom turned and left.

I waited until the bathroom door closed, then headed straight for my bedroom, my heart racing as I switched on my computer. Though Mom didn't know the half of what had happened on FacePlace, she was smart enough not to let me go near the computer today and she'd probably take the laptop from my room tonight.

Two minutes, that was all it'd take. Today was the day for tidying up loose ends.

There were messages from Penny and Alec. I was tempted to look but didn't have time. Besides, it was a pretty poor effort on their part to get in touch with me, especially after what had happened yesterday. They could've phoned. Or visited. It was another small hurt on top of all the others.

I stared at the screen. Brody was online. Which was what I'd wanted. Also exactly what I didn't want.

I'd composed all sorts of messages to him in my head. He didn't yet know that I had his real name and address permanently imprinted in my memory. I could taunt him. I could tell him I'd gone to the police with that information.

There were a lot of things I could do if I had it in me. But I didn't. Besides, I didn't even know if there was a law against what Brody had done. Lying on the internet wasn't illegal. He hadn't held me at gunpoint when I'd taken those topless photos. I was sixteen, after all, above the age of consent. And in the end, he hadn't forced me into anything.

One word. That was what I typed.

– *Why?*

A pause. He didn't reply. Maybe he wouldn't. Maybe he was thinking about it.

The words came up on the screen:

– *Because it was fun.*

The breath left my body. This was fun? Did it come down to so little? Could he still be enjoying the power he had over me?

I typed:

– *How could you do those things? This is my life.*

He shot back almost instantly:

– *So what?*

My mouth fell open, my hands trembling as I stared at the screen in front of me.

I did what I should've done a long time ago. I switched off the computer. My hands stopped shaking and I was surprised how liberating such a simple action could feel.

I left my bedroom and started chopping up onion in the kitchen as if nothing had happened.

Brody wasn't going to ruin everything for me, not when I only had another few hours and then the evening would be over. Then tomorrow would be a new day.

It had made me feel powerful turning off the laptop like that. It surprised me, in fact.

That was the answer. Switch it off. Switch everything off.

CHAPTER THIRTY-THREE

The Primary

Except I didn't get it right. Didn't get it wrong either. I ended up at The Primary instead. What's more, I am lucky to have been given this second chance. It beats the hell out of the alternative.

I also found out the words of that song weren't correct. Suicide isn't painless. It's a lot of things, and every single one of them involves a horrendous amount of pain.

It's nearly over though. My time at The Primary is coming to an end, one way or another. I'm certain of it.

Either that or I'm going to stuff up so badly I'll get incarcerated, sent to one of the labor camps Bridget mentioned or maybe even shot.

I'll take my chances. Sometimes you have to take a chance, especially when you've got nothing to lose.

I stand in the doorway of Mason's office and knock loudly. His dark, cropped hair and weathered face are softened by the gentle smile I don't trust.

He gets up from his desk, walks across the room like he's my best buddy, and slaps his hands onto my shoulders. "Where've you been, Sasha? I've been looking for you everywhere. Did Remy tell you?"

I place my hand on Mason's chest and push past into his office. "He told me."

Mason turns to look at me. "You seem different today."

I didn't come here to beat around the bush. "That whole thing at the training facility was orchestrated. You sent in three guys with baseball bats to break Bridget's leg. You knew there was going to be a real fire. You made sure the place was going to go up in flames."

He looks at me as if I'm an idiot. "Of course."

His calmness makes me angry. More angry than before.

"Do I look like a damn fireman?" I say.

"You're my best recruit, the top prime candidate at The Primary."

He smiles. I want to rip that smile from his face and shove it down his throat. I've never felt anger like this before, certainly not back home, but I feel it now. I know what it's like to be Sasha Rodriguez.

"You did all that just to test Bridget," I say. "To see if she had what it takes."

"No," Mason says.

"Of course you did. Don't deny it."

"You're wrong. It was a test for *you*."

"For me?"

"Bridget is expendable. I don't care what happens to her, but you're a different matter."

It takes my breath away. Bridget is a human being yet she's expendable. I'm Mason's best prime candidate yet it's okay to put my life in danger for some stupid test.

"What's more," he adds, "you exceeded my

expectations."

My mouth falls open. "How can you say that?"

"You were smart. You saved yourself *and* Bridget. It's more than I was expecting. The President himself is impressed with the result. He wants to congratulate you personally."

The President knows. And approves. At The Primary it's okay to put lives at risk for the sake of training exercises or to prove allegiance to country. It's probably okay to put a collar and leash around a girl's neck and make her eat dog food too. It's fine to humiliate and demean another human being as long as it's for the purpose of serving your country.

This is different from the abuse I endured back home. It's organized, orchestrated, institutionalized. All part of The Primary.

Well, it's not okay and someone has to show them.

At that moment, I know exactly what I have to do. It comes to me in a flash. And though I should feel fear at the magnitude of the task I'm setting myself, I feel remarkably calm. And certain. Not of success because there are no guarantees in life.

I'm doing the right thing. And that gives me strength. Back home, I may not have believed in myself but I sure as hell believe in Sasha Rodriguez.

"I'd like to meet the President too," I say. "When can I see him?"

Mason grins, pleased at my response. "Now, if you like. The President is at the Arena watching some training exercises. He's expecting you."

I'll give him something he's not expecting as well. A little surprise.

"One thing first," I say. "Before Remy and I went to The Ghettolands, before the tournament, something happened right here in this office. It was after you humiliated Bridget."

"Some people have to learn obedience. They have to learn where they stand in life." Mason's eyes glimmer with evil. "You know exactly what I mean, Sasha. You were part of it. You brought the dog food. You watched."

"Then retaliated."

I'm guessing, taking a punt. Something happened with Mason after that incident, immediately before Remy found me in this office.

"I made you see sense," Mason says. "Even if it took a blow to the head to do it."

That's it.

He hit Sasha over the head. That's the trauma that caused the body swap, I'm sure of it. Sasha confronted Mason, only she wasn't strong enough and now he has her in the palm of his hand. Or so he thinks.

Mason throws his hands up. "You were being ridiculous, ranting about the injustice. I pushed you a bit too hard and you hit your head. I left you here until you came to your senses which, thankfully, you did. I'm surprised you've even mentioned it again. Some things are best forgotten."

No apology, no remorse, no compassion. No, why would Mason be sorry when he has done nothing wrong?

His life is shallow and incomplete. Bridget and Remy both have friends and family. As far as I can see, Mason has neither, yet he's looking for some sense of family. I'm sure that's what he wants from Sasha even if he'd never admit it.

Though he is taller than me, I look down my nose at him. "Let's not keep the President waiting."

I usher Mason towards the door and we leave. I know I'm done for and I don't care. I have to see this through.

Mason's time is coming.

CHAPTER THIRTY-FOUR

Middleton

The day...

Mom looked at me across the breakfast table. "Honey, maybe I should take the day off work again. We can watch some more movies or go shopping or something."

We'd had a lovely, relaxing time together yesterday which was just what I'd needed.

But I knew what she didn't. Yesterday was the calm before the storm and today was something different.

"I've thought it through, Mom." I leaned back in my chair. "I'm going to school and you're going to work. It's a normal weekday."

"Honey, what happened to you at school the other day wasn't normal."

"It was a freak attack and it's over. The doctor said I'm fine, that the bruises will heal and there'll be no lingering physical injuries."

Mom chewed another mouthful of toast and washed it

down with some coffee. She tilted her head, warmth in her eyes as she caressed my cheek, then let her hand drop.

"I know my face looks bad." I was getting good at understatement. "And I don't care. Hiding isn't going to do me any good. I had a wonderful rest yesterday and now it's time to go out there and face the world. The sooner, the better. I'm sick of acting like a mouse all the time."

The irony didn't escape me. I had my little speech prepared and memorized, yet I knew my mother was one of the reasons I was so meek and mild. She was constantly putting me down, criticizing me at every turn and wearing away at my tiny reserve of self-confidence.

I was a victim of my mother's behavior and at the same time I was clever enough to work out what was going on. Also smart enough to know it didn't matter. Not any more. She was still my mom.

"You sound very certain," she said.

"I know what I'm doing."

"Okay, I'll give you a lift."

"Thanks but it'd be better if I take the bus," I insisted. "It's nothing I haven't done a hundred times before."

She tapped her fingers on the table. "I'll have my phone on all day. If anything goes wrong, call me right away and I'll be there in a jiffy."

"Got it."

I stood and picked up the dirty dishes from the table. "I'll take care of this. You've got to get into your work clothes."

She put her hands up. "Okay, okay, I get the message. I'll get dressed."

Mom shot out of the room and came back seconds later, placed my computer on the table and then went to her room. She'd taken the laptop last night just as I'd thought she would, and today I needed it for school. Supposedly.

I gave the kitchen a quick clean, then grabbed my laptop, took it to my bedroom and slid it in my bag with my other school things. This would be the world's shortest day at school ever.

I waited until Mom was dressed and out of the bedroom, then slung the bag over my shoulder and headed for the door.

"Love you," I yelled from the hallway.

"Love you too," came the reply.

It felt good to say it. And sad too. Maybe we should've said it more often.

I walked up the street and around the corner, stopping well short of the bus stop because I didn't want to go that far. Didn't want any kids on the bus to see me. An old lady went past, walking her dog. I smiled and she smiled back. I waited. Didn't want to make a mistake.

After sufficient time had passed, I headed back the way I'd come, unlocked the front door and stopped over the threshold. It wasn't cold feet on my part, far from that. No, there was one more thing I wanted to do.

Leaving my bag inside the door, I stepped off the porch and onto the grass at the front of the house. I closed my eyes and felt the gentle morning sun on my face, my neck, my chest. How strange that at a time like this I should feel I was coming to life.

Nothing stops.

Nothing was going to stop unless I made it.

That's what this was all about.

I remembered the terrible things that had happened at

my old school and how pleased I'd been when I'd earned a scholarship to Morton College. That hadn't turned out so well. New school, different kids, same bullying. I thought about the taunts and insults, about having my boobs all over FacePlace for the world to see. I thought about how Brody had lied and blackmailed me and the way his girlfriend had tracked me down at school and beaten me up. I thought about all those kids who'd watched and done nothing.

How much was one person meant to take?

I opened my eyes and squinted against the sun. Sunshine was supposed to mean hope, but I was all out of that.

I thought about that kid, Domenic Simms, the one from my old school who'd taken his own life. It had been his second suicide attempt. The first time he hadn't succeeded.

Tilting my head up, I raised my arms in the air and stood like that for a minute, reaching up to the sky.

Then I turned and crossed the threshold into my house. No turning back.

I'd had enough and there was only one way to make this stop, only one way out. I was smart. I wasn't going to fail.

Unlike Domenic…

I was going to get it right the first time.

CHAPTER THIRTY-FIVE

The Primary

The Arena. I'm standing in front of the President, Mason at my side.

Behind me, a couple of men are going for it inside the black octagonal cage. I hear the smash of a clenched fist against a man's face, followed by cheers from the small crowd of onlookers. Then the sounds of a scuffle, grunts, shuffling, a giant thud. The noises are distracting to say the least.

The President waves a hand. "Tell them to stop."

A bell rings and I turn to see the cage door fly open and a referee shoot in. The fighters stop immediately.

The President holds my gaze. "I've heard so much about you, Sasha. I've seen you in action, right here." He spreads his hands. "You were magnificent."

"Thank you, Mr. President," I say.

I'm surprised at how nondescript he appears. Average height and build, brown hair and pale skin. Large pores cover his nose. He's just a man.

"Mason has kept me informed about your latest success," he says.

I raise my eyebrows. "The training exercise with Bridget Simpson?"

He nods. "You exceeded all expectations."

"So I've been told."

"One more mission to go," he adds.

I know exactly which mission he means. *Country above all else.* I'm supposed to prove my allegiance. I'm supposed to kill Joey.

Mason turns to me. "Then you can choose whatever career path you like. You'll get first choice. The world will be your oyster."

Enough clichés. I don't even like oysters.

I look the President in the eye. "I won't be going on that mission. I have a proposal."

Mason says under his breath, "It's not your job to suggest proposals."

The President put his hand out. "No, I'd like to hear what she has to say."

"My mission is supposed to be to kill my little brother," I say. "I'm not going to do it."

Silence, only for a few moments.

The President's brow furrows. "You know what that means? One life will be taken, regardless. Do you want it to be yours?"

"I want to prove myself," I say. "I want a worthy opponent. Put me back in the cage now. With Mason."

Maybe I'm being reckless with Sasha's life but I need to do this. I can't change this world and its institutions and the way things work here. I can't make everything better.

But I can save Joey. I can do this one thing.

"What?" Disbelief in Mason's voice.

The President raises his eyebrows "You will fight to the death?"

I nod. "I will give you a life."

He points to the cage. "You and Mason. Now."

Mason glares. His muscular chest is heaving, reminding me how much bigger he is than me.

Remy strides towards us, two men at his side. He has been allowed entry but not without an escort. The anxious look in his eyes tells me he senses something is wrong, though he'll never be able to guess what.

I head straight for Remy, meet him half-way. I look into his gentle blue eyes, cup his chin in my hands and kiss him on the mouth.

"I love you and I'll come back to you." It's the truth. I'm talking about Sasha Rodriguez.

Shocked, Remy stays where he is while Mason and I head down the aisle toward the cage. Remy won't be able to help me, not with guards at his side. I'm on my own and that's how it has to be.

Mason stands at the foot of the steps that lead to the cage and turns to me. "I never thought it would come to this."

I don't say anything.

"I'm stronger than you," he says. "Smarter too. I'm the master and you're nothing. I'm going to annihilate you."

He's talking too much. He's worried or he wouldn't need to do that. And I am not nothing.

I am Sasha.

Mason takes his boots and socks off. I do the same.

My heart is racing so I breathe in deeply. Already my vision has narrowed, darkened at the sides. Blood pumps to my muscles, adrenaline and other hormones through my body.

He doesn't know what I'm going to do, that I'm not going to fight, that I'm taking a different path. Because maybe another near-death experience will get me back home.

I turn to Mason. "You're a shell of a man."

His eyes burn with pain. I've hit the nail on the head. I'm probably the only thing he cares about and I'm turning on him. Then again, that's not quite true. He only cares about himself.

I head up the steps and into the cage first, then turn to keep my eye on my opponent. Just as well.

The cage door hasn't even closed and Mason shoots in and tries to take me down. A murmur rises from the crowd. Remy yells for me to watch out. I sprawl my legs back to stop Mason taking me to the ground, my head over his.

"I'm not going to fight you," I mutter, then step off to get away.

The cage door clicks as it's closed behind us. I'm aware of noise from the crowd, of people watching us, aware of my heart thumping in my chest.

Then everything else disappears.

It's just me and Mason.

Hunched over, he straightens and stomps over. I hold my hands out, fight the urge to hit him before he hits me.

He comes at me with a barrage of punches. Pain shatters across my cheekbone. Blood drips from my face. I cover as best I can and shuffle out of the way.

Mason shoots in, lunges at me, then lifts me into the air and slams me to the ground. The breath leaves my body. I'm still down when he kicks me in the gut. I moan. Curl into a ball.

"Get up."

He paces the floor, gives me time. Breathing hard, I struggle to sit, then slowly stand.

"Fight," he says.

I stare at him.

Leaning over, he slams his right hand into my face. I see it coming and cover. Pain still blasts through my nose.

He grits his teeth. "Hit me."

I give a short shake of my head.

"I'll make you."

Mason walks away, gives me space, so I can get back to my feet. Then he bends over, pulls something out from under his pants leg. A knife. He must have a holster strapped to his calf.

My mouth suddenly dry, fear courses through me. And I know… No one is going to help. This isn't against the rules. There are no rules.

I try to get away but there's nowhere to run and he has me up against the cage, the blade against my throat. He snarls, his breath hot in my face, then nicks my ear lobe with the knife. It burns. Blood sprays everywhere.

"Hit me," he says.

I don't flinch. If he wanted to kill me, he would have. Instead, he slices the knife across my chest. A shallow cut but painful. More blood.

He lurches back. He can't do it. I see it in his eyes, written all over his face.

He can't kill Sasha, not without a fight, and I won't give him a reason.

The blade slips from his hand, clatters to the floor.

I'm smart. I'm quick. I'm Sasha. I scoop up the blade in one hand, run to the edge of the cage and hoist myself to the top of the fence.

Dropping to the other side, I point to the cage door and yell at the referee, "Get in there."

I look for Remy, for the President, for safety. I stagger up the aisle toward them. I'm covered in blood and bruises. And I'm alive. For now.

Remy and the President walk down the aisle to meet me. Remy steps closer but the President puts his arm out to hold him back. Lightheaded, I stop. I have no energy. Is it from the blood loss? Or something else?

I lay the bloodied knife flat across the palm of one hand. Shaking, I extend it to the President. "I said I would give you a life. Mason's life. My gift to you."

The President smiles, his mouth growing bigger, taking up his whole face. Am I hallucinating?

He nods for one of his escorts to take the knife from my hand, which feels suddenly lighter as if a great weight has been removed.

"The Primary cannot afford to lose me or Mason or my brother," I say.

He looks me up and down, then nods. "A clever approach."

People around him clap. I should be happy. That means Joey is safe. For now.

Suddenly heavy, my head lolls around on my shoulders. I feel strong arms around me. Remy's arms. If I'm going to go, then in Remy's arms is a good place to be when it happens.

I'm fading. I can feel myself letting go.

Remy is talking to me but I can't hear the words. The

world flashes black in front of me, then Remy reappears and I'm so glad to see him again.

My head feels like it's about to explode. My knees buckle beneath me. Remy's strong arms hold me up.

Maybe I'm going home now.

Maybe I'm going somewhere else.

Then everything turns black.

CHAPTER THIRTY-SIX

Middleton

My pulse pounds against my temples, my head throbbing. White light flashes behind my irises, then black, followed by a rainbow of swirling colors that ebb and flow before my eyes.

Have I died? Is that what just happened?

"Honey, you're as pale as a ghost. Are you okay?"

My mother's voice.

Slowly the world comes into focus but it's not the world I've just been in. I'm in my old lounge room, sitting on the sofa with my mother kneeling in front of me, her hands on my shoulders.

"Can you hear me?" she asks.

"Yes."

And it hits me. I can hear her. I can hear her because I'm here.

Mom straightens. "You don't look so good."

"I'm fine." I struggle to speak, my tongue sticking to the roof of my mouth. "Can you get me a glass of water please?"

"Sure."

I must be in shock. Still, I'm back. *It worked.* I'd faced up to the issues in Sasha's life at The Primary. Faced up to her biggest bully. That's what has got me back home. I know it is.

Well, I know it as much as I can know anything. It's probably not the sort of thing that would stand up to scientific scrutiny, but who needs science anyway?

Mom comes back and sits at the other end of the sofa, only she seems stiff and edgy, even more so than usual. I drain the glass of water and place it on the coffee table in front of me.

Was it all a dream? Or was I really at The Primary?

A pile of DVDs sit on the table. I reach across for them. There's a beefed up Arnie on the cover of *The Terminator*, a Vin Diesel smash-'em-up movie and a bunch of action films, each one seemingly more violent than the last.

The selection of movies makes me smile. Being back in my old familiar living room makes me smile too. I can't wipe the grin from my face. Inside, I feel relaxed and comfortable in a way I've never felt before. Maybe this is how it feels when you've found where you belong.

"Who chose the movies?" I ask.

"You did, darling," Mom says.

And I know.

Sasha Rodriguez chose them. She was here while I was at The Primary. I hope with all my heart that she's been catapulted back to The Primary, back to where she belongs, back to the people who care about her.

I press a hand to my temple. "My head is a bit fuzzy,

Mom. Can you tell me what things have been like around here these last few days? What I've been like?"

She shakes her head slowly. "Honey, you've been acting so strangely. I'd like to have things get to a more normal state and have the old Sasha back."

I shrug. "What's so strange?"

"I don't mind the early morning runs. A bit of exercise is good for you, but you've been taking it too far."

"Have I?"

Mom frowns. "I watched you in the park the other day. You'd set up a boot camp for yourself, doing stair runs, sprints, step-ups on the park bench, chin-ups from a tree branch, all kinds of things. Like you were in the army." Mom pauses as if she's trying to hold back but I know she'll come out with it. "To tell you the truth, I found it embarrassing."

I raise my eyebrows. "Embarrassing?"

"You don't seem to be fazed by anything now. When I caught you doing pushups in your room the other day, you weren't put out at all. It's a worry."

Go Sasha Rodriguez! Even when she was stuck in my puny Sasha Pierce body, that girl was making the most of things, organizing her own training schedule and doing who knows what else.

I'm sure of one thing. She didn't embarrass me. She did me proud. I only hope I took as good care of her body and life as she did of mine.

"And how have I been going at school this last week?" I ask.

"After the accident... I think..."

"It was no accident," I say. "I tried to commit suicide."

There, I've said it. I'm sick of hiding and not telling it

291

like it is. I've got to face up to the things that have happened if I'm ever going to deal with it.

I'm alive now. And glad, so glad. I'm so happy to be here I can't believe it. I also can't deny what I did.

Mom clears her throat. "It's time you got back into the school routine properly. Your teachers have been very understanding. They say it'll probably take you a while to get over the trauma and fit back in."

"I never fit in, Mom. That was the whole problem."

Her eyes widen. "You just haven't been yourself. It's as if you've been a different person."

Hope. Is that what I feel simmering inside me? Has it been so long that I find the emotion hard to recognize?

I lean forward on the sofa. "Maybe I need to be a different person. I'm sick of being pushed around and teased and taunted. You don't know what it's like."

Mom holds my gaze, her lips thin, and I feel a lecture coming on.

"It's been hard for me too," she says. "It's not easy being a single parent, being on my own. You were only in the hospital two nights before they released you. That first night was the longest night of my life. I sat there until you woke up. I didn't know if you were going to live or die. That's not something most parents have to go through. Every day, I thank goodness old Mr. Johnson found you before it was too late."

So Mr. Johnson from across the road found me? He must've seen me acting strangely that morning and investigated. How horrible for him to have made such a shocking find, especially since he's only ever been nice to me.

Also, what Mom says is true. I've put her through hell.

There's nothing worse I could've done, nothing that would've caused her more pain. There are some things you never get over. I'm sure losing a child is one of them.

I've caused my friends and the other people immeasurable pain too. Avoidable pain. I remember how cut up I'd been about Domenic Simms and I'd barely even known the guy.

It's killing me just thinking about what I did. And I know exactly how lucky I am to have got out of it. There's always another way. I can see that now.

I can't talk about that now, though, not when I have so many other things to sort out. My life has been hell too.

"I'm sorry, Mom, really I am," I say. "But you have no idea what I've been through either."

She shakes her head, looks truly pitiful. "I've always done what's best for you. Put my life on the backburner for you. Made huge sacrifices."

Time to face up to her. "I was trying to tell you about what I've been through, the bullying, the blackmail, the beating. Then you interrupted."

Her mouth falls open. "I-I interrupted?"

"That's right. This is about me. Only you're not listening. You never listen."

"I'm listening now, aren't I?"

"No, you've been talking about how hard it is for you. You haven't asked me how I feel or what I've been through and you certainly haven't been listening." I get to my feet. "We can talk later. I'm going to my room, then I'm going out."

I turn and head for my bedroom. It's only a small step but it's a step in the right direction because hopefully I've given her something to think about.

I'm not kidding myself that things can be perfect between us. Mom isn't going to start baking cookies and being warm and encouraging overnight. But things can be better and I can't keep letting her tread all over me.

For the first time in my life, I stood up to her.

And it feels good.

I stand in the doorway of my bedroom which is cleaner, tidier than before. The stuffed dog I used to keep on my bed is gone, as is the snow globe collection that sat on top of my bookshelves. Sasha must have been cleaning up.

I can't go anywhere without my phone so I grab it from my desk. I stare at my laptop. Later, I decide. I've got more important things to do.

Then an idea comes to me and I figure I can spare a minute. At The Primary, I'd kicked some serious ass. Now I wonder if I've still got it.

I drop down onto the carpet and do twenty pushups. Blood rushes through my veins. I'm pumped. Yes, I've still got it.

That's not enough of a challenge so I wait a moment until I've caught my breath and try some clap pushups. Magnificent. I remember what it feels like to use those fast twitch muscles, to be quick, to be powerful.

There's still a bit of Sasha Rodriguez inside me. She's given me a little something to help me along.

I hear a voice say, "Oh no. I hoped that was over."

Mom is standing in the doorway, poor Mom who probably thinks Sasha Rodriguez is back.

Swiping my phone off the carpet where I left it, I get to my feet. "Don't worry, Mom. Like you said, a bit of exercise can only be good for me." I kiss her on the cheek.

"I love you."

I mean it too, but I have to leave. I have more important things to do. One very important thing.

When I'm out the door, I call Alec and ask him to wait for me in a certain place. I tell him not to ask too many questions and that I'll explain everything later.

I know I should go to the police about Brody, but I'm not going to. Not yet.

I'm going to do something else.

CHAPTER THIRTY-SEVEN

The Primary

Dear Sasha

If you're reading this, it's because you found your way home and hopefully that means I did too. You're the only one who can truly understand, the only person I can tell because anyone else would think I'm crazy. I am a little crazy but that's not such a bad thing. Life would be pretty boring if we were all sensible, if we were all the same.

But I wasn't sensible. I was something else.

What's that old saying? Never judge a person until you've walked a mile in their shoes. Well, we swapped shoes and lives and everything else and I was listening all right. I didn't judge you. Or not very much anyway. I did my best to take care of everything. You gave me a hell of a lot to deal with. Talk about big shoes to fill.

I hope you're back. I hope you're safe. I hope I didn't stuff things up too much for you.

Which takes me back to the beginning because you're still the only person who can truly understand.

I wish you all the best and I don't even know how to make it sound like I mean it but I do. With all my heart.

Love

Sasha.

CHAPTER THIRTY-EIGHT

Middleton

Robert Bakowski.

I know his name now. Brody's real name.

His address too: 669 Light Street. I have an excellent memory. 669 – nearly the number of the beast. Light – the opposite of Dark. Years of study have taught me that creating patterns is a good way of remembering details. I remember his name, his address. I remember everything.

Alec is waiting in his car around the corner. I gave him the address and told him to call the police if I'm not back in ten minutes.

I walk up the front path, surprised to see a girl's bike, pink with white streamers on the handle, has been left on the lawn. A basketball is hiding under a bush in the far corner. Is it possible Brody has children of his own?

An old Jeep sits in the driveway, a motor bike behind it. His motor bike, the same one that was out the front of the house where I'd met Brody the first time.

There are two steps leading up to the front porch and

three more strides until I make it to the front door, my pulse racing, heart pounding in my chest.

You're not a mouse any more, Sasha Pierce. You're stronger than before and you can do this.

Deep breaths. I stand up straight, hold my shoulders back. I'm about to ring the bell when I decide against it. I bang on the door with my fist instead to make a statement.

From behind the door a voice says, "Hold your horses."

A woman pulls open the door. She's wearing jeans and a pale blue tee shirt, her blond hair pulled back into a ponytail. She looks…ordinary. She's not the woman who attacked me at school that day.

"Hi." She waits for me to speak.

I hadn't anticipated there'd be someone else home. Hadn't thought this through. Hadn't considered my personal safety either.

And I don't care. I have to do this.

"Is Robert home?" I ask.

"He might be." She frowns. "Are you sure you've got the right house?"

"Robert Bakowski?"

She nods.

"Then this is the right place," I say. "Do you mind if I ask who you are?"

She looks at me as if I'm an idiot. "His wife."

Brody has a wife? As well as the crazy girlfriend who attacked me at school. And he probably has kids too. Talk about a double life.

I wonder if this woman knows. Maybe I'm about to shake her world to its core. Maybe she has her suspicions. Only one way to find out.

"I'm Sasha," I say.

"Carly," she replies.

I reach for her hand and shake it. Always so polite, so well behaved. Not for much longer.

Confusion in her eyes, she says, "Wait here. I'll get Robert."

She turns and I follow. I'm not waiting for anyone.

The living room is beside the entry hall, a large room with sofas, a wide screen television, kids' toys piled in the corner and a comfortable level of clutter.

Brody or Robert – I'm not sure what to call him – slouches on an armchair, riveted to the baseball game playing on the television, a can of Coke in one hand. Light brown hair, brown eyes, medium build, he looks ordinary.

He turns to glance at us in the doorway, then does a double take. Jumps off his seat, literally. Coke spills onto the floor. He places the can on the carpet, then straightens.

He wipes at the brown stain on the front of his jeans. "What the fuck?"

"Surprised to see me?" I feel confident, powerful. I can do this. I can face up to him.

Carly glares at Brody, hands on her hips. "You know her?"

He looks to his wife. "I've never seen her before in my life."

"Don't give me that," she says. "I can tell by your reaction you know her."

"We've only met in person once," I say. "That was more than enough. He befriended me on FacePlace a year or two ago."

Her glare turns to daggers. "You made friends with this *girl*. Is that true?"

"No–"

Her chest heaves. "Don't lie to me. You're on that computer all the time. You won't let me near it."

I'd love to get my hands on that computer too but I don't fancy my chances. Maybe I should have thought of that earlier but I was only thinking of one thing. I'm still only thinking of one thing.

Besides, I'm sure the police have technological experts who can retrieve all sorts of data, even if he tries to erase it.

"There's a reason I was surprised to see you at the door, Carly," I say.

"What?" She's pissed off, angry that I've interrupted her, and she'll be angrier by the time I've finished.

"I didn't know Robert had a wife," I say. "I've met his girlfriend, you see–"

She raises her eyebrows. "You met his girlfriend?"

I can tell by her expression this isn't news to her. She knows. At the very least, she suspects. Brody has fooled around on his wife before.

I have her complete attention.

"I don't know her name," I say. "But I can describe her. She has long brown hair and a mole beside one corner of her mouth."

Carly turns to her husband. "Francesca King. You've been seeing that bitch again."

Francesca, I had a name now.

"No, no," Brody pleads with her, points at me. "That girl's making this up. I don't know how she knows this stuff."

"She sure as hell didn't imagine it," his wife shouts.

"She's been following me, stalking me," he says. "She's

warped. You don't know what she's done."

"So you do know her?" Carly asks dryly.

"No, no." Brody's head is in his hands.

Carly shakes her finger at him. "If this is true, if half of what she says is true, I'll make sure you never see those kids again. You won't so much as lay eyes on them." Her eyes narrow. "Not with your record, not after what you did before."

So that's the hold Brody's wife has on him. That's the reason he hasn't run away or lashed out or done something. That's why he's still standing there taking this. Because Carly will take his kids away from him.

A criminal record too, not something I'd considered. I wonder what else he has done, how I can be so calm too.

Carly turns to me, her eyes filled with tears. "Is this why you came?"

"No," I say.

I'm sick of taking the crap people throw at me. Sick of standing by while teachers and people in authority tell me it's going to be all right when it's not. Sick of leaving my life in someone else's hands.

Tears prick at my eyes, tears of anger and frustration. Fury too. I can feel it bubbling inside me and after my time at The Primary I know how to use it.

I turn to Brody. "No, I've come to say something."

Carly folds her arms. "Then say it and get out of here."

I look Brody in the eye. "You groomed me and took advantage of me. What you did is wrong in so many ways I don't even know where to start. You're a predator. You should be in jail."

"For fuck's sake," he mutters.

It feels good to stand up to him and say the words.

"That's it. That's what I wanted to say. I'm not afraid of you any more."

"You should be," he says under his breath.

He stands with his feet apart, his fists clenched. He looks bigger than before if that's possible. Scarier too.

My heart rate rises, blood pumps to my muscles, preparing me for what's to come. Fear runs through me.

Use it. Use the fear.

A giant, painful roar fills the air. It's Brody. His mouth is open. It happens as if in slow motion.

He lunges at me, his left fist heading for my face. I slip my head out of the way and stretch my right arm out. Brody walks into my fist. He drops to the ground. And stays down.

No one is more surprised than me. I didn't even mean to hit him. Maybe I still have a bit of Sasha Rodriguez inside me. More than a bit.

I head for the door, past Carly with her head in her hands.

From the hallway, I hear his voice. "You wanted it."

I turn. Brody splutters and says, "Besides, you're sixteen. You're legal."

Still, he can't get up. If he could, he would. Of that, I'm sure. I could kick him while he's down and he wouldn't be able to do anything. I could do a lot of things.

But there are other ways of hurting him.

"No, I'm not," I say. "I'm fourteen. I turn fifteen next month."

It's not the truth, but what do I care? I figure the fear of pedophilia charges will scare him to death.

Carly lets out a startled cry.

Though I feel sorry for her, I can't do anything for her.

I have to help myself.

I walk out of the front door and feel the sun on my face. I jog down the front path, then sprint as soon as my feet hit the pavement.

Alec is waiting for me around the corner. He'll be shocked when I tell him what I've done. And later he'll drive me to the police station and I'll tell them everything.

I run.

For the first time in my life I'm not running away.

I know exactly where I'm going.

CHAPTER THIRTY-NINE

I need time with Alec, time we don't have in a car while he's driving, so I ask him to take us to the garden next to the library.

This will only be our first stop. I think about the last time we met here and I'm grateful this is completely different. It's not dark. Neither of us has snuck out of the house and there's so much more that's out in the open now.

Not everything, though. Not yet.

We sit down on the bench and I throw my arms around him. He hugs me back, thank goodness, and at the same time I realize we weren't exactly on hugging terms the last time I saw him.

Alec is grinning. "Wow, you're really pleased to see me."

I lower my gaze. "Sorry if I was out of line. Just then, that hug, it felt right."

"It was right." He shrugs. "It's just you've been a bit weird lately. A bit distant. Not that I'm complaining. I mean, it's completely understandable after what you went through."

In the past hour I've been through more than he could imagine. He'll be shocked when I tell him. I should be in shock too. I should be shaking or in hysterics. I don't feel calm exactly. In fact, I'm not sure what I feel.

"Sorry if I've been hard to get along with lately," I say.

Alec holds my gaze. "No, I'm the one who's sorry for running away that night and for being a jerk and for not listening to you. I tried to tell you a few times but it was too late by then and I couldn't blame you for being pissed off with me."

I hope he doesn't catch the uncertainty in my expression because I still have to piece together what has happened while I've been away. That's one of the reasons I want to talk to him first before I tell him the full story and ask him to take me to the police station.

"I'm sorry for what I put you and everyone else through," I say.

"When I found out, I was a wreck. Couldn't stop crying. I didn't even know I could feel that way." A hitch in his voice, tears well up in his eyes. "It wasn't just me and Penny either. Kids I didn't even know were coming up to me and saying how sorry they were. We thought we'd lost you, Sasha."

My heart sinks at the way he must have felt, the pain I caused. 'Pain' is an understatement. It must've been agony for my mom, for Alec, for others. I hadn't considered what I'd be doing to the people around me. I'd thought there was no other way and I was wrong.

And as I look into Alec's eyes, it occurs to me that when I tried to kill myself, maybe I killed a little part of him too.

"Then we had you back but you were so weird," he says. "You hardly had any time off and then when you came back to school, you were like this new hard ass, army sergeant type. I didn't know what was going on."

"I hope I was nice to you."

His eyes widen. "I got off easy compared to the way you treated Madison and Aisha. That was amazing. It was only fair, though, after everything they did to you."

"Amazing?"

"Yeah, the way you cut them to shreds."

I have no clue what I'm supposed to have done. "Um, I didn't think I was that bad. Which bit, exactly?"

Alec's eyes which were sad are now gleaming. "When they were picking on you after school and you challenged them to a fight, then said if they had anything to say to you they should say it with their fists, that you'd take both of them on at once, and if they didn't want to do that then they should shut the hell up. Everyone was watching. It was really something."

"Whoa."

"I don't approve of violence, of course," Alec says. "But there wasn't any actual violence involved. It was so cool. And it shut them up. Madison and Aisha are both scared of you."

It was Sasha Rodriguez they were scared of, not that I needed to enlighten anyone on that matter. If something good has come of swapping bodies with Sasha, I'm going to make the most of it.

"How's Penny doing?" I ask.

"The same as ever," Alec says. "Are you two speaking?"

"I-I'm not sure."

"She was really upset when you said those things to her."

I try not to squirm in my seat. "Which things, exactly?"

"When you told her she was too conservative for her own good and way too judgmental, then told her to get a life."

"What? Um, I mean, well, some things just needed to be said."

Alec nods. "And you said 'em!"

All I can think is, *Go Sasha*. She really told it like it is. She gave me so much too, the strength and the skills to stand up for myself.

"I might have to apologize for being so blunt," I say.

He shakes his head. "Penny's the one who should say sorry to you after the way she abandoned you when you needed her. She knows it too, and said as much to me."

Yes, she judged me harshly, but sometimes it doesn't matter who's right and who's wrong. I can apologize to her first and that'll help pave the way.

"While we're on the subject of mutual friends," Alec says. "For the record, I still maintain Finn is untrustworthy and an asshole."

"He's definitely untrustworthy." I shrug. "I guess asshole is pretty accurate."

"That's what I'm most sorry about." Alec's face clouds over, his expression serious. "That night when I stormed off, you were trying to tell me you hadn't got together with Finn, but I wasn't listening."

"That's okay, Alec. I don't think you're an asshole."

"Gee, thanks."

I whack him on the shoulder and that raises a smile.

"Friends?" I ask.

"Always."

He clears his throat. "This is going to sound lame."

"What?"

"I feel like we're talking properly again. Really talking. Ever since you came out of hospital, I've been trying to have a decent conversation with you but it's like you haven't been there. As if you were a different person and we've finally got the old Sasha back."

"I feel much better now," I say.

Alec slaps his hand on his forehead. "Oh no, I've been doing this all wrong. I've been doing all the talking when I'm supposed to be listening. I told myself I wouldn't do that."

"Why would you say that?" I ask.

Another earnest look from Alec. "It's what the school counselor told me after…after what happened."

I slide my hand over his and give it a squeeze. "I made a huge mistake, Alec. I tried to kill myself. It's okay to say it."

My voice cracks, even though I've just told him it's okay. His lower lip is quivering and I don't want to make my best friend fall apart. Couldn't bear it. But I have done worse, so much worse, and I'm kidding myself if I think he's just going to get over it.

I press my eyes shut. "I'm so sorry, Alec, more sorry than I've ever been for anything in my life, but I couldn't take it anymore. And now I'm so grateful to be here, so grateful I can't tell you. It was a horrible, hideous thing I did. And so final. That's probably the worst thing of all. I know it sounds dumb to say that, but I had no idea how much it would affect other people, people I care about, people like you. I know that's not an excuse. I could spend the rest of my life apologizing and it wouldn't be enough."

Alec envelopes my hand in both of his and I'm brave enough to open my eyes again. Pain is still etched in his features but there's something else there too. Friendship. He leans closer and presses a kiss to my cheek, bringing a smile to my face that's both sad and hopeful.

And as I look into his eyes, I wonder how I can have gone for so long without seeing what's right in front of my face, a wonderful friend.

Maybe more than a friend.

"I'm not better yet, Alec," I say. "Not completely but I'm trying. It's like my head was in a vise and I can finally start to look around again."

"I'm here, Sasha." He swallows, his Adam's apple rising. "The counselor...she said you'd need friends and people to talk to. People to listen."

"I also need people to be themselves."

"Okay, I'll try." Alec settles back into the bench, his long legs crossed at the ankle. "I did a lot of thinking after you came out of hospital, especially about what you went through every day. I talked to Penny and some of the other kids and we pooled our information. I remembered you'd said things were bad at your old school too, so I figured this had been going on for a long time."

"It was bad, all right."

But I don't want to go there now when I have so much else I need to say to him.

"I'm sorry," he says. "It took me a while to work it all out."

"There's more, a lot more that I haven't told you yet."

He nods and I tell him about Brody and how he pretended to be my friend, how he was the one who spread the topless photos of me and then coerced me into meeting him. I tell Alec everything.

His eyes go wide. He asks a few questions. Mostly, he listens. When I'm finished, he wraps his arms around me and holds me. A hug is exactly what I need. It's what friends do for each other.

He strokes my hair. "You can cry on my shoulder."

I lift my head. "I'm not crying."

"What?" Alec stares at me, surprised. "I'm trying to be manly and sensitive and you just ruined the moment."

Maybe I've cried enough lately. Maybe I'm so happy to be home that it cancels out any tears that might be lurking inside.

"I didn't ruin the moment," I say. "We just created a new one."

"This is serious. What Brody did goes beyond bullying."

"That's another thing I wanted to talk to you about," I say. "It's kind of a part two to the story."

I tell him where I've just been and how I confronted Brody. I'm still not sure if there are laws against what Brody has done but I'll find out soon enough. If his wife follows through about not letting him see the kids, he's going to have other problems as well. And there's definitely a law against assault so his girlfriend Francesca King will pay for beating me up.

Then I say, "I'd like you to take me to the police station now."

Alec frowns. "So I just picked you up around the corner from Brody's house after you beat the crap out of him?"

I shake my head. "No, he walked into my fist.

Honestly."

Alec gets excited again. "Like that old fight. Anderson Silva versus Forrest Griffin. Griffin was swinging and couldn't hit Silva. Then Silva held his hand out and Griffin walked straight into it and dropped to the ground. Bam!"

With more than a hint of sarcasm, I say, "Yes, I'm exactly like this Anderson Silva person."

"How could you do that? You're not a fighter."

I am now. How on earth can I explain this? I'm not a bodyguard. I'm not a kickboxer. I'm a pushover. At least, that's what everyone thinks.

"Remember when I threatened Madison and Aisha?" I say. "It was as if someone else took over my body. The same thing happened today."

"Sasha, are you okay? You've been acting so strange lately and what you just told me is the weirdest thing of all."

"I stood up for myself."

"I know. In a minute, I'll drive you to the police station." Alec puts his arm around me. "Right now, just rest your head against my shoulder."

I do and it feels good. I've got my best friend beside me and maybe we're becoming more than friends.

I wonder if I gave something back to Sasha Rodriguez. I wonder if she can see how much more important friends and family are than her career.

I know what she gave me.

Something I didn't have before.

Hope.

Besides, every girl needs to kick a little ass from time to time.

Seeking Help

If you or someone you know is having suicidal thoughts or needs help, please seek assistance. Don't give up until you find the help you need.

USA
National Suicide Prevention Helpline
1-800-273-8255

Canada
Kids Help Phone
1-800-668-6868

UK
Papyrus Hopeline
0800 068 41 41

Samaritans
116 123

Australia
Kids Helpline
1800 55 1800

Lifeline
13 11 14

INFILTRATION (BOOK 1)

2120: A world ravaged by a devastating virus. Those healthy enough to live in New Nation lead a sanitized, orderly life where everything is tightly guarded by a brutal government. Lives, thoughts, information and emotions are all strictly controlled.

Now: Seventeen-year-old elite soldier Nicola Gray is sent back in time for an important assignment. She alone will stop the virus before it takes over the world – her mission, to gather intelligence, find the cause and stop the threat, whatever it takes.

She is trained to kill.

But the past is not what Nicola is expecting. Overwhelmed by an alien world, she discovers feelings she can't handle and a world with immense personal freedom and people who care for each other. She wants to stay. She wants to live. She wants a lot of things she can't have...

REGENERATION (BOOK 2)

Nicola Gray is a typical, slightly awkward high school student. Or so she appears. In reality Nicola is a hyper-fit, elite soldier from the brutal New Nation of the future. Her superior officers have given soldier Gray strict orders to eliminate their greatest threat, Ben Tanner. Her boyfriend.

And New Nation will not give up.

Nicola fights as only she knows how to keep Ben and those around her safe. Pushed beyond limits, she grapples with questions of love and loyalty, right and wrong, life and death. Nicola has a line she will not cross. But that's exactly what she must do...

VALIDATION (BOOK 3)

School's out for Nicola Grey but just as the party is about to begin, she is hauled back to the future to brutal New Nation. Suddenly she's hailed as a hero of the people when that's the last thing she wants and this is the last place she wants to be. *How did things go so wrong?*

Nicola is desperate to get back where she belongs – with boyfriend Ben, in the past. But that isn't going to happen, not when millions will die in a world decimated by a deadly virus, her country ruled by a despotic regime. Unless she can stop it.

It's Nicola versus New Nation. She has to change the future and save the world.

ABOUT THE AUTHOR

Susanna Rogers is the author of kick butt books for young adults. She also writes romance and at one point moved to a life of crime – you might be seeing more of that. She loves writing young adult, partly because she's an overgrown teenager and partly because she can write the kick butt heroines she adores. She's also a kickboxer and dreams of empowering girls and guys around the globe to believe in themselves, to take care and follow their own dreams.

Susanna believes in love and kicking ass and a little bit of murder here and there.

She would love to hear from you – susannarogers.com.

If you like her books, please post a review on Amazon or Goodreads. She'd like that a lot.

www.ingramcontent.com/pod-product-compliance
Lightning Source LLC
Chambersburg PA
CBHW030624110726
47901CB00002B/307